THE GHOST DANCE

INSURRECTION

A JAZZMAN NOVEL

BY JACK RANDOM

CROW DOG PRESS
TURLOCK CA USA

The Ghost Dance Insurrection

A Jazzman Novel by Jack Random

Crow Dog Press
1241 Windsor Court
Turlock CA 95380

This book originally published by Dry Bones Press 2000 (ISBN 1-883938-81-3). Original cover photo by James Mooney circa 1891.

Publisher's Cataloging-in-Publication Information
    FICTION
    Random, Jack. –
    The Ghost Dance Insurrection / by Jack Random.
    New Voices in American Fiction series
    p.   cm.
    ISBN-13: 978-0-9977883-4-1
    ISBN-10: 0997788341
I. Title. II. Author

THE GHOST DANCE

INSURRECTION

AUTHOR'S NOTE

Dry Bones Press originally published *The Ghost Dance Insurrection* in the millennial year 2000 on an on-demand basis. The publisher chose to label the work: A Jazzman Novel. Sadly, Dry Bones ceased operations sometime thereafter. The book has drifted into rare-book status and has been unavailable for many years.

Ghost Dance was my first novel and reflected some of my most fundamental themes, including politics, economics and the cause of Native America. The protagonist used the web moniker "Jazzman" and assembled a team of highly skilled and like minded individuals, including a retired Seattle detective, a business colleague, a corporate attorney, a law student, a woman of the night and a Native American tracker. Together they devise and execute a plan to expose and take down an organization of elites bent on world domination.

This edition has undergone a comprehensive revision. I've renamed my protagonist to bring him into alignment with the second Jazzman novel: *A Patriot Dirge*. While Ghost Dance focused on economic corruption, Patriot attacks the two-party system in American politics.

Ghost Dance was the precursor as well to a series of political essays called the *Jazzman Chronicles: Volumes I-X*. The chronicles found wide publication on the web during the catastrophic years of the Bush administration.

Jazz. December 31, 2016.

Prologue

THE ANCIENT ONE

If a stranger were to ask members of the Makah tribe on the northeastern sector of the Olympic Peninsula about the old Indian who lived near the Point of Arches, he would be told there was no such man. He would hear whispering as he turned his back and went his way.

But if you were known as a friend to Makah and the native people they would tell you much more. They would say that the old one was not a man but a spirit being. They would say he is a dream walker, a shape shifter and a guide to the spirit world beneath this world of waking beings. They would tell you he has lived many lives and his wisdom is beyond that of this earth.

They would tell you he is the crow, the coyote and the howling wolf. They would ask you to listen to the wind in the tall trees for there you would find his voice. They would whisper his name – Song of the Wind – for one does not speak aloud the name of sacred beings lest they be swept away in the madness of dreams.

They would speak of the old one's visions. They would tell you he was once a Ghost Dancer who stood with Sitting Bull, who smoked with Crazy Horse and held counsel with Big Foot. They would tell you of his promise that the Ghost Dance would rise again, that the earth would quake, the skies light up the night with thunderbolts and the waters would cover the land. They would tell you of his prophecy that the white man's rings of power would come crashing to the earth, that the native peoples would regain their sacred lands, that the salmon and the buffalo would once again be plentiful and that the people would live by the ancient ways once more.

They would tell you that the old one was crazy for he promised that this would come to pass in the span of a single lifetime. He promised and he swore on all that he held sacred that the time of the Ghost Dance was at hand.

Chapter 1

MURDER MOST FOUL

"Murder," Detective Jones said aloud with a glance to the pretty young widow who just appeared at the doorway to the study of the late William Miner.

"Murder most foul."

The detective was fond of Shakespeare and quoted the bard as often as he could.

"Murder most foul, strange and unnatural."

It was a sentiment he did not yet believe. He had not arrived at any conclusion in the case but he wanted to see if he could draw some reaction from the deceased business tycoon's wife. He did not and it surprised him. The case had been handed to him as a probable suicide. Had it not involved a prominent member of the Seattle business community, the investigation would have been little more than perfunctory. The department would certainly not have assigned their lead investigator to the case. But this reclining corpse, naked and undisturbed, a portrait in contentment aside from his absence of life, was Big Bill Miner. By most accounts he was one of the wealthiest individuals in the Pacific Northwest.

An empty vial of an unknown substance – most likely poison and the cause of death – was found on his desk next to a glass of single malt scotch.

If it was murder Cheryl Miner was the most obvious suspect. It's a familiar story: A wealthy older man marries a beautiful young woman. He catches her with one hand in the cookie jar and the other in the pants of a younger rival.

Before he can change his will, she acts in desperation.

Detective Jones had not had an opportunity to check the will but he was relatively certain she stood plenty to gain. He expected some expression of doubt or wonder at his pronouncement. When she did not react at all, he decided she was either dazed by the sudden loss of her husband or she would not be surprised if he had been murdered. In either case, she fell from the top of his suspect list.

"Oh, Mrs. Miner!" He raised his eyebrows in feigned surprise. "I didn't see you walk in."

"You wanted to see me?" she asked quietly.

He had ostensibly sent for her to ask her help in starting up her late husband's computer. In fact, her presence had already served its purpose. He would later apologize and explain that he was only hypothesizing aloud. He would express concern that she might have overheard and reaffirm the department's preliminary finding of suicide. For now, however, he was content to let it settle in her subconscious mind.

The widow calmly explained that she knew nothing of her husband's business or his computer and the detective excused her with a shrug.

"Just a shot in the dark. We'll figure it out."

"I'm sure you will."

He watched her, still dressed in her morning slippers, nightgown and an open silk bathrobe, as she glided down the winding staircase to the kitchen below. She did not look back. He thought how she might have played Juliet to a young man's Romeo or perhaps Ophelia to the tortured Prince Hamlet. He shook his head in reflection: Big Bill Miner to Hamlet was "Hyperion to a satyr."

His eyes narrowed in contemplation.

"Attractive, isn't she?" he asked no one in particular. Three male officers nodded in agreement.

"Attractive, highly suspicious and absolutely innocent."

He had come to his first conclusion: Cheryl Miner was

not the killer. She was capable of many unscrupulous acts – deception, fraud, greed and betrayal – but not murder.

He instantly arrived at his second conclusion: She was hiding something. She knew more than she would say. Why? Who was she protecting? Herself most likely. But why and from whom? The murderer most likely.

He had entered the case with one suspect and two possible leads. Already he had eliminated one suspect and diminished the importance of one lead. The will could wait. He could be sure it would point to the widow. Whoever the real killer was, he or she wanted the detective to believe it was Cheryl Miner.

That left the poison – probably strychnine, possibly belladonna. How and where was it obtained? Who purchased it and when? The murder weapon, if it was murder, no matter how common or obscure, always left a trail.

"Detective Jones?"

His eyes widened as if awakening from a dream. He appeared to return from the distant place of his thoughts.

"Yes, sir?"

"I think we have something here."

The detective followed the officer's gesture to an annoying green light emanating from Bill Miner's computer screen. He wondered how high tech geniuses could have selected such a stupefying tint of illumination.

"We found something in his business files," the officer explained.

"Well, what do you know?" the detective shrugged. He shook his head at the cryptic message displayed on the screen: *The Gods must fall! Jazzman.*

"Does this make sense to anyone?"

He waited for an answer he knew was not forthcoming.

"The killer goes to all this trouble to make us think the widow did the deed and then he leaves his signature on the guy's computer."

11

He threw his arms up in exasperation and pressed his fingers to his temples.

"Murder," he announced. "Murder most foul, strange and unnatural!"

Attorney Margaret Thomas had just entered the room.

Chapter 2

SOMETHING HAD TO GIVE

Lost in a state of awe and wonder at the ironic twists and bewildering turns that defined his life's journey to the present moment, numbed, stricken and paralyzed in a state of awkward transmutation, Roman Mason gazed absent mindedly at a brilliant west coast sunset.

His inspiration died in 1974. That was the year Richard Nixon ended the war. It was the end of all causes, the death of hope itself, the last insult and the penultimate message of despair. The system failed. The people were defeated. The cause was supposed to have prevailed but Nixon ended the war – the same Nixon who killed the protestors at Kent State and Jackson State universities, the same Nixon whose Nixonites killed JFK, Bobby and the King. The slaughters of Chicago, Detroit, Miami, Berkeley and Watts, the brutalities of every Westside or Lower Eastside or any side where concentrations of the poor – blacks, Latinos, white trash and gutter rats – rose from the madness of the great lie.

Where were they now? What had become of them? What had become of us? We were the generation of change. We were the creators of a new world order. We were the dreamers, the seekers and holders of the sacred flame, lovers of peace, freedom, equality and justice. Where were we now? Gone. Rechanneled into scattered causes of little real consequence in the swelling tide of humanity's slow passage through endless time: Abortion rights, El Salvador and Nicaragua, the Persian Gulf, AIDS, the New Age, the New Wave, the new and higher consciousness, sexual harassment in the working place, men from Mars and women who run with wolves, mythology and fairy tails, health care and free trade, welfare reform, gun control and crime. Images refocused through the eyes of a mystic crystal.

"Great causes all!" he tried to sell himself. "Worthy causes all!" he told himself.

Sold out. Hemmed in. He remained still. His heart would not be moved. He could not rouse himself to cry out. There was no passion. The cause of his soul was far more than the sum of these parts. He yearned for fundamental change – the essential cause without which all causes were little more than dust in the wind.

Now the world had begun a cataclysmic change, a long awaited reckoning of the human spirit, a realization of the promise and the possibility of peace. The wall we were up against had fallen. The wall that had locked and chained and bound our collective soul in a concrete prison had at last been brought down. The greatest single symbol of oppression in modern history was torn down in the blink of an eye.

The world had witnessed a massive breakdown of the communist-socialist system. In the Czech Republic the movement that sprang into worldview in 1968 and was struck down before the six o'clock news reasserted itself as if it had never been lost at all. In China the blood of a generation was offered up in martyred sacrifice. In Romania the heads of despots fell. The struggle for peace and justice continues around the globe while America sleeps in its position of power and dominance, playing politics with the cause of freedom, offering lip service in place of commitment, content to close our eyes and stand down. We want no part in systemic change.

Where are we now? We boldly challenge the motives of our militaristic leadership without threatening the leaders themselves. We question the integrity of our diplomatic maneuvers without maneuvering our diplomacy. We defend the right to burn the flag as the vindication of history. We

14

march for a woman's right to choose abortion and a gay man's right to life. We drink bottled water and use paper bags. We attack the poisoning of the air, the water, the earth and the plundering of forests.

Great causes all...but small. Within the grand view of an ever-expanding universe, they are of little consequence. The policies change but the ends remain the same. The lies are given a more presentable form – revised to suit the sentiment of the day.

Flags burn when there is not enough fuel to warm the soul. Judges will always fall for sympathizing with the disenfranchised. The poisoning of our air and water will go on as long as the heart of power and the souls of the greedy are poisoned. Forests will be plundered as long as the privileged require redwood desks and maple cabinets. Abortion is economics. Gays will continue to die until a sufficient number of the new aristocrats join them.

Where are we now? We gaze through mystic crystals at a planet in decay. We hold hands to signify our awareness of a new beginning without ever wondering what that new beginning brings. Will it bring a rebirth of transcendental consciousness? What will it transcend? Where is the truth in all this mystery? Can we see it through the vision of a mystic crystal? Can we absorb it through the holding of hands?

Roman tried. He tried long and hard to believe as they believed in the path we were on but he could not. He could not hold out on the meager offerings of spiritual guides. His vision had long been altered not by crystal but by jade. His spirit was poisoned and his soul infected. He could not keep faith with the shallow promises of hope his contemporary colleagues had to offer. Something had to give.

It was time to act – even out of desperation and fear and the loneliness that comes from struggling too long with one's own conscience. That long, lonely silent night, as he drifted in and out of sleep, his plan came into being. In the morning he would set the wheels in motion.

Jazz, he thought. He would set it to a jazz beat. Jazz is the music of rebellion. Jazz is the beat the powers despise. They cannot control it. It directs itself.

Who can say what part a man's dreams play in the waking world of thought and action? For the jazzman, dreams were essential. He came to rely on them for more than inspiration. The separate worlds of conscious and subconscious reality seemed to fuse in the hours of his nightly ritual. He welcomed the powerful spirits of the nocturnal world into his sleeping soul and looked forward to his daily rebirth.

Tonight, as he overcame the anxiety that accompanies a moment of transformation, he was enveloped with a sense of contentment, almost euphoria. The spirits would not let him down.

He awakened to the brightest, clearest, most glorious morning of the century – or so it seemed. He stepped out onto the deck where the cypress opened to reveal the shimmering, pounding waves of the eternal Pacific.

The seventh wave, he thought. He counted them, taking care to appreciate their subtle differences. One. *One must pull oneself up by one's own hair.* Two. A seagull soars overhead in all its grace and beauty. How simple the world must seem through the eyes of a gull. Three. *See the world with fresh eyes.* He recalls the eyes of youth when all things large and small were clear and simple. Four. He smiles. His life had waited for this solemn moment of commitment. *The decisive action of one man can change the world forever.* Five. 1972. Decades of germination, frustration and despair. Twenty-six years on an island of isolation, alone in a faceless crowd, a prison of one's mind. Six. A deep breath. Seven. The saltwater air cleanses his soul and fills his spirit with passion as a smile of satisfaction evolves into determined resolution. *Jazz.*

Chapter 3

MOUNT OLYMPUS

Detective Myron David Jones of the Seattle Police Department did not look the part. His gray streaked brown hair was a little too long and a little too wild. His stubble of a beard, speckled like a chessboard, violated department regulations. He got away with it by arguing that his disheveled appearance contributed to his effectiveness as a detective.

To the department brass he was a little hard to take and even harder to deny. He earned his reputation as the best in the Great Northwest. In twenty-five years as a detective he had never failed to solve a case. He stuck to a trail like a bloodhound on a hunt until he brought the responsible party to account. Like his beard, it did not endear him to his commanding officers. On more than a few occasions his chief pleaded with him to drop a case but he always endured. There would be no unsolved murders on his watch.

The beard strengthened an otherwise weak chin and rounded out his gaunt features. His face recalled Freud, as did his general disposition. He looked more like a professor of literature or philosophy at a liberal arts college than a police investigator. He was not the sort of man you'd pick out of a crowd but he was the kind you would approach to get directions. Strangers at pubs and funerals would engage him in conversation. He possessed a gift for establishing a connection within the wide spectrum of humanity.

He possessed another gift that he preferred to describe as his method. He employed dreams in the solution of crimes.

It first came to him during a baffling case involving the death of a local artist. It appeared to be a simple love triangle but the detective could not shake the jealous lover's alibi. He came as close as he ever had to giving up on the case when a dream directed him to a particular piece of art. That revelation led to a rival artist in Chicago who had stolen the early work and used it to create a series that established him as an artist. When the now deceased artist learned of the theft, he threatened exposure. The rival then contracted a hit man. The connection was sufficiently remote and the evidence so scarce that he very nearly got away with it.

He did not share his dream methodology with his fellow officers in law enforcement. They already derided him for his eccentricities. Fanning the flames of madness would not serve his cause if his cause was to continue working as a detective. His investigations on the topic led him to believe that he was not alone in employing dreams to an earthly purpose. Exceptional talents in a variety of fields, from artists and scientists to political leaders, often hinted at such an approach. The most notable advocates of dream research were of course Sigmund Freud and Carl Jung. The most notable user of dream inspiration was Albert Einstein.

The detective learned to direct his dreams by focusing on a given aspect of the case he wished to explore. He would sit motionless, sounds of nature on the stereo and a single candle burning in the darkness, until he achieved deep relaxation and receptivity. He would then climb into bed and drift into a deep sleep.

He did not always employ the method. It had not been necessary in some time. His career had entered a new phase and one that he found particularly gratifying. Considered semi-retired, he reported to work two or three days a week to consult his fellow detectives on any troubling cases. The arrangement seemed to please everyone involved. Detective Jones had grown tired of the mundane everyday crimes. Now he would only handle the most interesting cases. It offered the additional advantage of providing time to write his memoirs, correspond with other professionals, read case studies, reread Shakespeare and generally explore the spiritual side of life on planet earth.

He was just about ready to conclude that his days with the Seattle Police Department had come to an end when he began to have a recurring dream. It came to him almost every night. It always began at the Point of Arches on the Olympic Peninsula. He knew the place. There he notices the shadowy figure of an old Indian who guides him without words toward Mount Olympus. Each time he would get a little closer to what he knew by raw intuition was his destiny. At last he comes to a cave shrouded in shrubbery. He makes his way inside, kneels and uncovers a small wooden box. Dusting the dirt from its cover he reads the eloquently carved initials: WM.

That was the dream. He didn't open the box. He never saw anyone other than the old Indian. He heard the caw of a raven or a crow and he awakened.

It left him baffled. The dream was not clear or focused enough to enable him to locate the precise location without further assistance. He knew with a certainty that astounded him that this dream would connect him to his most important case. He would have to wait for the next clue to propel him forward. Knowing that it would come lightened his step and his perspective brightened. Some of his friends struggled to explain the change in him. His in-laws wondered if he was having an affair. Fortunately, his wife had helped guide his spiritual awakening. She understood him better than anyone.

How does one explain the joy of knowing one's destiny? He would only shrug and suggest that he was experiencing a rebirth that he hoped would last forever. His wife only smiled as he confided in her his latest and most powerful dream.

His heart quickened when the William Miner case crossed his desk. The initials WM left little doubt that the moment was at hand. He stepped into action with the energy of a young athlete primed for competition. He felt the drive of an angry bull and the enthusiasm of a teenager in love. His entire life had been a rehearsal, an elaborate preparation for the path that led to this crossing. He would not fail.

"This is the case. There is no other."

He said it to himself as he had at least a hundred times before. It became his mantra as well as his guiding philosophy. This time, however, he really meant it.

Chapter 4

THE MINER AFFAIR

"Good morning."

A faceless voice spoke, signifying normal routine. Nothing in her life had changed – nothing of significance.

Attorney Margaret Thomas was a strikingly beautiful woman beneath a staunch business-like demeanor. Years of practice could not obscure the attraction she held for the common lot of men. Her eyes brought out the worst in them. Rosy metaphors rolled from their tongues like idiot name tags stapled to their foreheads. It took years of practice to rise above. *Transcendence,* she thought.

While other women had always envied her for her appearance, dedicating much of their lives to the application and maintenance of outward beauty, Maggie had mastered the guise of sincerity. She yearned for the respect of a Barbara Walters or Margaret Mead. She succeeded beyond expectation.

"Good morning, beautiful."

Joseph Thomas walked in as if he owned the place. He did.

"Good morning, Mr. Thomas."

"I thought I'd check in to see if everything is in order before I resume my R & R."

"The Miner case?"

"Is there another?"

William Miner was a very important client. He was a man of great means and powerful influence. Maggie expected her father's visit. She handed him the brief.

JACK RANDOM

"We need a break," she said. "We've got more character witnesses than we can use. We can line them up from here to Vancouver. We have three witnesses of questionable character prepared to provide an alibi. Best-case scenario: It's a push. They either believe us or they believe the other side."

"Even odds?" His eyes avoided hers. He always attempted to shield his disappointment – never successfully.

"That's optimistic," she replied. The prosecutor's chief witness was an exemplary university student who had no apparent motive to lie.

He let his thoughts run their courses, gazing out the windows into a perpetual sea of gray, high above the city skyline. He sighed and turned to confront his daughter face to face.

"What do I tell him?"

"The truth," she said. The words echoed in the chambers of her mind. She was a slave to the truth. She was unable to deceive and unwilling to put a positive spin on what was clearly a disintegrating situation. She literally said what she meant and meant what she said. It served her well when defending an innocent client but was otherwise a liability and one she was working hard to rectify.

It seemed an eternity before her father spoke again in a tone of helpless resignation.

"Okay, Maggie."

He tossed his blessings and perhaps his forgiveness over his shoulder as he walked to the door. "I know you've done your best." He tried to smile as he turned back. "See you at dinner."

Thoughts raced through her mind in ever-expanding circles. Never before had she arrived at these crossroads. She had no way of knowing what to expect. She had always admired her father but she didn't know the limits of his code. She hoped she never would. The one thing she knew beyond all doubt was that the Miner case was far more important to him than it should have been. She reviewed the case from the basement up at least a dozen times.

William J. Miner was a very successful businessman with diversified interests: an import-export business, a financial firm, a gold mine in Nevada, holdings in platinum and uranium, a chain of restaurants and a great deal of real estate centered in the Pacific Northwest. He had engaged in more than a few shady business deals but this was new ground.

Sara Kent was a promising law student who took a part-time job at a Miner real estate operation to defray the cost her education. She chanced upon some damning information. It seemed Bill Miner had a habit of bribing local officials to obtain favorable outcomes on zoning decisions, government contracts, local ordinances or import fees – whatever he needed to gain an advantage over his competitors. What he spent on bribes he made up in tax evasion.

Incredibly, Ms. Kent not only blew the whistle, she provided the district attorney a complete case, including memos, correspondence, emails, bank statements, phone records and financial transactions. It was everything the DA needed minus the closing argument.

At first no one could believe that Ms. Kent was what she claimed to be but a team of highly motivated detectives could not shake her story or her background. She was a highly skilled, highly principled and exceptionally resourceful individual. As a result, William J. Miner was about to fall.

When Maggie drilled deep, she was not all that surprised. Bill Miner was a friend of her father. She knew and liked him but they were not near and dear. What really stunned her was her father's apparent involvement. His business interests were entwined with Miner's. If Miner fell the shock waves would run through the entire Northwest. To what extent it would affect her father she did not know. The best she could do now was to prepare and mitigate the fall-out. Unfortunately, she didn't have a clue as to where to begin.

Chapter 5

A NEW RECRUIT

Sara Kent tossed in her sleep. For several weeks now she had a recurring nightmare of being pursued by a shadowy figure. He chased her through tunnels of darkness, brief flashes of light moving her forward, stumbling and out of breath when she fell into the arms of her hero: a tall, handsome man with long flowing hair and the kindest eyes she had ever seen. Strengthened by his presence and the warmth of his arms around her, she turns to confront her pursuer only to recognize him as her own father. His face is frozen in horror. She slowly turns back to her hero, knowing that a transformation has taken place, and awakens in a cold, shivering sweat, gasping for air and paralyzed with fear.

Sara had come a long way from her rural, small-town community where she had once been vice president and secretary of the chess club. That was the most prestigious honor of her young life. Through the turbulent and stimulating years of the late sixties she watched from the grandstands of a little town that never advanced beyond the Rockwell image of the forties and fifties. She yearned for adventure. She wanted a part in the great drama beyond the white picket fence, the riveting history that was only a footnote in the local paper.

By the time she graduated high school she found nothing but traces and shadows of what might have been. The sixties were gone. The upheaval was swept away by a silent majority that wanted nothing more than to turn the clock back. She mourned the passage of time and the bitter twist of fate that released her from the prison of her childhood into a world only slightly more stimulating than the one she left behind.

To the dismay of her kind but uninspired parents, she rejected the local college and accepted a scholarship to Seattle University where she enrolled as a political science major. Within a semester she switched to business law and within a year she became what she had always held in lowest regard: self-centered, ego-driven and financially oriented with a strong drive for power and influence. The late sixties were dead and all but forgotten. The world of the nineties was all about money: independence through financial innovation. Self-sufficiency replaced self-sacrifice and a higher standard of living replaced a higher level of consciousness.

Welcome to the age of the ego and the deification of the self. A whole generation had fallen to gratuitous nihilism. Still, there were times when she recalled how it once was and how it might have been. There were times when she still had hope that the great pendulum of social consciousness would swing back once more.

That was when he entered her life. He was her hero, the white knight and the father figure of her dreams. A sage of the sixties, he had been a part of the history she so admired. He saw it all from the vantage point of direct engagement. He had traveled to Haight-Ashbury during the reign of the flower children. He was a leader in the Berkeley free speech movement. He dropped acid with Timothy Leary, smoked the magic weed with Jimi, Janis and the Dead. He shook hands with Jack Kerouac. He survived the communal movement. He went to Woodstock and drank from the cup of free love. He went to Selma and marched with the King. He cheered Abbie Hoffman and the Chicago Seven. He went to LA when a crazed gunman shot down Bobby and pronounced an end to the generation of hope.

He was everything she had ever dreamed of being and

she placed her trust in him completely.

"Jazz," he said with a smile that lit up a moonless night, a smile that knew the past and looked forward to a brighter future. "Jazz," he winked.

Plans were being laid.

Chapter 6

CIRCLE OF POWER

The jazzman was obsessed. Reborn with the kind of drive and energy that only a madman or a zealot possesses, he had undergone the transformation of a man who has found his calling. He no longer slept for rest. He slept only for the dreams that uplifted his spirit and guided his actions. He felt alive and he cherished every moment of every day. The plan was in motion.

The first element was to make a mark in the world of unfettered greed and avarice. He figured he was half there. He anticipated the urban migration from Seattle to its surrounding area well in advance of his competitors. He had observed the pattern in central California. The price of real estate in the greater San Francisco bay area rose so dramatically and so swiftly that it priced the working force out of the market. Longtime residents, unable to afford property taxes and rising mortgage payments, sold out and bought new homes at inflated prices within the ever-expanding reach of the daily commute. Real estate agencies secured zoning arrangements with local governments eager to cash in on the bonanza. The first wave hit Concord, Walnut Creek, Pleasanton and Dublin. The second washed over Tracy, Manteca, Patterson, Stockton and Modesto.

The army of commuter labor took root and grew in the fertile farmlands of the central California valley, ninety miles east of the bay.

Those who anticipated the sprawl and had the resources to capitalize made a killing by buying land at pre-migration prices and selling them at two to three times their investment. It was a virtual gold rush. Never mind that it displaced masses of the valley working class. Never mind that it initiated a decline in the American dream of home ownership. Never mind the loss of prime agricultural land. Fortunes were made. Mostly those who already possessed more than their share took advantage.

A handful of neophytes got in on the action before the window of opportunity closed and Roman Mason was among them. It would hardly qualify as a fortune but it was enough to buy a stake in the Pacific Northwest. Aside from a natural attraction, the Seattle area featured a relatively preserved landscape and still undeveloped sections of the rugged Washington coast. He recognized that the pattern of eastward expansion would soon develop here. Seattle was among the fastest growing cities in America and it was attracting capital.

He recognized early that his stiffest competition would come from the Japanese who were more than eager to invest their yen in American real estate. As a businessman, he welcomed the anti-Japanese propaganda and restrictive trade agreements that pushed back foreign investment. He celebrated when the yen and the Tokyo stock market took a hit.

Meantime, he bought land: Northbend, Cedar Falls and Monroe to the east; Buckley, Eatonville and Alder to the south; Shelton, Union and Belfair to the west. As the expansion reached his holdings, he sold and bought outward, multiplying his profit in a cozy, geometric pattern.

He became a force in the Great Northwest, a man to be regarded with respect. But it was hardly enough. For his plan to advance he needed to make a leap. It was no longer about money. He had already accumulated more than he could spend in a thousand years.

He was an intensely private man. He lived in a rustic wooden structure on the harsh north coast, a two-story lodging overlooking the Pacific at the Point of Arches just south of the Makah Indian Reservation at Cape Flattery – no more than twenty-five miles as the gull flies from Vancouver Island. Despite its size, immense compared to the modest dwellings of his Native American neighbors, it blended seamlessly with the landscape. It was the design as well as his influence that allowed him to build and settle here. The place was inaccessible by road and he promised to keep it that way.

He maintained a small fleet of helicopters, two of which were on the premises at all times. Without staff at his private abode, he took responsibility for maintenance as well as piloting the aircraft. The only other access, aside from a long hike across rocky and difficult terrain, was a modest boat ramp to which he tethered a small motorboat. The lack of access allowed him to feel safe despite minimal security measures.

He thrived on isolation. He envied the simple lifestyle of his neighbors. He loved the sense of oneness with the earth it afforded him on a daily basis. He felt a kinship with nature and all its creatures: the spotted owl, the gray wolf, the North American brown bear, the deer, the gull, the great humpback whale, the seal and the sea wolf.

The affection he harbored for animals was something he rarely felt for humankind. There were only a few with whom he shared his thoughts. The Makah were distrustful and generally stood at a distance whenever he approached. He managed to make a connection with an elder who lived apart from his tribe. Rumor held he was once a powerful medicine man, a shaman, in a previous life.

Once a month he visited the old man's secluded dwelling. He looked forward to it and treasured it. It allowed him to break out of an otherwise lonely existence.

He did not mind the loneliness. He embraced it as a young man embraces his first romance. He loved his life at the Point of Arches. He could manage all his business deals by computer transaction. His telecommunication system was linked by satellite to the information pipeline, giving him access to the world. He had no need to leave his private paradise. He was content.

He should have remained so, bidding the world adieu and living his life separate and alone, just as the old man of the Makah did. He would have enjoyed an occasional sojourn into the city of lights, a taste of jazz at his favorite haunt, perhaps an occasional romance, but for the most part he would have remained alone at his coastal retreat, alone with his thoughts, alone with his immense library and alone with his growing memoirs.

In time it was not enough. He had a need that was central to his being, a need to make a lasting mark and to write his page of history. His social consciousness was born in the late sixties. His generation wanted nothing short of fundamental, systemic and revolutionary change. He was determined to climb that mountain at last.

Jazz, baby, jazz.

Wealth and the wealthy had long fascinated him. His studies went back decades. First from the perspective of a student activist at UC Berkeley who had just read *Das Capital* and *The Wealth of Nations*, then from the markedly different view of a capitalist. Seduced by an opportunity that unfolded in his lap, he had joined the enemy. He became a part of the monster he and his revolutionary comrades had wanted so desperately to take down. He rationalized: To know the enemy you must become the enemy. Infiltration was a classic revolutionary tactic. But it no longer rang true. The movement was dead. The new age was something entirely separate and distinct. The sixties were dead; long live the sixties!

He often reflected on the days of glory. Like an acid flashback the images came without warning. They held to his subconscious like a midday shadow in a cloudless sky. The image that came to him now was that of Patty Hearst in her Simbianese Liberation Army guise. Was that how it happened? Was that when it first grabbed him? He could not tell. The events of his past fused, leaving no real sense of order or chronology. It no longer mattered.

He became intrigued with those who accumulated great wealth, especially those who did so without gathering attention. Their names were not listed in Forbes magazine or any other public accounting yet their holdings – in real estate, stocks, bonds, art, precious metals or other entities of value – were of the status of empires.

To some they were known as the illuminati. Beneath the shadows of obscurity, they were said to be an inner sanctum of immensely wealthy individuals intent on enslaving the planet with a New World Order. Others held they were the stakeholders of the military-intelligence-industrial complex that Dwight Eisenhower foreshadowed in his farewell address. Masters at concealing their wealth and influence with intricate chains of ownership and control, they seemed to operate separate from the flock. They were above the rules of trade and traditional business operations and for a time Rome longed to be one of them.

Once, while representing a multi-national corporation based in Los Angeles, he had an opportunity to meet Governor Ronald Reagan. He soon became convinced that the former actor destined to become president was incapable of anything greater than the most basic philosophical line of thought. He became even more cynical about the political system that would elevate him to the pinnacle of world power. He realized that the Reagan power circle did not include Reagan himself. The circle of power brokers managed him. They transformed his modest holdings into a fortune and provided the best political analysts, strategists, operatives, consultants, speechwriters and public relations specialists money could buy.

Reagan might have lived out his years as a cantankerous old actor in a Hollywood rest home. Instead the power circle invented an American hero. They controlled him as surely as the puppeteer controls the puppet.

The individuals who comprised that power circle interested him the most. Who were they? Who if anyone did they serve? The more he investigated the more illusive they became. Years of research uncovered little more than a short list of names shrouded in mystery. One of those names was William J. Miner whose financial empire was headquartered in Seattle.

Chapter 7

AN EMPIRE FALLS

Bill Miner was atypically early in arriving at the home of his friend Joe Thomas, his representative in legal affairs and head of a thriving Seattle law firm. Officially, he was there for dinner and friendly conversation. To those who knew him well he was Big Bill. By most accounts he was a decent man. Given his success in the merciless world of finance that alone was remarkable. Traditional business logic held that no one could reach his lofted position of power and influence so rapidly without cutting more than a few corners and stepping on a few heads. Until now Miner had appeared an exception.

In three generations the Miner Empire rose to become the monster of the Great Northwest. John W. Miner had set the wheels in motion, turning a Sierra Nevada gold mine from a bust to a major find. The grand patriarch did not trust the banks and so put all his holdings in gold and silver, secured in a secluded cave of granite. His associates thought him eccentric but when the Great Depression hit and the banks failed, they fell and he was left standing.

He soon recognized the opportunity at hand. He was in a position to buy controlling interest in major companies at rock bottom prices. Just as the prohibition would do for the Kennedy's and countless others, the depression elevated the Miners to the class of the nouveau rich.

John's oldest son, William Sr., multiplied the family fortune through a series of shrewd investments and corporate manipulations. William Jr. was responsible for an early and advantageous move into technology, thus securing the family's empire. In short, the Miners were major players in the money world.

On this night, however, Big Bill did not look like a major player. He was worried. He wore a scowl that could not hide the fear in his eyes. This was not a social gathering. Among the warning signs, it was not his lovely young wife who accompanied him to the Thomas household tonight. It was a business associate, Roman Mason.

Mason was a highly regarded consultant. Big Bill hired no one but the best. Striking a contrast to the general atmosphere of gloom, Mason was calm, icy calm, giving the appearance of emotional detachment. His specialty was damage control. He supervised the fall of titans and the demise of empires. His presence was an omen and a clear indication that all hope for a favorable legal disposition was fading like smoke in an autumn wind.

Joe Thomas greeted them at the door, wearing an artificial smile that did little to comfort his friend.

"Bill! Come on in! You're early."

"I thought we might have a private talk, Joe. This is Roman Mason. Maybe you've heard of him."

"I have indeed."

They shook hands, their eyes meeting intently, as if sharing a private understanding of what would follow.

"I know Mr. Mason by his impeccable reputation. Welcome to my home."

"The pleasure is mine. I only wish the circumstances were more conducive to friendly interaction."

Mr. Thomas led them to his private study and poured drinks around. Big Bill was a scotch man, straight up. He lit a Cuban and downed his drink in one gulp. Joe looked at Mason who remained stoic.

"Go easy, Bill. You've got to make it through dinner."

"To hell with dinner! Rome tells me it's a lost cause. A done deal! The only thing we can do now is cut our losses.

Cop a plea. Scrap the whole operation and start over!"

Joe gazed into his whiskey. The ice reminded him of Mason. He recalled the studies of subliminal imagery that revealed devilish and evil spirits the ice of alcoholic beverages.

"Is that your conclusion, Mr. Mason?"

"I'm afraid it is. At this juncture it would be in Mr. Miner's best interest to negotiate a settlement – unless of course you have some new information that would offer a reason to believe we would stand a chance in court."

Joe Thomas walked calmly around his executive redwood desk. Sitting in his plush leather swivel chair he took a stiff drink before he spoke to his old friend.

"I guess that's a vote of no confidence."

Miner's spirit dropped like a stone from a tall building. His heart rose to his throat, his gaze downward and his despair palpable. He cleared his throat and grumbled in a tone just barely decipherable: "You've no idea."

His collapse touched Joe deeply, pushing him beyond the scope of common words. They went way back. In many ways, Bill Miner made him what he was. As a young attorney he had successfully pressed a lawsuit against one of Miner's companies. Big Bill inexplicably took a liking to him, picked him up and sponsored him in putting together his own firm. He owed everything to Bill Miner.

Now it seemed his old friend was at the end of his rope and there was nothing he could do to save him. For the first time since this drama began, he sensed the inevitable end. It was a strange sensation.

Bill Miner would not spend a day in confinement. He would not live without the comforts of his elite lifestyle. His personal wealth would not be threatened. His punishment was the end of his empire, his loss of prestige and personal pride. Until it happened he didn't know how much it meant to him. It was his bloodline. It was the legacy of his great, great grandfather. It was his obligation to his children and grandchildren.

Big Bill excused himself from dinner early. He drank too much and needed to lie down in his own bed. Not even Maggie, for whom he had a special affection, could lift his spirits. They discussed the case and the possibilities of a settlement. It would cost him. He accepted it. But he appeared resigned to his course of action. He was convinced that someone was behind it. Sara Kent could not have acted alone. He was certain of that much but time was running out.

Chapter 8

CRASH IN B MINOR

On a cold September night, near the witching hour, the north wind whispered sweet melodies to a yellow moon, a lone wolf howled in the sacred moonlight and the sound of laughter was heard by the sea mammals at the Point of Arches.

The jazzman sent a message via email to a small army of freedom fighters:

The emperor is fallen! Long live the empire! Long live freedom! CRASH! in B minor! – Jazz.

Having tapped William Miner's email account without his knowledge or consent, the jazzman recorded the following interactions.

SUBJECT: Miner.
MESSAGE: Sell, sell, sell!
SOURCE: Encrypted, Seattle.
RESPONSE: Access denied.
RECEIVER: Encrypted, Laguna Beach, CA.

It was not difficult to decipher the meaning. "Sell!" meant the tycoon had been sold out. His stock would soon fall hard and fast. Investors would be wise to get out now. "Access denied." meant it was a done deal. Negotiations were closed. The long reign of Big Bill Miner as a lynchpin of the Pacific Northwest financial empire had come to an abrupt halt. Whatever his role in the greater power structure, his power and influence had dried like a shallow pond in the

Sahara desert.

The jazzman smiled at how easily he accomplished his objective. "Too easy," he said aloud. Miner must have been further removed from the circle of real power than he imagined. Either that or he was too close. He could not tell. He needed a great deal more information. He needed to uncover the source and receiver of these messages. He needed to identify the players.

As he mulled over the possibilities to the tune of Charlie Parker's ingenious sax, he was startled to see a new message appear on his computer screen:

SUBJECT: Miner.
MESSAGE: Dear friends and family, I have let you down. I have let myself down. I'm sorry. Bill.
SOURCE: Encrypted, Laguna Beach.

While easily interpreted, this message was more difficult to absorb. Someone was placing it in Miner's personal emails to be read by the detectives who would investigate his untimely death. Those who had gathered at the Thomas household would confirm that Miner was despondent that night. Friends and family might protest but the case would be open and shut: Suicide.

The person or persons responsible for this message were without doubt also responsible for his death. It was already too late to alter the chain of events. They left no window of opportunity between the message and the deed. They were as cautious as they were deadly. That much was certain. But why had they taken such a drastic measure? Were they afraid that Miner would turn informant? It seemed unlikely. Bill Miner lived by the code: Honor among thieves. His friends and partners counted him as loyal to a fault.

Charlie Parker played on, a soulful strain of melodic and anti-melodic tones. Charlie Parker played and the jazzman mourned the fall of an enemy. He envisioned the crime: The big man rising from his leather swivel chair in the study of his palatial mansion, pouring himself one last drink, gulping it down before stumbling down the hall and crawling into bed beside his beautiful young wife. She would pretend to be asleep as she always did when her husband had too much to drink. In the morning, she would notice the coldness of his skin. She would speak to him, shake him and try to stir him but he would not awaken.

Why? he wondered. He tossed it around, over and over, through and through, as if the answer held the key to his long-suffering soul. He wandered as a blind man in a foreign environment until he found himself gazing at a reflection of the moon in the waters off the Point of Arches. It came to him with a thud. This was a warning. It had to be. It had nothing to do with loyalty or mistrust. Miner was the victim but he was not the target. He was.

They were on to him. They didn't know who he was but they knew how to deliver a message. He had taken the necessary precautions. Even the most sophisticated system could not trace his hack beyond the web of satellite connections. They knew he was out there. They had detected his presence and they were warning him: This is the consequence of your meddling. The blood of Big Bill Miner is on your hands.

If they wanted to back him down or weaken his resolve they had miscalculated. It had the opposite effect. He now knew his enemy was both cunning and ruthless. They didn't know who they were dealing with. They thought he was a rival businessman, not a warrior on a cause. Their move was calculated so that the risk of further action far outweighed any potential profit. A simple businessman wouldn't hesitate to withdraw.

But he was not a simple businessman. Their arrogant disregard for life and the warped values they demonstrated enraged and motivated him. He would respond in kind. They had shown their colors and the hideous nature of their

39

being. Now he would show his.

He sat down to his computer and typed a simple message: *The Gods must fall! Jazzman.*

With the stroke of a few keys it was loaded with a short-fused trigger and sent to Miner's computer. The enemy would have an opportunity to read it seconds before it disappeared. They would be unable to trace it. Within moments every bit of information stored on Miner's system, including the fake suicide note would vanish.

There was no defense against the jazzman's virus. It had never been used before. It seemed there would be an investigation after all.

Chapter 9

SONG OF THE WIND

The long hike to the old man's hut was invigorating. Like an old fisherman he arose with the sun to admire a brilliant northern Pacific sunrise. He took in the fresh saltwater air and set out on foot up the rugged coastline. The hike would consume most of the day. He would find his pace and struggle to free himself of all thought. He wanted to be aware only of his immediate surroundings, the smell of the pines, the ocean wind, the gulls flying overhead.

He had only begun to master the skill that the old one assured him would come with time. Today the task was more difficult than usual.

The old one's name translated to Song of the Wind for it was said his voice could be heard in the wind through the tall pines. He christened his wide-eyed visitor: White Man who Lives Apart and Thinks Deeply. A deep bond grew and strengthened between them.

Rome saw him as a father figure, a mentor, guide and purveyor of wisdom. He was everything hc would have wanted in his own father, a good man who was always too busy to spend time with his son. He came to depend on the old man for spiritual guidance.

Their first encounter mystified him. On his way back from a visit to the Makah reservation he stopped to savor a rainbow sunset. The moon was full and he was enchanted. The red and purple glow of the descending sun diving into the calm rhythmic waves of the ocean gradually gave way to a silver glow of moonlight. He sat motionless on a rocky overhang, aware of all around him but conscious only of breathing. He'd never felt more at one with the earth. He remained there for hours, scarcely moving a muscle except to gaze at the heavens. He sensed something imminent. Something indefinable rose up within him to announce that an event of great importance was about to occur. A loud caw shattered his glow of enchantment and a crow appeared in the white of the moon.

He did not know the way of the forest yet he knew by instinct this was an extraordinary creature. The crow is not by nature a nocturnal bird nor is it capable of graceful flight under normal circumstance but this magnificent bird appeared to hover in the moonlight with a thunderous clapping of its wings. In the blink of an eye it vanished.

As he searched the skies he heard another caw directly behind him. Gales of laughter followed as he turned to view the moonlit face of the old one, deeply wrinkled and with a broad, knowing smile.

The old man invited him to spend the night at his simple shelter, nestled in the pines not more than a hundred yards from where he sat gazing at the sunset. He had hiked this trail at least a dozen times and never caught the slightest glimpse of its existence. That night his life changed and his spirit became entwined with that of the old Indian.

"My friend the crow told me you would cross my path this day."

Rome smiled. "Your friend the crow is very wise."

"His eyes are open."

"His eyes are your eyes, my friend."

Song of the Wind smiled that wide smile that spoke a thousand thoughts of true knowledge – the knowledge that exists beneath and above the surface of all things. The white man was only beginning to understand.

The old one did not rise to greet his new friend. He remained seated Indian fashion on his rust red and brown woven blanket, spread out on a bed of pine needles outside his hut. With a tilt of his head he signaled the white man to sit beside him. The view was breathtaking, a harmonious balance of land, sea and sky. They sat for a long time without words to break the spell. Rome would learn it was the old one's way. At length, when he finally gave up trying to formulate his thoughts, the Indian spoke.

"A man with sorrow's eyes spoke to me. He said: *I have been to the mountaintop. I have seen the rings of power. They appeared before me, one after another, forming circles to the stars. They called to me and I traveled through them on the wings of my spirit being. As many as I left behind that many appeared before me, without end, until I could go no further. It was then that I heard the voice of our fathers and our father's fathers. It said: You have been to the mountaintop and seen the rings of power. Return now to your people and tell them what you have seen that they might continue the journey.*

"He did as he was told. He returned to his people and told them about the rings of power. Then he left to seek new mountaintops, those of his own making."

That was the end of Rome's vision. It would be a long, long time before he understood its meaning. But he did not doubt even for a moment that understanding would come.

Chapter 10

OLYMPIC REALTY

Sara Kent's life changed the night she logged on to the university law library's massive computer information system. She was startled to find a message waiting for her.

"We'd love to change the world but we don't know what to do. Jazzman."

Somebody had gone to a great deal of difficulty not only to contact her anonymously but also to uncover who she was and what moved her. The message was a reference to an old song by Graham Nash. It was a song she knew well and felt deeply – at least she had at one time.

The message contained a warning that this and any further communications should be erased within minutes or a virus would be released that would utterly destroy all files in the library system. An attempt to save the message to disk would have the same result. She decided against testing the warning's validity and resisted her impulse to report the message to the authorities. It intrigued her.

She received a series of messages from the same mysterious source in the following weeks, culminating with detailed instructions for gathering information to be used in an indictment of William Miner. The jazzman submitted that such a blow was a necessary step to bringing down what he called "the rings of power."

In the last year of law school, her complicity in collecting incriminating evidence against her employer came with great risk. It certainly threatened a promising career. Even the most scrupulous firms would hesitate to hire her now. Such firms were rare as diamonds on a public beach.

Still, she pressed on. She possessed a mind for the law, an innate understanding of how the system worked and how it could be exploited for justice or injustice. She considered it a form of chess: the pieces moved in predictable ways and the player who could envision the possibilities would almost inevitably win. She remained confident that her value as an attorney would overcome any doubts an employer might harbor.

Her optimism was validated when she was offered a position with a firm representing a conglomeration of business interests immediately upon graduation. She was assigned to a thriving company specializing in real estate. Olympic Realty was everything she could hope for: interesting and varied work in a comfortable and supportive atmosphere of like-minded individuals. Her salary far exceeded her expectations.

It seemed at last that the scattered pieces of her life were falling into place, bringing together the adventurous and idealistic spirit of her youth with the sophistication and professionalism of her career. She felt alive and carried a golden glow of energy and warmth with every step she took.

That golden glow caught the attention and captured the interest of Jake Marshall. He had engaged her services in researching and summarizing the laws and regulations governing land use and ownership on the Olympic Peninsula. She dove in headfirst. To complete the assignment she had to study not only public land use policy but also the regulations governing the Bureau of Indian Affairs and the separate treaties of the Squaxin, the Quinalt, the Hoh, the Quillayute, the Ozette, the Makah, the Skokomish and other tribes that claimed the peninsula as their home.

Mr. Marshall explained that his client, an emerging real estate baron, had two objectives: First, he wanted to uncover opportunities for investment and, second, he wanted to protect the tribes from investors less scrupulous than himself

– most prominently, the Japanese.

Sara engaged the client but retained a healthy skepticism. She would have no part of any business venture that exploited Native Americans. She reserved the right to refuse any assignment that compromised her values or offended her sense of fair play. She left it up to Jake Marshall to secure her trust, to convince her beyond doubt that his client's intention was to uphold and protect the interests of the tribes. If she caught wind of any exploitation or double-dealing, she warned him that she would switch sides in a Manhattan minute.

He laid out his client's strategy. The pattern of urban expansion was set in concrete. The growth rate of the greater Seattle-Tacoma area was phenomenal. Expansion in a north-south direction along interstate five had already reached capacity. The ninety-mile stretch from Olympia to Everett was solid development. The eastward migration had begun in earnest but would eventually be halted by the Cascade Mountains. The Olympic Range on the peninsula side would present a similar barrier but further incursion was inevitable. It was only a matter of when, how and how much. His client foresaw a suspension bridge over Puget Sound. Inevitably, urbanization would come to Olympic Peninsula.

Japanese presence throughout the Northwest had already become pervasive. The mega-corporations of the Tokyo Stock Exchange – Mitsubishi, Sony, Honda, Samsung and Sansui – had staked their claim. They owned the Seattle Mariners, the major league baseball franchise. Their ties to the locals, the land or its natives were shallow at best. Their expansion would be restricted only by strict enforcement of government regulations.

Olympic Realty's strategy was to buy or lease long-term available properties at a reasonable price on the one hand and to hold back the cash-rich Japanese on the other. Sara would be their expert on the Olympic Peninsula. She would be given a free hand in representing tribal interests. She would join a controlled development team to devise plans for environmentally sound communities with controlled growth. To be sure, no growth on the peninsula would be ideal but that would not be sustainable. Limited growth, controlled by individuals who cared about the land and the people who inhabited it for a thousand years, was the best the modern world could hope for.

Sara drilled deep into Jake's warm brown eyes and sensed her guard dropping. The professional persona that allowed her to do business over a candlelit dinner with an attractive if older gentleman was gradually slipping away. She lowered her gaze, sipped her wine and recovered her demeanor. This was a new experience.

Jake smiled instinctively and in a manner that suggested more than strictly business. He sensed that he was finally making progress. He was winning her trust. He chose his words carefully, knowing that they came at a critical time. Reaching across the table, he gently lowered his hand on hers and recaptured her soft brown eyes.

"Sara," he said just above a whisper, as if addressing royalty or an enchantress, "I've told you all I know. I've been as open and candid as I know how. What more can I say or do to assure you?"

She wanted to take hold of his hand. She wanted to give her warmth to him and allow his to warm her soul but she held back. Too often in her life she had been too quick to trust. Too often she had been betrayed. She couldn't help feeling that Jake's generation, the generation of hope and enlightenment, had betrayed her by holding forth the promise of a brighter world only to see it crumble and fold with the swiftness of an assassin's bullet. She felt betrayed by her father as well when he left her mother for a younger woman as soon as Sara left their home. She had not been able to forgive him.

She withdrew her hand, leaned back and took account.

"I want to believe you, Jake. If it's everything you say it

is, I'd like to be a part of it. But I can't take your word for it. I want to meet your client face to face. If I'm going to dive in, I want the personal assurance of your boss."

He leaned back and bit his lower lip. Only a moment ago he thought this could be avoided. Now he realized it was the only way but the way was blocked.

"I wish I could arrange that, Sara. I do."

He sighed as if to inform her how difficult this was and observed the disappointment on her face. He was losing her and feared he would not be able to win her back.

"He's a very private man. The fact is: I don't meet with him myself."

"I respect that," she replied in resignation. "I value my own privacy. But I don't think I'm being unreasonable. He doesn't have to make a public appearance. I just want to look into his eyes and get a sense of the man's character. I have my own interests to consider."

"I understand," he said sincerely. He had wrestled with the same question before he gave in. "Look, he said to tell you, if it came to this, that he'd like nothing more than to meet you someday. He admires what you've done and thinks the world of you. We all do. Still, he can't meet with you now. Not yet."

Sara instinctively recoiled. She could conceive no honorable reason for this level of secrecy. She could think of several dishonorable reasons. She stood to leave.

"I'm sorry he feels that way."

As he helped her with her coat, he played his last card, whispering in her ear, "Jazz."

It stopped her cold, as if a light clicked on and all the pieces suddenly fell into place. Now she understood why they had given her an interview so easily, why the terms were so ideal and why everyone at Olympic Realty had treated her so well. The entire process was a formality. They wanted her. They targeted her. She smiled when she recalled that a portrait of Lady Day adorned the wall of her prospective office. She loved Billie Holliday. Now she knew why she felt so comfortable and at home. These were her people and the common thread was jazz. The mysterious jazzman had orchestrated it all.

"Why didn't you just say so?" she smiled.

He returned her smile and helped her to remove her coat. They sat back down and enjoyed the evening. She wanted to know more and she wanted to know now but it would have to wait. Everything would have to wait.

Everything in time.

Chapter 11

THE YOUNG WIDOW

Margaret Thomas was no more convinced of the Bill Miner suicide theory than she was by the single gunman theory of the Kennedy assassination. The facts did not fit. First and foremost in her mind, Miner was a survivor. He was famous for it. When everything around him turned to mush he stood strong. He had survived the death of his first wife, who he loved dearly, and weathered the storms of a dozen financial crises. When everyone else scrambled for cover, he held his ground. It was not conceivable that he would cash it all in no matter how bad the circumstances.

The autopsy revealed traces of strychnine in the bloodstream. The coroner surmised he had ingested the poison with the massive quantities of alcohol he consumed that night. Scotch con muerta. Not a novel trick but neither was it a pleasant way to go.

The police initially suspected the family. In addition to his wife of four years, the victim left behind two sons and a daughter who ranged from their mid-twenties to thirties. His first wife and the mother of his children died tragically of breast cancer. While all of the survivors were well provided for in Miner's will, each stood to gain a great deal upon his death. While he lived the patriarch wanted the family fortune to remain intact. After his death most of his wealth would be distributed among these four. A sizable amount was set aside for Miner's favorite charities.

In short, while all had some degree of motive none of the children seem to have the inclination.

Cheryl Miner, the young widow, was an actress, a model and a sometime receptionist at twenty-seven, the wife of a multi-millionaire at twenty-eight, and the wealthiest widow in the Great Northwest at thirty-two. *Free at last. Free at last. Great God Almighty, she was free at last!* She alone was a natural suspect. She had the most to gain, the least to lose and, unlike the others, she had a clear opportunity. The police pressed her but after three interviews they decided she was incapable of planning and executing a homicide of this nature. By all appearances, she was the prototypical blonde and the police were inclined to accept the generalization.

Maggie Thomas was not so sure. She made an appointment with the young widow soon after the funeral on the pretense of cleaning up some legal business. As it happened, Roman Mason was leaving just as she arrived. She was pleasantly surprised.

"Damage control, Mr. Mason?"

"Life goes on, Ms. Thomas. I wouldn't make too much of it."

"Actually, I wanted to see you. I intended to call."

"Really? Any particular subject?"

"The same subject: Bill Miner."

Mason pulled out his appointment book and drew a line through an entry. "How's three thirty at my office?" He handed her his card.

"That would be fine. I appreciate your making time."

"My pleasure. As a matter of fact, I expected you to call. You're not the kind to leave things unresolved."

"Is it unresolved?" she smiled.

He returned her smile before his face yielded to an expression of genuine concern.

"She's in the bedroom," he said as he pointed upstairs and turned to make his exit.

Maggie raised her brows in mock disbelief.

"She's been there since the funeral," he said.

He took a moment to admire Maggie's finer qualities, her

51

style and form. In some ways, he thought, they were very much alike.

"Good luck, Ms. Thomas."

She moved to the windows and watched him depart. She waved when he looked back. It was an astonishing exchange of thoughts. Rome Mason had nearly been candid. That was a first. He had always been a rock, an iceberg, a stone-faced monolith. On the many occasions she had observed him not once had she been able to determine what he was thinking. She felt a curious attraction that she quickly tucked away. She looked forward to their meeting for more than strictly business reasons but she did not quite understand why. He wasn't her type. Then again, what was her type?

She shifted her thoughts and climbed the broad staircase that circled above a magnificent ballroom with lush, modern furnishing. She had observed a transition from Victorian to modern since the arrival of the new bride. She didn't know and never asked if the change was motivated by Cheryl's taste or Big Bill's desire to leave the past behind. They appeared reasonably happy together.

Miner hired Cheryl as a part-time receptionist a brief eight months before the wedding bells – two years after the passing of his first wife. She soon began accompanying him to formal dinners and social gatherings. There were the usual rumors of gold digging but Maggie never paid attention to gossip. The elite were always suspicious of those who joined their ranks without a pedigree. Cheryl was not particularly extravagant and if she was unhappy with her marriage she kept it to herself. She had sacrificed her interests in acting and modeling soon after the wedding, keeping herself busy with theater parties, benefits and social affairs. The plain and simple fact was: Bill Miner adored her.

It was almost noon yet when Maggie came to the open door of the master bedroom, she found Cheryl in her nightgown. Despite her disheveled appearance she remained extremely attractive. She reminded Maggie of a high school cheerleader, fun loving, carefree and without a serious thought. Scattered on and around the bed were half empty bags of chips, pizza boxes, popcorn, magazines and discarded wrapping. The television blaring in quadraphonic sound, Maggie signaled her presence with a loud knock. Clearly startled, Cheryl pulled the sheets around her before she recognized a familiar face. Maggie shook her head, partly in amusement and partly in dismay.

"Mr. Mason let me in," she announced. "If you'll recall, we had an appointment."

"Sorry, Maggie. I've forgotten a lot lately. In fact, I've forgotten everything."

"It's been two weeks, Cheryl. It's about time you pulled yourself together."

Disappointment registered on Cheryl's pretty face and Maggie regretted saying the obvious.

"I know, Maggie. I will. It's just that I didn't realize how much I depended on Bill. I don't have many friends on my own, you know."

Maggie did know. It never occurred to her that Cheryl wanted friends independent of her marriage. She'd seemed more of an appendage than a fully functioning human being.

"As soon as you get out of bed and start answering the phone, you'll have more friends than you could ever need."

She cleared the debris and sat at the foot of the bed. For the first time since the funeral, she felt sorry for the young widow. At thirty-two years of age, she seemed little more than a child. She possessed that innocent charm that made men want to take care of her. Her little-girl smile melted away any lingering suspicions Maggie may have harbored.

"That's what I'm afraid of," said Cheryl with half a smile.

Maggie felt a sudden urge to hold her and comfort her. She wanted to reassure her that their relationship was that of friends. Cheryl looked into Maggie's eyes and sighed.

"I wish I could be like you, Maggie."

She received the compliment as best she could. Cheryl's candor disarmed her. The last thing she anticipated was a heart to heart exchange.

"Be happy with who you are, Cheryl. Most of the women I know spend their whole lives trying to be exactly like you. You're young, rich and beautiful. I have a suspicion you're talented as well. The world is opening its doors to you. You can do anything you want."

"No, I can't. I can't be Maggie Thomas, the brilliant attorney who can hold her own in a man's world. I can't do that."

Maggie shook her head and smiled. She was normally immune to flattery but she enjoyed it coming from Cheryl. She wondered if there was more to the young widow than she imagined. She thought it possible they could be friends after all.

"Do you jog?" she asked.

"I could learn."

"It's not something you learn. It's something you do. I'll pick you up tomorrow at six thirty."

"Gee, I'll see if I can fit it in."

Maggie studied her for any cracks in the façade. She wondered if Miner had really known and fully appreciated his young wife. She was a fascinating character, her eyes sparkling with inner joy and excitement. Her off-key sense of humor was delightful.

"By the way," said Maggie, "what *was* Mr. Mason doing here anyway?"

"He wanted to look around Bill's office just in case the police missed something."

"Would you mind if I did the same?"

"Not at all."

"There are a few things I'd like to clear up."

"Anything I can do to help."

Maggie started out but held back at the door. She hesitated to show her hand but she decided to place her trust in this woman.

"Do *you* think it was suicide?"

Cheryl bit her lip and directed her gaze downward. It was a question she had been asked repeatedly and one she had considered. She knew the rumors and understood the wrong answer could place her in jeopardy.

"The police say it was."

"But what do you think?"

She wanted to be honest and candid with Maggie and so she discarded her doubts and cautions.

"Bill wasn't afraid of anyone or anything. He wouldn't have left me alone."

Maggie looked into the soul of Cheryl Miner and knew she was telling the truth.

"See you tomorrow."

She turned and walked down the hall to Bill Miner's office. She glanced around the familiar room and went directly to the computer on his desk. She started it up and opened a file labeled "Business Correspondence." She noticed something curious. Her office had been in constant communication with Miner, at least three or four times a day for several weeks, yet there was no record of any such communication for the two days preceding his death. It seemed certain that someone had erased them. The only message that survived the expungement was one from an unknown source. It read: *The Gods must fall. Jazzman.*

Something was clearly wrong. The message stuck out like a red winged dove. She recalled her interview with Detective Jones. At its conclusion, he asked her if the name "jazzman" meant anything to her. Facetiously, she had replied, "W.C. Handy." Now she understood.

Whoever this jazzman was, it seemed he was being framed for a murder he did not commit. It appeared the cops were being sly with their finding of suicide. They didn't want to alert their prime suspect. If they uncovered his identity, he would probably be booked for homicide. She would take it upon herself to discover his identity and contact him before the authorities did. What he knew could lead to the real killer. It was the breakthrough she needed to spur her to action.

Chapter 12

DOUBLE CROSS

Rome lay in a hammock on his front porch overlooking the coast, his legs crossed at the ankles, hand behind his head, swinging slowly to the rhythm of Lady Day's Strange Fruit. A storm was starting up in the distance.

The news was bad. Very bad. His cover was blown. Until he rectified the situation, his primary means of gathering information over the internet was cut off. To make matters worse, he was being sought for questioning by the Seattle Police. It seemed probable he was the prime suspect in the murder of Bill Miner.

Worse still, it seemed possible if not likely that Bill Miner had been an ally, not an enemy. In the wake of his death it came to light that one of his endowments was to the Makah reservation. Somehow Miner had connected him to the tribe and wanted to warn him. It seemed possible he wanted to contact him. Maybe he held key information to aid the cause. It all seemed far-fetched but what other explanation could there be?

He surmised that Miner had somehow detected his presence when he was monitoring Miner's communications. He may have wanted to signal his intentions but someone else was listening in as well. The endowment to the Makah was one way of announcing his allegiance in the event of his death. If that was the case, his attempt to contact an insurance magnate in Laguna Beach was his way of marking a trail. It also sealed his fate.

Rome pondered the words of his Indian friend. They

came to him, as they often did, as if channeled from a higher source: *On the path of righteousness the good of heart will fall. The warrior must struggle on. He must not look back until he stands upon the mountaintop and tells what he has learned.*

He came to the conclusion that his adversaries, whoever they were, had used him to attack their own enemy from within. He would not look back but he would take greater caution. He now knew the danger the enemy posed. He would have to learn more. The lords of power are cunning. Like the shape shifter he would become even more so. He would pierce the circles of deception surrounding and protecting them like clouds of ocean mist. He would deceive the deceivers. He would become one of them and he would strike at their very heart.

He had a new name: Edward Kramer of Laguna Beach. With his extensive insurance interests, he was vulnerable. While catastrophic fires in southern California spared his oceanside estate, an estimated $750 million price tag on insurance claims put a substantial dent in his net worth. The companies would eventually absorb the cost but in the meantime his standing in the business world took a hit. It was the precise condition that made Bill Miner vulnerable. Kramer, unlike Miner, had no reputation for fairness or integrity. There was no chance that he was a secret ally. Given the right kind of persuasion, however, he might give up what he knew or who he knew, adding yet another name or two to the lords of power and avarice.

Given the circumstances it was entirely possible if not probable that Kramer would be replaced in the organizational structure. Rome needed to be in a position to observe the transition. Clearly, he could no longer trust either the phone or the internet without greater security measures.

He was reasonably sure his adversaries knew that he and his friends were mounting an attack. The whole Kramer situation might be a setup. It was a risk he was willing to take.   He contacted his good friend and skilled detective Jimmy Longbow to arrange surveillance of Kramer's estate.

Meantime, he targeted one of Kramer's insurance companies and began buying stock at an increasing rate.   It would raise an alarm.   Kramer would assume that someone was making a play.   Raise the pressure and something has to give.   He would ask for a meeting, bringing his people into direct contact with Rome's people.   They would gain access to his business connections.

Neither Kramer nor his superiors would ever suspect that Rome Mason was the jazzman.   As far as they knew, he was one of them: a player in the world of finance.   As far as they were concerned, he was only interested in money and the power it bought.   Individuals of great wealth did not engage in radical politics.   It was inconceivable.   Indeed, it was the perfect disguise.   Jazz.

Chapter 13

AN UNEASY ALLIANCE

All the years of carefully planned obscuration of her physical attributes could not hide the fact that Maggie Thomas possessed a body that rivaled the Madonna and a face that reminded of Liz Taylor. It did not escape the eye of anyone in her sphere, certainly not the discerning eye of Roman Mason as he engaged her in a discussion of the Miner case. She wondered who had access to the dead man's office in the hours after his death. Someone had altered his files. The suspicious nature of her inquiry was obvious.

"Come on, Maggie. You don't need to be in his office. You only need access to the internet, the appropriate software and the knowledge to crack the system."

Her face wrinkled with doubt. The web was still in its early stages of development and her knowledge of its vulnerabilities was limited.

"You can do that?" she wondered.

"Absolutely."

"You can erase selected files and create new ones over the internet?"

"Of course."

He could see that she remained skeptical. He would have to educate her. This was an area of expertise.

"In this case, I think it's more likely the hacker erased everything. He or she or they reloaded the files from a backup. Unfortunately for them, Miner hadn't bothered to back up his files for a couple of days. That's why there's a gap between the everyday communications and the last message."

"The jazzman message?"

"That's right. It's an obvious fake."

"Why jazzman?" she wondered.

"Who knows? It's a tagline or an internet identity. It might be a group of people."

"Whoever he or she or they are, they know more than we do at the moment. I'm planning to hire a detective to find out who we're dealing with."

"I'll make inquiries on my own," he said. "If I find out anything, I'll let you know."

"Good."

Rome took note: she did not reciprocate. She gave no ground. He would have to try harder if he intended to form any sort of bond with her. He decided to bait her.

"What about Sara Kent?"

"What about her?"

"Is she a suspect?"

"She's on the list."

"Who else is on the list?"

"The widow, of course."

"You don't think she did it."

"I don't. No."

Maggie hesitated. She straightened papers on her desk and glanced at his face. It was clear he expected another name, a familiar one. She gave it to him.

"And you, of course."

Rome smiled. He liked the way her mind worked. She considered all angles before she spoke. She would not have added his name to the list if she believed it.

"Fair enough," he replied. "What about Joe Thomas?"

Turnabout is fair play. Maggie sighed. Her father had been less than enthusiastic about pursuing the investigation. Miner was a close friend, a partner and confidant. His hesitation was curious. He clearly knew more than he was saying. She believed it was for the family's protection but she didn't know why and she couldn't be sure. Her father was on the list.

"Fair enough," she conceded.

Rome wrapped up the discussion as Maggie rose to take her leave. "We'll pool our resources and see what we can uncover." He stopped her at the door with a stern voice that he hoped conveyed his concern.

"Maggie," he said, his eyes drilling into hers, "be careful. We're on shifting ground. It could get dangerous."

For the first time she sensed his sincerity and the depth of his feelings. It was more than professional courtesy. It was more than respect for a colleague. It was personal and from the heart. She nodded her acknowledgement and departed.

He called her later just to chat. When she became impatient, he admitted that the real purpose of his call was to ask her to dinner. She told him she was very busy, it was a bad time and it would have to wait.

"It's just dinner, Maggie," he said. "You have to eat."

She told him she would think about it.

"Sometimes it's best not to think at all."

Indeed. It was her policy not to become involved with anyone in her professional circles but, frankly, it was a policy that didn't leave a lot of prospects. She accepted against her better judgment.

Rome smiled and sensed the importance of the moment. It would be the beginning of a most interesting relationship.

Chapter 14

LUCKY IN LOVE

From the moment they met Jake and Sara felt a powerful connection. The jazzman revelation was like a break in a floodwall. What began as a crack, imperceptible to the common eye, grew and widened until the full depth of Sara's emotions, long contained to protect her image, came spilling forth. It would not be denied.

The first time they shook hands she felt an electrical charge, a tingling sensation that started at the base of her spine and flowed outward to the palms of her hands and the soles of her feet, traversing all territories, crossing all boundaries and crying out for more. She wanted him as much as he wanted her.

Jake Marshall was a lucky man – lucky in business and now, lucky in love. He was the kind of man people wanted to be around. In his mid forties, he was single and had been most of his life. An early marriage lasted less than a year. As a result he did not trust long-term relationships. It might have been his upbringing. His parents stayed together just long enough to see him through high school. If they were ever in love, Jake did not witness it. He had more than his share of relationships but nothing that endured.

His connection with Rome Mason went way back. They grew up in the same central California town, went to Berkeley to join the revolution in the late sixties and eventually gravitated to the Pacific Northwest. A self-taught attorney and a shrewd businessman, his lifestyle was more than comfortable. He had an apartment on the coast and another in the city. The dual residency suited him. He enjoyed the best of both worlds and he loved jazz.

It did not take long for Jake to recognize the impact his relationship with Sara would have. He felt it at first glance. He knew – if only they could overcome her initial hesitation – she would be his second wife. Only this time it would last a lifetime. Once they gave themselves over, nothing could stop it. The attraction was so strong it would take a monumental break to pry them apart. Jake was a man who did not hesitate to place a bet when he liked the odds.

When he offered to drive her home that cold and rainy night, she accepted without hesitation. When she asked him in for a nightcap he did not wonder. When she put Coltrane on the stereo and offered a glass of zinfandel, he smiled and the walls came tumbling down.

They would never know who made the first move. They could only say they never touched their wine. They only recalled being wrapped in each other's arms, engulfed in a feeling of liquid warmth. They only knew that the floodwall of longing and unbridled passion broke wide open, releasing them into a world of erotic awe that neither had known before this moment.

Stripped of hidden agendas and ulterior motives, they found themselves naked and free to act on purest instinct. Sara's honey colored flesh, delicate but firm breasts and perfectly proportioned hips appeared to glow in the soft light of her bedroom. He appeared to her as a god, towering above her, his full chest tense, abdomen heaving, alive and pulsing with desire.

They became as one, floating on waves of ecstasy, further and further from the world of earthly concerns, to the land of dreams where all is rhythm and harmony. As Sara arched her back, like a bow coiled for release, Jake released a gasp, pleasure and pain, sealing their sacred bond for eternity. Coltrane orchestrated a soulful background as they regained human consciousness and melted into each other's arms once more. They would never forget this sensation. They were floating on the edge of existence.

Exquisite, lovely and heavenly jazz.

Chapter 15

THE TRACKER

Jimmy Longbow sat at the bar, sipping a non-alcoholic beer, admiring the dancer's poise. He could tell a lot by the way she moved her hips, the way she eyed her customers, the way her nipples stood erect with or without prompting, the way she admired her own form in the wall length mirrors reflecting her naked image. This dancer was especially adept at the pelvic thrust and appeared to take a special interest in the hunch shouldered private detective at the bar.

He was on a job and preferred to remain unnoticed. She was good and he was not above admiring her special talents but tonight was not the night and this was not the place.

A direct descendent of the great chief for whom the city of Seattle was named, Jimmy was what some would call a mestizo. His mother still lived on the Skokomish reservation at the southeastern foot of the Olympic Mountains. He never knew his father but it was said he was an Irishman and a sailor. He set out to sea one day, when his son was just a babe in his mother's arms, and never returned. No one knew what became of him. White men were like that.

Jimmy did okay. He left the reservation as a young man to attend the white man's university in Seattle. When he tired of law school, he settled for a career as a private investigator. He soon discovered that white folks were eager to engage the services of a native, believing that his ancestry provided him with an innate tracking ability. After all, it was a band of Apache scouts who finally tracked down Geronimo in the Chiricahua Mountains.

Who knows? Maybe they were right. Jimmy was good at his job. He established a reputation as one of the best in the Great Northwest and his services came at a premium. Were it not for his habit of disappearing into the woods for long periods of time he would probably be pretty well set by now. As it was, he was comfortable. He saw to it that his mother was provided for and he managed to take care of his needs just fine. At the moment, however, he needed a quick infusion of cash.

Maxwell's was a high-class strip joint. He was hired by a suspicious wife to tail her husband and document his fall from grace. He was on the job for three days and he knew all he needed to know. The unfaithful husband was as predictable as sweat on a workingman. He worked at a brokerage house within walking distance of Maxwell's. At five o'clock he took a leisurely stroll down to stripper's paradise where he would whet his appetite for erotic fantasies for about sixty to seventy-five minutes, leave a twenty on the bar and walk back to his car for the drive home.

He told his wife about his daily ritual of patronizing a local pub, neglecting to note the dancing artists around a silver pole. He explained that he wanted to wait out the traffic before the commute.

It seemed logical enough but the wife grew suspicious. Their sex life did not exist and she was certain he was having an affair. It turned out he was only cheating on her in his mind. Some guys are like that. Jimmy felt sorry for him in a way and thought about tossing the assignment aside but he needed the money. If not him, someone else would take the estranged wife's money.

He could tell by the strange silence behind him that Maggie Thomas had the entered the premises. The clientele was not accustomed to her kind of class.

"Hello, Maggie," he said without looking up.

"Hi, Jimmy. I see you're still keeping quality company." She took the stool next to him and laid a twenty on the bar.

"A man's got to make a living. Sorry to put you through it though."

The bartender approached in a revealing blue velvet bunny costume. She was a dancer on break.

"I'll have what he's having," she said without a beat. "It's nothing I haven't seen before."

Maggie was a busy woman and this was a matter that couldn't wait. Jimmy told her on the phone he planned to leave town for a while but she pleaded with him. There was no one else she could trust. So she agreed to meet him here. It was either that or catching the ferry across the sound and driving out to the reservation where Jimmy was visiting his mother.

"So what's on your mind, Maggie?"

"Someone who goes by the tag of jazzman."

"Jazzman?"

"Yeah. Apparently it's an internet thing. Ever heard of him?"

Jimmy wrinkled his forehead trying to come up with something. He'd run across a lot of jazzmen in his line of work but none of them specialized in the internet.

"I can't say that I have," he replied.

Maggie ran down the basics: This mysterious jazzman was connected to the Miner case. The police wanted to talk to him as a suspect. Maggie was certain they were wrong about that. He was being framed. She needed to find him before the police did. She surmised he was a prominent businessman in the Seattle area and he or his people knew a great deal about technology.

Jimmy knew all about the Miner case. He had worked on it. He assumed it was closed.

"The coroner said it was suicide."

"It's a cover, Jimmy. It was homicide. They know it, I know it and, whoever this jazzman is, he knows it as well." She handed him a card with a list of names and their businesses. "He may have ties to one or more of these people. That's all I have."

The names were familiar to Jimmy: Roman Mason, Cheryl Miner and Joe Thomas. His brow wrinkled at the last name and he gave her a hard look that she returned in kind.

"Whatever you find out," she added, "make sure I'm the first to know."

"Understood," he replied, tucking the card into his shirt pocket. It did not sit well. He knew Maggie's father. He liked the man. He was one of the few white men who was honest and straightforward with him. If there was a hidden agenda he let Jimmy in on it upfront.

"I'll do it, Maggie. I think I'm the man for the job but I've got to tell you: I'm working on another case."

She stared at him blankly and shot a glance toward the stage where a dancer writhed like an erotic serpent.

"Right. How much?"

He chuckled, careful not to let the dancer think it was directed at her. Dancers can be sensitive to that kind of thing. "Not this," he said. "I'll wrap this one up tonight. It's a serious case. It'll take some of my time."

She conveyed her desperation in a glance. It was an expression he rarely if ever saw in her so it made an impact.

"Can you handle it?" she asked pointedly.

He gave it due consideration before answering. He would not take a case if he could not give it the attention it needed.

"Yeah," he answered. "I can handle it."

"Good," she said with relief. "I wouldn't trust anyone else on this one." She pressed his hand with five crisp one hundred dollar bills. "It'll get you started."

She rose to leave but he held on to her hand.

"Did anyone follow you here?"

"I don't think so."

He could see by her expression that the possibility hadn't occurred to her. He didn't want to sound condescending but she needed to be on alert.

"Listen, Maggie, if I had a client who wanted to identify someone called jazzman, there's a good chance I'd be tailing you right now."

"Thanks, I'll keep an eye out."

She turned and walked out to the same reaction as when she walked in. Along with every man and some of the women in the joint, Jimmy admired her form. He watched to make sure no one followed her.

As the door closed behind her the dancer with the pelvic thrust approached him with a look of envy.

"So Jimmy. Who's the classy broad?"

Jimmy stuffed the century bills in his pocket like it was chump change and pulled out a twenty on the return motion. He placed it in her palm.

"Ever heard of a cat called jazzman?"

"Lots of them. But no one in particular."

"He left her behind. Can you imagine?"

One thing Jimmy had learned is that you never know where your leads might come from. He cultivated his connections like a gardener cares for plants.

"Maybe he's gay," she purred. "Maybe she is."

"It takes all kinds."

She pressed her body to his and got a rise.

"What are you up to tonight?"

He took a moment to find his balance.

"Got a date with my mother. Otherwise…"

"Sure. Anytime. You've got my number."

"Thanks, babe."

The dancer went about her business and Jimmy got back to his. He took a deep breath, downed his beverage, pulled a five spot from his wallet and strolled down to the unfaithful husband at the other end of the bar. He slapped the bill to the bar and whispered so no one else could hear: "Your wife's on to you, buddy. Do me a favor. Don't tell her I said so."

The guy's face reddened to his ears.

Jimmy walked out of the bar feeling better about

everything. Life had a way of getting interesting just when you needed it most. This was the opportunity he'd waited for. He could feel it in his bones.

"Jazz," he said aloud. Jazz.

Chapter 16

AN OCCASIONAL RENDEZVOUS

Cheryl Miner was an infinitely better actress than anyone assumed. In the morning she jogged with Maggie. In the evening she entertained her father. Not often. Not yet. It was too soon after her husband's death. Aside from the matter of taste, it would raise suspicions. She was already a suspect. An occasional rendezvous at a remote location somewhere out of town was the best they could manage.

She realized it was only a matter of time before Maggie found out. That would be unfortunate. Cheryl liked Maggie and Maggie was beginning to appreciate the subtleties of her character – her off key wit, her southern charm and disarming smile. All that would change soon enough.

Maggie would learn that her father was not alone among Cheryl's romantic conquests. Either she was a gold digger or she had an inexplicable taste for older gentleman of wealth and influence.

She got away with it by exploiting the special talents that older men found irresistible. She had plenty of time for recreation and entertainment. She batted her eyelashes and struck a Marilyn pose: head tilted slightly back, her enchanting aquamarine eyes nearly closed, her lips alternately pursed and smiling, the tip of her tongue playfully flicking her upper front teeth. Men looked at her and believed whatever she wanted them to believe. They believed in her innocence and vulnerability. They believed in her honesty and loyalty. They believed because they wanted to believe, because not believing would mean an end to the pleasures she gave them. Even if they did not believe deep down where the truth is laid bare, they considered it worth the price. They did not know that the price could be death.

Joe Thomas was not a fool. He'd been alone for more than a decade. His wife of twenty years left him for neglect. It led him to rediscover his true values but it was not enough to save his marriage. He had a habit of flirting with beautiful young women without regard for their marital status. He thought of it as harmless, the eccentricities of age. When Cheryl reciprocated he was amused, then enticed and finally seduced. He knew there were others and figured Bill must have known as well.

There were no pretenses between them. There was no fantasy of a life together now that Bill was out of the way. There was, in other words, no motive for murder. If anything, Miner's death was an inconvenience. It sounds heartless but it was true. Everything was easier and much simpler when he was alive.

He lay back on the canopied bed of a rented cabin overlooking the sound. He had no thought of the outside world as he admired the soft, flowing lines of his lover's firm young body in all its naked glory. Was it any wonder he found himself in this compromised position? Was it any wonder he yielded to this temptation? At this moment nothing mattered except the lines of her feminine grace. Nothing mattered except the feeling of rejuvenation and the surge of energy she gave him. She was an angel of erotic joy. She delivered champagne in long-stemmed glasses and teased his thigh with the inside of her knee.

"Joe?" she purred. Her voice took on a breathy quality when she was at her seductive best. He knew it was an act but it never failed to arouse his senses and soften his heart.

"What is it, sweetness?"

She teased his body, sweeping the tips of her fingers from his upper thigh to his chest.

"What's wrong with Maggie?"

She draped her leg over his body and huddled up close so that he could feel the pointed warmth of her breasts and the heat between her thighs. He melted like butter on a skillet and sensed his rising to the occasion.

"Nothing's wrong with Maggie. She's a go-getter. She always has been."

"Something is bothering her. I can tell."

He didn't want to talk about Maggie. He didn't want to talk at all but it was understood, like an implied contract: first they would talk; then he could have his way.

"She doesn't believe it was suicide," he confided. "Neither do I."

"That makes three of us."

She swept her hand back and forth across his chest and felt him harden to the point.

"You don't think she suspects me?"

He laughed, almost breaking the spell.

"Maggie's the consummate attorney, my dear. No one is above suspicion. Not you and not me. She won't cross anyone off the list until the case is closed."

His mind wandered briefly. The thought of losing his daughter's respect almost spoiled the moment. Cheryl brought him back with her delicate lips.

"Maybe we should stop seeing each other."

"Why?"

He held her tight and gazed into her enchanting eyes for more than a moment. He was mesmerized.

"We're innocent," he pleaded. "We didn't do it. I have every confidence that Maggie will figure it out. Along the way she may find out a few other things that could make life uncomfortable but she'll get over it. She's a grown woman. She'll understand."

Cheryl straddled him, planting her knees on each side of his hips. She leaned forward to whisper in his ear: "Promise?"

He smiled and ran his hands firmly across her svelte backside. "I promise," he said. He would have promised her the moon.

She took him in and sheltered him from all worries and cares. In waves of writhing pleasure they drifted together to a far away place where there is no past or future. There is only the moment and the moment is pure ecstasy.

Chapter 17

CASE CLOSED

The detective arrived at Maggie's office unannounced and confronted her secretary.

"Did you have an appointment?"

"I'm afraid not," he explained patiently. "Could you just tell her there's a Detective Jones here to see her? I'm sure she'll find time in her busy schedule."

"Detective Jones?"

"That's right."

He flashed his winning smile and displayed his badge discretely, leaning over to whisper: "Seattle Police."

Despite Hollywood depictions of his profession, he had learned that discretion went a long way where bravado came up short. The secretary pressed a button on the intercom.

"Ms. Thomas? I'm sorry to disturb you but there's a Mr. Jones here to see you."

"Mr. Jones?"

"*Detective* Jones."

"Send him in."

The detective thanked her politely and was greeted at the door of her expansive office.

"Nice," the detective observed as she guided him to her desk. It was an office designed to advertise success in a tasteful manner, featuring impressionist artwork and hand carved hardwood furniture.

"Thank you."

She sat at her desk and the detective took his seat before her. The Miner file lay open in clear view. She made a conscious decision not to conceal her active interest. There was no point. Since Jimmy's warning she had become aware of being followed and she was certain it was the police. It was strange having eyes on you wherever you went – like a rash or a persistent salesman. It left her feeling uneasy, bothered and too often distracted.

"What's on your mind, Detective Jones?"

"I'm afraid I have some disappointing news. I say 'disappointing' because I believe you're as interested in solving this case as I am."

"The murder of William Miner?"

She was exercising her gift for sarcasm though it went against her nature. She was reminding the detective that the police initially considered this case a suicide, open and shut. That didn't bother her but the fact that the police were trailing her did and she held the detective responsible. It was an invasion of privacy and to her way of thinking it was unjustified. The detective was suitably rebuffed. From his perspective they were on the same side and his presence was as much for her benefit as his.

"You understand, Ms. Thomas, that I'm here of my own accord. I'm only interested in the truth."

"I understand. I also understand that I'm being followed. I don't believe I'm a suspect in this case and I don't appreciate being treated as one."

Detective Jones leaned back and wondered for a moment if he'd wandered into the wrong office. Eliminating that possibility he was at once perplexed and pleased. He had already learned more than he expected. She was not a suspect and neither was she given to bouts of paranoia. If she was being followed he was all but certain it was not the police doing the following. He had given no such order. If it wasn't the police then who was it?

"Ms. Thomas," he said at length, "I'd very much like to put your mind at ease but I'm afraid that might be difficult. You are not being followed on my orders. As a matter of fact, I'm here to inform you that the department is closing the case."

Now it was Maggie's turn to drop her jaw. This was the last thing she expected to hear.

"You're dropping the case?" she intoned with absolute incredulity.

"The department is satisfied that Mr. Miner's death was self-administered."

"Surely you don't believe that?"

He sighed in a manner he hoped would convey an appropriate level of consternation. He was not convinced but it was not his call.

"I'm afraid the evidence is persuasive. It seems Mr. Miner purchased the instrument of his demise: rat poison. You've been to the Miner estate, Ms. Thomas. Would you ever imagine a rat infestation?"

"I've seen a lot of rats around Bill but not the four-legged variety. Are you sure?"

"We are. He used his credit card and made sure his image was captured on the security camera making the transaction. It seems to me, Ms. Thomas, that he wanted to make absolutely certain his young wife wouldn't take the rap."

"So it *was* suicide."

Again he hesitated. He seemed reluctant to arrive at a conclusion that did not satisfy his sense of justice and truth. It troubled him.

"It's a fine line, Ms. Thomas. When is a suicide murder? If I hold a pistol to your loved one's head and offer you a choice: him or you? Is that suicide or murder or both?"

"So you're not convinced."

"Convinced?" he shrugged.

He constantly struggled with words that did not conform to meaning. "I'm not satisfied. I can tell you that much. There are some very unsettling questions."

"Who is jazzman?"

"Exactly. And who is following you, Ms. Thomas?"

"And why?"

The unanswered questions hovered like puffs of smoke in still air while the two of them, the corporate attorney and the eccentric detective, came to a mutual understanding. They were after the same thing: the truth. They were allies in this venture and that seemed critical to their cause. They would need each other to solve this case and bring it to a just conclusion. Neither could find words to explain but they knew by instinct they had to work together.

"May I call you Maggie?" he asked.

She nodded her consent.

"What should I call you?" she countered.

"I prefer to be called Detective if you don't mind. My birth name is Myron David. For the first twenty years of my life I was known as Myron. Do you know what it's like to be a Myron in this world? It left a bitter taste. I could change it I suppose."

Maggie smiled.

"I'll call you Detective. What next?"

Well, Maggie, the first part of any case – especially a complicated one like this – is to identify all the players. Once we do that, we'll have to distinguish the good guys from the bad. My sense is that might be a difficult task."

He stood to depart and turned back at the door.

"Do you believe in dreams, Maggie?"

She smiled again. It seemed the detective was full of surprises. "Of course," she replied.

"So do I," he said with a conviction that struck Maggie as profound. A tip of his fedora and he was gone, leaving her dazed. She had not yet told him about Roman Mason or Jimmy Longbow. He didn't ask.

She suddenly realized the position she had placed herself. The detective singled her out as his connection. He informed her that some unknown party, probably the killer or the force behind the killing, was following her. He warned her in so many words not to trust anyone. Did he include himself? Maybe it was best to keep her alliances separate and distinct – at least until things settled. She had to proceed carefully. As the detective suggested, the first step was to identify all the players. She pulled out a pad and pencil and began mapping the case.

Chapter 18

DREAM TRAVEL

He could not be sure when it began. He was not one to write down his dreams but something strange was happening between the hours of sleep and awake: visions of tall stone mountains shrouded in layers of clouds or mist, voices in the wind, howl of the wolf, fluttering of wings, caw of the crow and cry of the raven. It was a mystical magical world that honored no laws of nature and no sense of traditional order.

He would awaken in a cold sweat and know: the old Indian was visiting his dreams. With each visitation the images grew starker and more vivid. Each time the words beyond the vision became clearer. Song of the Wind said it was possible to travel in the mind, to take on different forms, to traverse space and time. He said it was not a gift – not in the usual sense.

He believed that people who opened their minds to the spiritual world were chosen. He believed the spirits of the forest chose him. He believed the White Man who Sits Apart was also chosen. But it was not a gift; it was a skill like any other, like totem carving or buffalo hunting or operating the white man's machines. Like any skill it could be learned and refined through meditation and practice.

As the old one demonstrated his remarkable ability to travel in dreams, Rome began to understand as a man on the mountaintop understands his place in the world and his understanding led him to realize how useful it could be to his cause. His adversaries had effectively countered his electronic eavesdropping, turning it to their own advantage.

It was their methodology, like choosing pistols to dual a marksman. He would choose a new methodology. They would not know how to deal with spiritual transference. They had no frame of reference for dream travel.

He began meditating on a regular basis, each time diving deeper and deeper into the void beyond consciousness. He became more comfortable with the old one's visits. Soon he would enter a new realm. Where now he only observed his dreams, he would soon be able to engage. Where now he only listened, he would soon learn to speak. Where now he sat apart, soon he would interact.

The next step was to see himself apart from his physical being. Song of the Wind smiled and nodded his approval. Rome understood. He was a warrior in training and he was getting closer every day.

The day would come when he would visit the old one's dreams. The day would come when they would share consciousness in a waking state. When that day arrived he would know how to employ the technique against his enemies. He wondered how the natives had lost their own wars against the invaders. Perhaps their spiritual powers were limited to a chosen few. Perhaps they had not had time to develop their skills. Perhaps the knowing could not prevent the happening.

It was a different world that required a different kind of war. In the modern world the knowing is power in itself. Maybe they had not been defeated at all. Maybe the war was still being waged and the tribes were gathering allies such as himself. Maybe this was but one small battle in a greater war. Who can tell?

He decided it was time for a little jazz. He flipped on the radio and approved the modern, ethereal syncopation of Jaco Pastorious. Sitting on a pillow shaman style, he looked out on a silver moonlit Pacific ocean and counted the waves. Closing his eyes, he slowly drifted away.

Chapter 19

CONNECTIONS

It was a stone gray day. The rain hammered the wood shingle roof of the Kingfisher Café where Rome awaited the arrival of Maggie Thomas. He ordered a bottle of vintage Shiraz and stared like a monk into the flames of a fire, alone with his thoughts, his musings on the mystery of murder.

It seemed the police were obsessed on the question of how. They knew Bill Miner was poisoned. They knew the poison and they knew it was mixed with the victim's scotch. Whoever his murderer was, he or she had to have access to the house and had to be familiar with Miner's habits. Whoever it was probably knew he would be drinking heavily that evening. There were no indications of forced entry and no reports of strangers in the neighborhood or unusual visitors.

Had it not been for the jazzman message and the fact that his computer files were tampered with, the evidence of suicide would have been compelling. As it was it all seemed to point in one direction: Cheryl Miner. She had motive and opportunity.

The problem was: Why would she tamper with his files and leave anything but a suicide note on his computer? It did not add up. Fictitious or real, there was no reason to implicate someone else. Or was there? Maybe she was smarter than anyone thought. Maybe she knew the suicide theory wouldn't hold. Maybe she wanted to throw suspicion in another direction just in case. If she was the killer, was she working alone or was there someone more powerful pulling her strings?

It was a maze of circular reasoning, leading everywhere and nowhere at once, like Theseus in the labyrinth of the Minotaur without a ball of thread.

He shifted his musings to the question of motive. Miner did not seem to engender fierce enemies. Even competitors who lost millions to his manipulations appeared not to hold a grudge. They were simply outplayed. Miner made it a point never to crush anyone. There were a number of occasions when he helped his defeated adversaries get back on their feet. He played hardball but he played by the rules. So a personal vendetta seemed unlikely. That made it strictly a matter of business. Whether cash, influence or power it all came down to the profit motive.

The police would not have eliminated family. Indeed, there was a great deal of inheritance money at stake but there was no indication that any one of them was in danger of being disinherited. None of the children had shown any interest in making money as Miner had. Consequently, they stood a better chance of increasing their net worth with their father alive. As for Cheryl, even if their marriage had secretly been in trouble (and there were signs it could have been had certain infidelities come to light), after four years of marriage the divorce settlement would have been more than adequate to take care of her in style for the rest of her life.

Rome tossed it over in his mind and arrived at the same conclusion he walked in with: it came down to connections – most likely business connections. Connections that were not commonly known. Connections that may be responsible for all of Bill Miner's problems, including his untimely death.

If he was right, Miner had made a deal with the devil whether he knew it or not. As the entanglement grew and the implications became clear, he would have wanted to get out. He may have tried.

But who were they and what was their game? He felt certain it was somewhere in Miner's files. The connection was there. Maybe it was something Miner said in his drunken rambling that fateful night when he had cursed an unseen enemy like a madman in the final act of an epic tragedy.

"I'll get them!" he had said. "I'll nail them to the goddamned wall!"

At the time it was perceived as the ravings of paranoid delusion. "They're all out to get me!" Maybe it was pure instinct. In any case, it was all witnessed and recorded.

These were the questions that Maggie Thomas was asking herself and he went through them as much for her benefit as his own. Perhaps more. He had already arrived at the conclusion that other forces were at work. If Cheryl was involved at all she was acting on behalf of someone else. Who and why were the remaining questions.

He was entranced in the dance of flames when Maggie approached his table. She startled him.

"Hi," she said with a tone of near indifference.

"Maggie!" he replied.

He cleared his head and straightened his tie. He didn't like wearing one but the occasion called for it.

"I'd nearly given up on you," he confided.

"I hope it was a good one," she smiled.

"What's that?"

"The dream or the fantasy."

He returned her smile. Her charm commanded his attention and brought him swiftly back to earth.

"It was," he said. "Enchanting."

She was checking him out. There was no mistaking it.

"Sorry I'm late."

"Please have a seat."

He poured wine and focused on the woman who sat before him. They toasted without words and drank.

"I had a talk with Detective Jones," she announced. "He says they're dropping the investigation."

The news hit like a winter thunderstorm.

"Why would they do that?" he inquired.

"It seems he purchase rat poison on his card."

"Anyone could have used his card."

She shook her head and studied his reactions. It seemed he was genuinely surprised at the news.

"They checked it out. The transaction was recorded on the security footage. He looked straight at the camera. He didn't want to leave any doubt."

"I don't believe it," he said.

"Believe it, Rome. Bill Miner committed suicide. The question now is: Why?"

Maggie examined his dark brown eyes, the curve of his face as it transformed from expression to expression. She looked for signs of affect or insincerity. She found none. Finally, she said: "I thought you might be relieved."

"Relieved?"

His expression now registered deadly intensity. It was a side of his character he rarely showed and one Maggie did not suspect existed.

"Maggie, I think Bill Miner was on to something. I think he threatened to expose a powerful organization. I think they killed him. If they didn't do it, then they pushed him to it. I want to solve this crime as much as you do."

He made an impression. It aroused something deep within her, something she was not entirely sure she wanted to confront. Whatever it was, it would not prevent her from thinking clearly.

"The question remains," she challenged. "Why?"

He leaned back and relaxed. He carefully scanned the surrounding tables and the people seated at them. He picked up his wine and returned his gaze to the fire. He spoke slowly and calmly.

"Things are frequently not what they appear to be. I've cultivated an image of indifference because it serves my purpose. It's good for business. But I am not indifferent. Someone put the squeeze on my client. It doesn't matter that he was someone I could talk to over a glass of wine. It doesn't matter that we were friends or that I cared about him as a human being. What does matter is that he was my client and no one puts the squeeze on my client and gets away with it. It's bad for business."

He sipped his wine and Maggie let the silence sit a while. She was trying to decide how much she could trust him. It was obvious – so obvious it almost made him smile.

"Okay," she said. "I've got a man on it. He's a private investigator and the best tracker in the business. The next five hundred is on you. Whatever he finds out, we share it. That's the deal."

He gazed into her eyes and felt genuine warmth. The ice slowly melted. He raised his glass and she raised hers. Clink!

"You're on!"

They drank to a new alliance and allowed the warmth of the fire to envelop them like a mother's love or the first day of spring.

"Do you like jazz?" she asked with an inquisitive grin.

"Who doesn't?" he replied.

Chapter 20

MEETING AT THE MONASTERY

It was open mike night at The Monastery in the market district. A mix of fringe and mainstream poets took the stage, one after another, eager to spend their allotted fifteen minutes of glory – mostly on what they wrote in place of last night's dinner. Each hoped to catch a majestic wave that would catapult the chosen to a jazzman high. For every pearl there are a thousand dives.

The real attraction was the jazz trio. It was down to a bass and a sax for this evening's program of beat poetry. The sax player was an old time Chicago blues man, reduced by the bottle and the winds of change to providing scat back for would be Kerouac's. Had nobody heard? Kerouac was dead. They were only here to provide old jazz players a chance to keep their chops up.

Jimmy Longbow sat back to the wall as close to the corner as he could get. He had just returned from Laguna Beach where he set up a surveillance operation. He could feel a powerful presence beyond that of the old blues man and he wondered if the jazzman was in the building.

Jake Marshall walked in, hiding behind a pair of small round shades. He took the waiting chair next to Jimmy. It was a perfect place to meet. Anyone who did not belong stood out like a steel guitar in a jazz ensemble or a black rose at a wedding.

They skipped the small talk and kept their eyes dead ahead where they could view anyone who walked in the front door. The poet on stage, sporting long dark hair, tied back, in a deerskin jacket, blue jeans and moccasins, started a chant.

"We cannot be free / We cannot be free…"

A portion of the crowd picked it up on cue and carried it under his litany. The sax man started an improvisational scat and the bass player flipped his standup around to simulate the tom-tom of an Indian drum: 1-2, 1-2-3, 1-2-3, 1-2, 1-2-3…

"We cannot be free / We cannot be free…"

"As long as snakeskin boots trample the sacred hunting grounds…"

"We cannot be free / We cannot be free…"

Jimmy listened with acute interest. He knew the poet, a mixed breed like himself. Funny, he thought, how all the mestizos had returned to their native bloodline. Where once they were ashamed of their heritage, even to the point of hiding it behind white man dress and white man ways, now they wore the markings like ceremonial war paint and swore their allegiance to the Indian nations.

"We cannot be free / We cannot be free…"

"Until the rings of power are worn again by mother earth and father sky…"

"We cannot be free / We cannot be free…"

"Until the white man's gods are fallen and the paleface masters die…"

"We cannot be free / We cannot be free…"

Jimmy's interest intensified. It seemed the jazzman was here at least in spirit. This was his poetry. He published the piece on the web under the name of Gray Hawk.

Jake tried to break the spell but it would not be broken. Jimmy would wait until the poet finished.

"Howl of the wolf and the eagle's cry; caw of the crow and song of the wind. I have been to the sacred mountain. I have walked the plains of buffalo. I have swimmed the stream of salmon. I have danced the song of the whistling pine. I have ridden the smoke of the ancient flame and talked with the tallest trees. I have heard the voice of our ancestors cry out: We will be free!"

"We cannot be free / We cannot be free…"

"We will be free!"

Only when the applause had fallen to the random sounds of clinking glass and the buzz of conversation did Jimmy turn his attention to Jake.

"How'd it go?" asked Jake, still looking straight ahead.

"Fine," said Jimmy without skipping a beat. He was talking about the stakeout of Edward Bates' estate. "I can't say it went smoothly but it's all set up. There are a lot of construction crews in the area and we're one of them. We're keeping track of everyone who comes and goes. There's a lot of rental cars and taxis so we spend a lot of time tracking down the ID's. That's all we can do. We can't get inside the place. Security is too tight."

He reached into his shirt pocket and pulled out a pack of Native Spirit cigarettes. He offered Jake one, which he refused, lit one up and left the pack on the table.

"There is another matter," he said.

"What's that?"

He took a drag and blew a gray cloud of smoke that drifted over the crowd as the next jazz poet whispered something into the sax man's ear, leading him to play a soulful Billie Holiday type blues.

"Maggie Thomas," said Jimmy.

"What about her?"

"You won't believe this one. She hired me to track down someone operating under the name of jazzman."

"Hasn't she heard? The case is closed."

"She's heard. She wants it reopened."

The poet onstage dove headfirst into a dark erotic fantasy – something about a leathered goddess with her knees apart. His voice was low and slow, blending nicely with the multi-layered texture of the blues man's sax.

"What did you tell her?"

"I said I was the right man for the job."

Jake didn't like it and it registered on his face. He knew

90

that Jimmy was his own man. He did not take orders from anyone and he would not be pressed. Jake objected to bringing him in and Jimmy knew it. It didn't matter. Rome had his loyalties and the Indian tracker was at the top of the list. He earned his keep in half a dozen cases, including the Miner case. There were only a few who knew who the jazzman was and Jimmy was one of them.

"What do you have in mind?"

Jimmy looked into the eyes of Jake Marshall and Jake looked away. He had a gift for reaching into a man's soul and reading him like an open book. To Jake it felt like a root canal of the psyche. He wanted no part of it.

"I want to level with her," replied Jimmy.

He grabbed his cigarettes and replaced them in his pocket, leaving a folded square of paper exposed on the table.

"Tell him I want to talk to him about his poetry," he said as he prepared to leave

"I don't think that's a good idea."

"Just tell him."

Jimmy slid out and vanished into the crowd before Jake could raise his eyes. *Indians*, he thought with a shake of his head. He palmed the note and reached into his pocket, producing a couple of bills to leave in its stead. He knew what the note contained: A list of names, businesses and phone numbers from the stakeout. He was anxious to see who made the list and how many of them were familiar. At a certain level the business world is a close-knit group and a mere thousand miles was not enough to separate them.

It would have to wait. For now he had a date with Sara. The evening was young and filled with promise. With a glance at his watch he settled back and listened to the old sax player and the sad-eyed poet. The rain had begun again. Welcome to Seattle. It was a gentle beat that seemed to soothe his mind and free him of his troubles if only for the moment. He pulled out another bill, laid it on the table and walked out into a misty Seattle evening.

Jake did not notice the older gentleman with the close-cut beard who followed him out of the bar. He did not notice the cab that followed him to Sara's apartment.

Detective Jones was moonlighting and his list of players was growing every day. He was aware of Sara's involvement but he did not know she was connected to the jazzman. Now he did and he sensed that the jazzman knew about him as well. He looked forward to the time when they could meet face to face. For now, he was content to gather names and add them to an expanding chart on his wall labeled: The Jazzman Connection.

Chapter 21

VISIONS OF HORROR

Jake knew something was wrong on the drive to an Italian restaurant for a candlelight dinner. Sara was too quiet. When he inquired she only said, "I haven't been able to sleep." She offered no more and he opted to let it rest. He knew she was working hard and assumed that whatever troubled her was work related. He was only partly correct.

Sara's nightmare had returned with increasing force and clarity. Later, over dinner, unable to maintain her interest in casual conversation or business talk, she opened up and told him about it: how she was pursued through a deep forest by an unknown predator, how she fell into the arms of her savior, a glowing figure of Christ, how she turned and recognized her pursuer as her father, his face etched in unspeakable horror, peering into the eyes of the figure behind her, how she awakened, trembling, her face streaked with tears, her body covered in sweat. Try as she may, she could not rid her mind of the horror and she could not sleep.

She gazed once again into his caring, giving eyes. She wondered if she had been wrong about him. She could not bring herself to tell him how the dream actually ended. It was a measure of trust and at the moment she came up short. In the dream she turned back to observe the transformation of the Christ figure. It was Jake. He wore an expression of calm detachment. As she continued to observe she sensed a growing sadness within him, as if he knew something she did not know and its implications were unthinkable.

It haunted her. Why was her father terrified? Was there

a hidden family secret buried in her subconscious? Would Jake ultimately reveal the truth or was he the villain in disguise? Was her father's fear directed at him and what he would do to her? Was it really her father or a symbolic representation of a father figure? Could it be the jazzman?

For the second time in her brief career she had come across incriminating evidence. It appeared to be a double set of figures estimating the value of a strip of land belonging to the Skokomish tribe. She ascertained that one set of figures had gone to the tribal leaders for the purpose of determining an appropriate rate for a long-term lease. She deduced that the alternate set, substantially larger, represented the true value of the land.

Had she been set up once again? It had taken so long to trust anyone and now that she had found her community, her circle of common cause and faith, had she been betrayed? Who was the jazzman? Why did he wish to remain anonymous? Why did he hide even from those of proven loyalty? The whole situation began to emit the odor of deception. Who could she really trust? Just as her life, her plans and dreams seemed to be falling into place, everything scattered like dust in the wind, like hope in the eye of a storm.

She prayed that Jake's touch would bring her back from the darkness. Confusion born of hope, hope born of love, she wanted desperately to believe. She longed for him to fill the void with a need that sprang from deep within the core of her being. She wanted him to hold her like her father never had and he wanted nothing more than to take her in his arms until the warmth returned.

"Take me home, Jake," tears welling in her eyes. "I want to feel you next to me when the rain stops."

He felt as though the weight of a granite mountain lifted from his shoulders. His spirit soared on the high winds of another world.

"Don't worry, baby," he said. "I promise it'll be okay."

She believed him. In spite of the facts, in spite of her dreams, in spite of the terror, she still believed and she gave thanks to god or whatever forces of nature rule the human heart. She gave thanks to Jake for being there.

The rain came pouring down, pounding the pavement like ancient drums, while their hearts beat as one. Within the hour they were enfolded in each other's limbs on the satin sheets of Sara's feather bed. She rolled over onto a hard pillow and beckoned him to follow. There was no need. Their bodies melded together like yin and yang, like waves on a shore, like petals on a rose or the monoliths of Stonehenge – a divine and perfect coupling. Their love was born in heaven, undeniable and as natural as rain in Seattle. With the swiftness of a breath everything became clear.

Within the hour, when their journey of joy had crested and settled into a profound peace, she told him everything. He soothed her and assured her all would be well. He assured her the villain behind this scheme and the demon in her dream was neither he nor the jazzman. He assured her they would do nothing to harm or deceive the tribes of Olympic Peninsula. He assured her they were allies. He assured her they would find and expose the perpetrators of this fraud. He did not need to reassure her of his love.

The rain softened and fell silent as Sara drifted into a deep and peaceful sleep.

Chapter 22

COMMUNION

Jimmy went into the woods to seek communion with his mother, the earth. This time it was a part of his job. He parked his Cherokee off the unpaved road to Ozette, concealing it with pine boughs, and set out across the rugged, moss covered terrain under the cover of darkness. Only a sliver of moonlight in the cloud-filled skies, he hiked toward Snag Peak on his way to the Point of Arches where he would make camp.

Few could negotiate a path through the dense forestland of Olympic Peninsula at night and none were white men. He had to make sure no one could follow. Though it was only ten miles as the crow flies, the hike would consume the better part of two days. He would reach the peak just before dawn. He would set up camp, eat, sleep and meditate before resuming his journey at sunset.

Rome did not know he was coming. There was no way to contact him except through Jake and that was a path he chose not to use. He knew that Jake would oppose a meeting but he had to talk to his friend face to face. Too much was at stake. He had to warn him about Jake's betrayal. The only way was through the forest at night. Even if their enemies hired a turncoat Indian, like the scouts that tracked Geronimo, he would discover their presence before the second leg of his journey.

The sun was just appearing on the eastern horizon as he settled on a ledge where the rock formations concealed a small cave. Here he could view and listen to the life of the forest and the mountain. As always, he greeted the rising sun with a prayer: *Father sky, mother earth, spirit of the ancestors; brother crow, sister salmon, song of the wind and voice of the tall trees, guide and protect your faithful child.*

He sat still, watching and listening as a hawk soared overhead, circled and departed, as deer grazed and a gray squirrel gathered seed, until at length his eyes could no longer bear the light of day. He then retreated into the cave, laid out a blanket of deerskin and reclined, eyes to the heavens. He freed his mind of thought, closed his eyes and welcomed the world that visits those who walk in their sleep.

It was not the first time the old one came to him in his dreams. As always he appeared in the form of a large black crow, hovering in flight with a great fluttering of wings. The image frightened those who were not prepared to greet him. It had frightened Jimmy at first, so many moons ago. Those who were strong in heart and mind gazed at the vision in wonder and watched as the old one transformed from crow to human: Song of the Wind.

The old one's face revealed an inner peace, a sense of contentment, as if celebrating a great victory. They offered each other thanks and exchanged greetings in silence before the old one spoke.

"Have no fear," he said. "You are not followed."

Jimmy nodded in relief. The old one was never wrong. He continued.

"White Man who Lives Apart knows you are coming. He welcomes you and bids you a safe journey."

Jimmy acknowledged his gratitude without words as the old one transformed once again into a great crow with fluttering wings. A song of the ancients whistled through the pines, a strong wind swept through the canyons, wolves howled, the crow cawed and Jimmy awoke at twilight. A crow feather lay on his chest.

He smiled and tied the feather to a leather strip that he wore around his neck, binding it to his medicine pouch. He ate a meal of dried apple and venison and meditated on the meaning of his dream vision for half an hour, though it seemed a full day. He packed and set out for the Point, his mind filled with wonder, his heart filled with questions and his body with renewed energy.

Chapter 23

THE SANCTUM

Since the 1950's they referred to their select members as the Sanctum. The value they placed on security and secrecy was surpassed only by their high regard for money, influence and power.

They contacted Cheryl Miner when she was a dancer at a low class strip joint in downtown Seattle. She danced to finance classes in acting and modeling at a local school for the dramatic arts. The Sanctum offered a better life and a more direct route to her ambitions – or so she thought.

There was a time when almost any attractive woman of liberal persuasion, a good-looking stripper, a high-class call girl or quality escort, well placed at a local bar, was entirely adequate to their purpose. As long as the woman had an appealing style the task was easy. Those days were gone. In the age of safe sex, media exposure and family values, they needed women who could close the deal and sign on the dotted line – not only mistresses but wives. They chose women specific to the job.

Cheryl was a prime example of the new breed. With her slim, athletic figure and hypnotic Marilyn eyes, the Sanctum chose her to fit the sexual-erotic taste of Big Bill Miner. No one could have been better prepared for a job interview than she was when she applied for an opening as a receptionist in Miner's office. They provided credentials, experience and recommendations. They rehearsed her on what to say and how to say it. When she landed the job they knew it would not be long before he took the bait. Within a month they were having an affair. In eight months they were married. That was the hard part of her assignment. The rest was easy: she observed and recorded his affairs, communications and connections, reporting what she learned to the Sanctum.

The organization had marked Bill Miner as a prospective associate. His meteoric rise in the business world was promising. They needed new blood to keep the reins of power viable. Once they committed to a candidate he or she would be confronted with the choice of their lives: If he chose to accept the invitation, he would be welcomed to the fold and his business interests would prosper. If he declined he would be eliminated. They could not afford to allow anyone outside the circle to know of its existence. The Sanctum depended on anonymity.

Certain that he would recognize that the benefits far outweighed the costs they counted on his acceptance. No one had refused. At the highest level, their members included the world's most generous philanthropists, men who had donated billions to worthy causes around the globe without publicity. These men had no political or philosophic agenda. They had no direct connections to organized crime. They were bigger than the mob and the cartels combined. They had no need to profit from illicit drugs, prostitution, the slave trade, gambling or any other illicit ventures.

They did not buy politicians – not in the usual sense. They contributed to both parties as well as an occasional third party. They were not interested in buying elections or tipping the balance one way or another. No matter who claimed the presidency or congress, they would surround the winning party with advisors and consultants who would do their bidding.

Their past was not as clean as their current operation and they made sure the trail was covered. The past is buried, dead and gone. No one would be allowed to dredge it up.

Their new methodology was simple and beautiful: They converted knowledge into money. It did not matter what decisions were made in the business, legal or political realms as long as they were the first to know. It was like being able to freeze a horse race moments before the finish line so that bets could be placed. To the world outside the circle it appeared that they were exceptional businessmen when in fact the game was rigged.

They had turned enormous profits from every major military operation since the Korean War. They made fortunes on the rise and fall of gold in the seventies, from the oil crisis, the stock market crash of the eighties and, more recently, from the collapse of the Soviet Union, the savings and loan scandal, the healthcare crisis, the El Nino disasters and the collapse of the Asian markets. They loved disasters; they thrived on them.

It's one thing to be able to forecast events from economic and social trends. It's another to be able to predict with absolute certainty the precise moment and magnitude of impact. Every event has winners and losers. Knowing in advance guaranteed they would be on the winning side. The bigger the stakes, the better the profits.

Nothing in the financial world was beyond the reach of the Sanctum and no one who came within its grasp was left untouched – certainly not Cheryl Miner. She was a pawn in a colossal chess game. She did what she was told without a second thought.

Cheryl waited by the fire in a secluded cabin north by northeast of Seattle, on the western shore of Lake Goesiger between Monroe and Granite Falls. She was about to give up and head back to town when she heard Jake's four-wheeler in the distance. She watched him approach from behind the curtains of a small window. She smiled when she saw him step out of the jeep. He wore jeans, hiking boots and a red flannel shirt. She had never seen him in casual dress. Their prior meetings were always covert but under the prevailing conditions they had to be twice as careful.

She liked Jake. He was younger and so much more interesting than the other men she knew in the business world. They also had something in common. Jake was her connection to the Sanctum. She had known him for over a year now. It seemed much longer. For a time they were lovers as well as conspirators. His predecessor, an older man, was transferred when things got a little hot. She figured the same was about to happen to her. Her newly acquired wealth offered no security and gave her no protection. She knew what happened to those who tried to get out. The only escape was in the same manner as her late husband.

She greeted Jake at the door and led him inside. They exchange niceties and settled in front of the fire with a half-pint of brandy and a couple of snifters before getting down to business. Jake initiated.

"As soon as the dust settles, they want you out of town."

"I figured," she said.

Jake took a sip of brandy.

"It's a good assignment, befitting your status as a wealthy young woman."

Cheryl took a drink and nodded. Her doubt was palpable. Why would the organization treat her any better than anyone else it dealt with? Besides, she liked Seattle and the friends she made there. She didn't want to relocate.

"Where am I going?"

"New Orleans. The Big Easy. An enterprising young entrepreneur has made a mark with a consortium of business interests throughout the region. Mid forties, good looking, he comes from a long line of Louisiana charm."

"Why me?"

"You fit the profile, sweetheart. He won't even look at anyone without your kind of money. They'll set you up in his social circles and let nature take its course."

"When do I make the move?"

"There's no hurry. They don't want to rush it. The last thing they want is someone on your trail."

She tossed it around, looking for angles they might not have considered. Jake took a hit of brandy. Her apparent reluctance made him a little uneasy.

"What do I tell people?"

"Tell them you need to get away. Tell them you always wanted to live in the Easy. Whatever it takes."

He cleared his throat and refilled his snifter.

"Remember Melissa Wilson?" he asked.

"Sure."

Melissa had been one of her few female friends. Like herself, she was married to an older and less attractive man.

"She moved to New Orleans," she recalled.

"That's right. Give her a call. Start a correspondence. She's your ticket to the places you need to go."

Cheryl shrugged. She was thinking of Maggie and realized for the first time how much she would miss her. It surprised her. She was not sentimental and she tried hard not to form attachments.

"What about Joe?"

He almost laughed. It would not have occurred to him that Cheryl would give a second thought to Joe Thomas. If anything, she should be relieved to be rid of him.

"Listen," he confided, "the lid is about to blow on that one. Maggie's got a private eye working the case. He's good. He will find out. That's another reason to get out of Seattle."

She reflected before responding, half to herself: "What a shame."

She was out of questions and her mood was shifting from pensive to playful. For Jake's amusement, as well as her own, she offered her best Marilyn pout and spoke in an enticing, seductive voice: "Well, it looks like our days of working together are about to come to an end."

Jake smiled and nodded.

"Be a pity to waste such a warm, cozy cabin."

She rose, blew a kiss and walked with a swaying motion

that reminded him of the tides to sit on the side of the bed. Kicking off her shoes, she leaned back and slowly dragged her hands up her thighs. Where they came to rest had been a source of great pleasure to him in the not too distant past. He recalled her lovely body in exquisite detail. Making love with Cheryl was like climbing aboard a mechanical bull. It was hot and heavy and unforgettable. She should have been the death of both Joe Thomas and Bill Miner. Their hearts must have been stronger than their age allowed.

"Not today," he sighed.

She sat up and smiled a knowing smile. She was slightly disappointed. She knew he was seeing someone and she wanted to test the strength of their relationship.

"She must be someone special."

"She is."

He stood as if anxious to remove himself from temptation. A man can only take so much before the tides sweep him away.

"I'll be in touch," he said in parting.

She blinked and he was gone. She took a hit of brandy and reclined on the bed with a sigh.

"New Orleans," she said. "Not bad. Not bad at all."

Chapter 24

THE MAKAH REVELATION

It was another stone gray day. Maggie sat in her high-rise office taking in a spectacular view of the space needle and the Seattle skyline. In the distance a layer of mist lingered above the sound. She struggled to keep her eyes open. She had deprived herself of sleep for several days now and it was catching up to her.

Since their last discussion, her father sat her down for a quiet reckoning. He explained that while he could not prevent her from pursuing the Miner case on her own time no matter how much he might wish that he could, he reminded her in a manner that conveyed only the warmth of concern that it was no longer an official case of the firm.

He was right of course. Since William Miner's death her standards of excellence had gradually declined. She attended fewer conferences. She missed important details. She handled her usual caseload but she was less diligent and less engaged. Her clients were beginning to notice. After her father's gentle admonition, she made a concerted effort to make up for lost time and reputation. She worked twice as hard, often remaining in her office to the early hours of the morning. It was not what her father had hoped for. She was frazzled and exhausted, her thoughts scattering like dandelion seeds in four strong winds.

Compounding her restlessness and growing frustration, she had been unable to find anything of interest in Miner's papers. She had not heard from Jimmy and she was unable to contact Roman Mason. Consequently there was no one with whom she could share her thoughts. The absence of new information, speculation and conjecture was like a dull chord at the back of her skull, a constant reminder that something dark, unreachable and deeply disturbing remained to be discovered. It hounded her subconscious like the ghosts of a distant past.

Jimmy had returned from his assignment out of town and informed her that he was on the job. He said he would contact her when he had new information. He asked her to be patient but she was clearly having a rough go.

Rome had not been in his office. She called several times. That was unusual. She knew he only handled special cases like the Miner case. Otherwise he preferred to work out of his home on Olympic Peninsula. He answered to no one and worked at his own pace and in his own peculiar manner. He checked in at the office from time to time and insisted on no distractions. He too had left a message that he would contact her when there was something to reveal.

That was all. His receptionist refused to give her his home phone or private email. "Strictly forbidden," she said. "He never takes business calls at home."

Though she would not admit it, it angered her that she was not an exception to the rule – if not because of their agreement then for other more personal reasons as yet undisclosed. She knew and understood his need for privacy and she respected him for insisting on it but it nevertheless gave her a feeling of unease. She wasn't sure how to interpret her feelings. This was new ground and she found it both engaging and disarming. She resented being relegated to outside his personal realm though she was fully aware that she had not invited him into hers.

She stood at the windows, staring off into the gray mists of the sound. Beyond the sound was Hood Canal and Dabob Bay on the eastern side of the peninsula where she had spent some of her most memorable summers as a child, running barefoot through the trees, playing Pocahontas, creating fantasies of wilderness kingdoms where animals spoke and goddesses reigned. Those summers represented a carefree and sheltered existence that always left her wistful in remembrance.

Beyond Dabob Bay was the national forest, among the richest and densest in North America. Beyond the forest were the high, rocky peaks of the Olympic Mountains with Mount Olympus towering like a Titan over the northern Pacific. Beyond the mountains were the rocky cliffs of Cape Flattery at the Straight of Juan de Fuca and the Makah Indian reservation. In her frazzled state of mind, she did not make the connection.

She had come to a decision. For reasons she did not fully understand, she was committed to the Miner case. It was not like her to obsess. She had become indifferent to the daily, media amplified spectacle of tragedy and misfortune that passed for mass information, education and entertainment in one. At any other time in her adult life she would have let the case go. She would have fought for a time and yielded. It would have become an anecdote at a cocktail party: "Do you really think he killed himself?"

Everything had changed. Her passion was renewed and her sleeping soul awakened. The cry for justice was no longer an intellectual exercise but a pulsing presence that struck to the heart.

She decided to take a leave of absence and was preparing to announce her decision when her secretary announced the arrival of Detective Jones over the intercom. She felt the anxiety of a schoolgirl being asked on her first date.

She ordered coffee and invited him in. They exchanged warm greetings and the detective settled in for polite conversation about the weather (rainy), the Mariners (another losing season), a jazz club he'd recently discovered (Monk's) and other matters of personal interest.

Just when Maggie arrived at the conclusion that this was a social visit, his tone dropped a register.

"I've come to give you an update on the case. I've taken a leave of absence from the department."

She was struck by his timing and confided her own similar decision. His reaction surprised her. Rising and strolling to the windows, he admired the magnificent view. He pulled a pack of Native Spirits from his coat pocket and politely asked if he could indulge.

"I don't normally allow it but I'll make an exception."

The detective gazed at the still closed pack for a moment and replaced them in his pocket. "Nasty habit," he reflected. "It seems to have attached itself to me." Again his tone changed to reflect the seriousness of what he would say next.

"Maggie. Can I call you Maggie?"

She nodded and wondered if this was a part of his famed detective act. He disarmed her and set her mind adrift.

"I don't think that's a good idea," he said.

The depth of his conviction struck her with curiosity. What did he know that she didn't?

"Why not?" she replied.

He scratched his head and rubbed his temples as if he was cursed by severe headaches.

"For reasons that will soon be obvious but I must have your assurance that what I'm about to say will remain between us. I'm prepared to give you all the information you need but you cannot share that information or reveal its source. Not now. As we proceed in this case you will have to understand that there are things I will not share with you and that my motive is to protect the innocent."

She took a moment to comprehend the conditions of his confidence. It was more or less unconditional yet she trusted him as she would her own father.

"Understood," she said. "Your reasons?"

He took his time with the explanation, pacing around the office, sipping his coffee, handling various objects and inspecting others. He spoke in a halting manner, almost as if reflecting on each syllable before releasing it.

"There is a lot more involved here than any one person or any one business. There is a powerful organization the full nature of which I am only beginning to realize. These people are aware of your interest in the case. They've had you followed. Your lines are very probably tapped. For now, they are content that you know very little. It would not be wise to alert them that you are intensifying your efforts. For myself, it's only logical that I should take a leave. I'm near retirement. I've signed off on the case. It's been signed and sealed: Suicide. Case closed. For you, however, it would be altogether too obvious."

She reflected on each and every word. The implications were mind blowing. It all hinged on the existence of a secret organization and a conspiracy of unprecedented proportions. She was not convinced but the detective was a man of sound mind and established reputation. She could not dismiss the possibility so she decided to go along.

"What do you suggest? I can't continue to represent my clients half-heartedly."

"You're depressed. It's normal. It's understandable. You lost someone close to you. You've been working too hard for too long. You need to delegate more cases – especially the more challenging ones. Take a cut in pay and begin to enjoy the finer things in life. These are natural behaviors. They will not arouse suspicion. In fact, they may have the opposite effect."

Maggie sensed a quickening of her heartbeat. It aroused a deep indignation at the intrusion of some unknown beast not only in her life but also in the lives of those she loved. Were they responsible for Miner's murder?

"Who are these people?" she demanded.

"That's what we need to find out," he replied. "I can tell you this: They are rich and powerful beyond imagination and they have formed an alliance the likes of which the world has never witnessed. They are disguised, protected, shrouded in an intricate web of secrecy and deception."

She began to realize the position he was putting her in and the danger it entailed. She would be his connection to the case while he would remain behind the scene like a shadow or a ghost. She needed more information. Why had he chosen her and what purpose did it serve?

"What would you have me do?" she asked pointedly.

"Be yourself. That's all. Be discreet, be cautious and do what you think is right. Nothing more and nothing less."

"Why me?"

"There are more things in heaven and earth than are dreamt of in your philosophy," he smiled. It was a quote from *Hamlet*. "The why you cannot know. Not now. I promise you'll understand in time. I suspect you already know more than I do or soon will. Then *you* can play the cat and mouse with *me*."

"You've given me a lot to think about, detective, but not much to go on. I'm already going crazy trying to find a clue… something I can move on."

"It's right in front of you, Maggie." He wore a wry, knowing grin that conjured a fatherly image. She gazed down at the file on her desk, opened to the last will and testament of William Miner. Detective Jones smiled, nodded and turned the page. He placed his finger on a heading entitled Endowments.

"Happy holidays," he said over his shoulder as he headed for the door. Turning back he imparted another entry in his words of wisdom: "Truth is truth to the end of reckoning." It was a quote from the bard's *Measure for Measure*.

Maggie took it all in as the detective closed the door behind him. She scanned the list of Miner's endowments and one entry stood out. There it was like a brisk jolt of whiskey on a cold winter's night: The Makah Indian Reservation. It was a relatively modest endowment but its significance far outweighed its monetary value.

If Miner left a clue as she assumed he had, this was surely it. Why the Makah? There were at least a dozen reservations in the surrounding area. Why not the Ozette, the Skokomish, the Quinalt or the Hoh? Why this one tribe and none of the others? To her knowledge, Bill Miner had never spoken of the tribes or Native Americans in any context other than commenting on a movie or television documentary. His ancestry was European and he had not been involved in any Indian causes. Maggie had once spearheaded a fundraiser for the tribes of the Northwest yet Miner neither contributed nor commented in her presence.

Beyond the scope of reason she had a strong gut feeling that this was the clue she was waiting for. She felt an imperative to determine its meaning. The detective's parting words pressed down on her: *Truth is truth to the end of reckoning.* She needed to speak to Jimmy Longbow. How right he had been when he told her he was the man for the job. She felt the same need to speak with Rome as well now that she had something of substance to share. The good detective cautioned her about sharing the information he gave her but he had allowed her to discover the Makah endowment on her own. She surmised he meant for her to share it.

For the moment she would be content to muse on the discovery and uncovering everything she could about the tribe on Cape Flattery.

Chapter 25

BLOOD BETRAYAL

Every cause and every movement must eventually pass the test of subversion if it is going to survive. The successful cause would recognize the betrayer and anticipate his or her actions before they could do irreparable harm. Jimmy considered it his good fortune that he had recognized the traitor before he could do significant damage but now he faced the challenging task of informing Rome before Judas realized his cover was blown.

He reached the coast at around sunrise. Not far from where he stood the jazzman still slept in the early morning hours. Jimmy lowered himself on a high cliff and peered out across the open sea. Down below, seagulls swept the ragged coastline; a family of sea mammals reclined on sea worn rocks and a Great Blue Heron dove into the waters and emerged with his morning meal. He watched until it vanished into the waters in the misty skies behind the northern cliffs. His journey across the peninsula brought him closer to the earth, to the cypress, fur and cedar, to the fern and moss, to the deer, the wolf and the vanishing elk.

He was at peace with the world. He gave thanks to the Great Spirit for guiding him to this place and prepared for quiet meditation. He opened his eyes at the squawk of a raven that now appeared before him with a fluttering of wings, its eyes of black fire peering into his own. In an instant it vanished below the cliff and a loud "crrruck" sounded behind him. He sprang to his feet and turned, pulling his knife from its casing in one movement.

There at a safe distance stood Rome Mason. Jimmy relaxed, replaced his knife and embraced his friend.

"Song of the Wind told me you were coming," said Rome with a smile.

"Did he tell you to greet me on this cliff at this precise time?"

"That much I gathered on my own."

Jimmy smiled at that and knew his friend had learned a great deal since their last meeting.

"You've come a long way, white man. When we first met you would have laughed at such a notion."

"The old one is a great teacher."

"I believe he is that and more. He has walked the same path as Sitting Bull and carries his spirit."

It was high praise. Sitting Bull was among the most powerful warriors, chiefs and spirit guides of the Oglala Sioux. Along with Crazy Horse, his death at the hands of his own people gave impetus to the Wounded Knee massacre, where men, women and children were disarmed and slaughtered for dancing the sacred dance, the dance of Wavoka, what the white man called the Ghost Dance. The return of the ancestors as promised died with them. Sitting Bull was a Ghost Dancer.

They walked together back to Rome's lodging, breathing the crisp saltwater air, taking stock of all they saw and giving thanks for the glories of a new day.

As they neared the front entry, well below the main structure and climbing to its center, their mood shifted to focus on matters of grave concern. Rome spoke first.

"I have something to share with you," he said as they climbed the stairs to the door. Jimmy watched as he punched in a combination of numbers on a keypad and pressed his thumb on a scanner to open the door.

"You've added security."

"I've had to, Jimmy."

They made their way to his study on the second floor.

"Word of the jazzman has spread."

"I've noticed. That's what I've come to talk about."

Rome picked up a printout from his desk and handed it to Jimmy with an expression of foreboding.

"It's the list from the stakeout. Give it a look."

He obliged and realized their minds were on the same track. He had compiled the list he was looking at.

"Jake send you this?" he asked.

"That's right. Any names missing?"

Jimmy pulled his own copy from his pocket, unfolded it and held it next to Rome's printout for comparison.

"Just one," he replied. "Robert Bates of Chicago."

He handed both papers to Rome who gave them another look. He didn't want to believe what it said about his oldest friend in Seattle. Jimmy sensed the sting of betrayal struck his boss deep. He had felt the same sting at the betrayal of his own native brothers when they teased him about his white father. It taught him a valuable lesson: Human prejudice is not the exclusive property of any one race.

"How did you know?"

"Honestly, I didn't. But after what happened in the Miner case, I don't trust anyone without confirmation. Not even Jake. You'd be wise to do the same."

Jimmy waited to get a measure of Rome's composure. He looked into his eyes and felt they were sharing their thoughts without spoken words.

"You trust me," he said cautiously.

"I know your spirit, my friend. I'd trust you with my life."

A heavy and profound silence descended as if the two men inhabited the same spiritual plain. They understood each other at a level that few ever experience. Rome broke the spell.

"I have a message for Maggie Thomas. Tell her Miner is only the tip of the iceberg. Tell her that knowing more would put her life in danger. Tell her the jazzman is an ally.

He is aware of her interest and will contact her when the time is right."

"She wants your identity."

Rome shook his head with finality. The jazzman's power was in his anonymity. He existed only on the web. It would not serve their cause to unmask him.

"Tell her he serves the cause."

"She will want to know what the cause is."

"Tell her everything, Jimmy. We have identified a powerful, malignant organization, an organization that undermines everything America stands for: the free market, the rule of law and our democratic institutions. Tell her we're fighting for the tribes and all Native Americans. Tell her what she needs to know. Before this is over, we'll need her."

Jimmy was familiar with the cause and the core of it, the part that won him over, was the return of native lands to native peoples. It was not enough to defeat an evil enemy; there had to be a positive goal and this one was dear to his heart.

Rome gripped Jimmy's shoulders, looked into his eyes and waited to give emphasis to what he was about to say.

"There are things not even you can know," he said. "This enemy is cunning like the fox and sly like the coyote. His eyes and ears are everywhere. He knows what cannot be known."

Jimmy conveyed his understanding with a nod. Rome spoke wide-eyed as if guided by a vision.

"Right now only you and I know that Jake Marshall works for them. Let's keep it that way. There is a lot to be learned by this betrayal. Jake would not do it without reason. The name of Robert Bates is proof enough."

Jimmy understood. He would continue to use Jake as his contact. They would learn by his omissions, evasions, and misstatements. Rome provided an alternative means of communication: an electronic bulletin board used by thousands of web walkers. His code: WMWLAATD.

"White Man Who Lives Apart and Thinks Deeply."

Rome nodded with a grin. No one knew his Indian name but the old man and the two of them. The plan was set. They would speak no more of it. They shared breakfast and spoke of the forest, the old one and walking in dreams.

At length, Jimmy wished his friend well and set out across the peninsula once more. As he found his pace he could hear the voice of the old one saying: *You have done well, Seeker with Two Souls. May the Great Spirit go with you.* A large crow flew overhead and cawed. He cupped his hands over his mouth and cawed back as it vanished beyond the tall trees, like a desert mirage or the ghost of his ancestors.

Chapter 26

ACCESS DENIED

Edward Kramer's appearance belied his reputation as a ruthless business executive and fierce competitor. Slim, pale, slightly hunched and wrinkled, his thin silver brown hair slicked back in the style of a former age and his thick round glasses on gold metal frames made him look older than his sixty two years.

An avid golfer who always asked for strokes without regard to the skill level of his fellow players, he always played for money and rarely played twice with anyone who bettered him. He played the insurance business like he played golf: he liked a stacked deck.

He was soundly beaten this time and he wasn't taking it well. Already smarting in the wake of a series of natural disasters – earthquakes, floods, mud slides and fires carried on a Santa Ana wind – he had taken a chance on a quick fix and now he braced for the consequences.

He should have been patient. The insurance business is always prepared for disaster. It is in fact the bread and butter of the enterprise. Short-term loss is long-term gain. After all, disasters are the reason people lay down their hard earned cash for whatever protection they can buy. After all, the bulk of Kramer's business and much of the country's wealth is concentrated on top of one of the world's most dangerous fault lines: the San Andreas where quakes, fires and floods are a frequent occurrence.

Kramer made his fortune on the fear of impending doom. However devastating on the surface, the fires should have been a blessing in disguise. But at the time it presented a problem of cash flow and a window of opportunity for enterprising entrepreneurs – anyone with large cash reserves eager to enter the insurance business. Within a week of the fires, while the insurance companies doled out hundreds of millions in claims, a Seattle consortium purchased large lots of stock in several companies under Kramer's control. They filed with the Securities and Exchange Commission stating their purpose as purely speculative. Kramer doubted the veracity of that statement.

Certain that some unfriendly entity intended to take his business over, he reached out for help. It was not the first time the Sanctum offered him a tip to bail him out of trouble. It was a sure thing. They were never wrong. He had no doubt they were privy to inside information. The practice was illegal but the Sanctum had refined it to an artform. As far as Kramer was concerned, there was no risk involved.

So when he received a message by email from a Chicago connection advising him to sell a Texas Biochemical company short, he didn't hesitate to sink all his cash holdings into the deal. To his astonishment, the deal went south. Texas Biochemical merged with Exxon, producing the exact opposite of the expected effect. The stock went through the roof. Within hours Kramer was broke. Within a day he was hopelessly in debt. Someone had sold him out big time. Maybe they were looking for younger and more promising candidates. Maybe they found his loyalty wanting. Maybe they just didn't like the looks of him. In any case, he was targeted for replacement. There was no way out and no one to turn to. The Sanctum was everywhere.

He sat quietly in his expansive office in downtown Los Angeles, a desperate man contemplating his next move. Closing in on midnight, the lights of the great metropolis danced in the background like stars of fallen angels in a city that always seems to slumber but never sleeps. Kramer did not notice. His eyes were glued to his computer screen.

He reached for a handkerchief to wipe beads of sweat from his oily brow and glanced at the wall clock above his trophy case. It housed memorabilia from his past conquests but he took no notice.

He had received a message during business hours that simply said: *RE: Bates. Contact New York, midnight.* He erased the message immediately, according to instructions, in order to prevent a virus from being released in his system.

It was more than curious; it was suspect. Contacting the Sanctum under any circumstances was forbidden. But then this was an extreme emergency. There were guidelines and always a go-between. Otherwise he would wait for the organization to contact him. He was not to contact another member directly. But Kramer figured this was the exception. After all, if the message was legitimate, then someone had betrayed not only him but the Sanctum as well. The usual contacts were not reliable.

He knew it was a gamble but it was the last chance he had. If he was wrong, he was wrong for the last time. But he couldn't be wrong. No one but his broker and Bates knew of the transaction. Only the Sanctum had the resources to find out what went wrong. In any case, he had no choice. The organization did not look kindly on the redistribution of wealth. It wouldn't matter that someone played him for a fool. The Sanctum didn't have fools. He had no choice. Something had to give.

Twelve hundred miles up the coast, Rome Mason sat poised at his own computer screen. He had gambled that Kramer would take the bait. He had sent the false tip under the name of Robert Bates. He was gambling that Kramer had a New York connection.

Why wouldn't he? It was clear that the organization was worldwide and New York was the center of the financial universe. Kramer had made an enormous bet on the New York Stock Exchange. Maybe Kramer would contact his broker and his broker would contact someone else. Every name added to his knowledge of their organizational structure. He was hoping to add the name of another member.

He logged on thirty seconds prior to midnight when the exchange would take place. He would monitor for no longer than sixty seconds. If they caught on to his tap, he could not allow them an opportunity to trace it.

Kramer had his message typed up and ready to go. It read: *Contact as per instructions. Kramer, LA.* He now typed in the contact information: *Logan 212-598-7324.* At the stroke of midnight, he pressed the enter key and waited. Leaning back in his chair, he removed his glasses, wiped the perspiration from his eyes and reached inside his suit pocket for the airline ticket to Buenos Aires he had purchase under an assumed name. He replaced his glasses just as the reply appeared on his screen: *Access denied.*

He felt his face go pale with embarrassment. Once again someone had played him the fool. It felt as though he was out hustled on the golf course by someone who was just toying with him like a cat with string until the eighteenth hole. In this moment he would have killed someone if someone were there to kill. But Kramer was all out of choices.

He clicked off his computer, called a cab and picked up his briefcase. It contained a large sum of cash and a small travel bag. He would have to leave his attractive young wife behind in their Laguna Beach estate. She wouldn't mind but he would miss her. Before he left he smashed his computer and trophy case with a Ping putter.

Edward Kramer was a poor loser.

Twelve hundred miles away at the Point of Arches, as the cold winds announced a change of seasons, Rome Mason smiled and settled back for a little Charlie Parker. Jazz, baby, jazz.

Chapter 27

WORLD DOMINATION

The Sanctum was an entity not unlike the towering redwoods of the northern California coast. The sheer magnitude inspired awe and its roots reached back hundreds of years, spreading in all directions to satisfy an insatiable thirst. The redwoods thirsted for water and nutrients; the Sanctum thirsted for power and wealth.

There was a time when power and wealth were virtually anonymous. At that time the Sanctum stood alone atop the power elite but that time was past. In the age of technology information was king. The Sanctum survived as only one of many branches in what some called the Shadow Government. They did not exist. They were the creators, the origin and the heart of the beast. They could not exist. They were content to share the glory with their counterparts in the military, intelligence and the inner sanctums underlying all facets of economic and social order. They were content to be at the forefront of the financial empire.

Historically, they were the western Europeans who migrated not for religious freedom but to find a new outlet for stolen treasures and to escape retribution for past indiscretions – a euphemism for high crimes and treason. They were the profiteers of the American Revolution who thought nothing of skimming a layer of profit from contributions to the cause of independence. They were the northern industrialists who perceived the South as an untapped resource for exploitation. They were the agents who corrupted organized labor when they could not break them at the turn of the last century. They were the military-industrial-intelligence alliance that formed to fight the war to end all wars when their actual intent was perpetual war. War was and always will be good business. They were the wealth that survived the Great Depression and thrived on the folly of Prohibition. They were the brain trust that catapulted America into worldwide prominence in the wake of Pearl Harbor. They were the minds that made the Cold War the multi-trillion dollar industry it became.

Yet it was not until President Dwight D. Eisenhower alerted the world to their existence in his farewell address to the nation that they became the Sanctum. Ike coined the phrase "military industrial complex" and warned that it was an existential threat to the republic. Like a doomsayer of the darkest dimension, his warning brought them together for the first time in a cohesive, highly structured unit. To them Ike was the existential threat. Until then they had existed as a scattering of powers and authorities moving to the same rhythm. Such are the ironies of the well intentioned.

In the early years they met frequently, defining loyalties, formulating plans and laying the groundwork for future prosperity. America had already emerged as the dominant world power and they would be poised to control it by controlling its economy. They formed international alliances but their operational base was and would remain within the United States of America. With their support America would rule the world.

The Eisenhower warning served as a cautionary message. They could have no connection to the underworld – that is, the underworld of organized crime. If you joined the Sanctum you were required to sever all ties to criminal enterprises. The new order of power required anonymity as well. They were not interested in money as an end. They needed wealth as a means to power. They wanted to determine the shape of the world to come. They were confident in the capitalist system. They were certain that

America would become the heart and soul of the global economy. If they could control the American economy, the rest of the world would follow.

They were not *solely* responsible for the end of Camelot. They knew that the young president's vision would not allow for their existence. They knew that the president's younger brother, Bobby, had identified them as an element of organized crime and vowed to attack them just as J. Edgar Hoover had attacked the mafia.

Back in those days the elite could buy most politicians but they could not buy the Kennedy's. Joseph Kennedy was one of them but he could not control his own children. They were raised apart from their father's business. They were raised on idealism and groomed for political careers. Neither Joe nor any other member of the Inner Sanctum foresaw that his children would attempt to destroy the power that created them.

If the Sanctum did not kill the Kennedy's, it could not have happened without their consent. No one but the Sanctum had the connections linking business, government, intelligence agencies, the military, law enforcement and the media that were necessary to pull off the assassination of a president without repercussions that would have shaken the world to its core. No one but they could have buried the truth until the end of time.

Since that fateful day in 1963 the Inner Sanctum met only sporadically. They grew cautious and more secretive than ever. No one on the outside could identify them. No one could link them together. They had Swiss bank accounts to hide and shelter their wealth. In the modern age there was rarely a need for physical gatherings. As long as they could be assured that their communications were secure, they were safe and their meetings could be remote.

When financial markets became computerized they discovered the perfect method of raising unlimited capital without risk. It no longer mattered which way the pendulum swung. No matter what happened in the worlds of finance or politics, the Sanctum would be the first to know. They would place their bets and take their profits.

When the market crashed in 1987 they were the first to sell out and the first to buy back after the market bottomed out. Investors would note that the market came to a standstill for more than an hour as the Dow Jones Industrial Average plummeted. The explanation that it was a computer malfunction always seemed specious. It was.

The truth was far more sinister and the Sanctum was the prime beneficiary. In a single day, the organization made more money than nations were worth. Using the same method, they capitalized on oil shortages, the rise and fall of gold and uranium, the collapse of the savings and loan industry, the Gulf War, the opening of trade with China, the crisis in the Asian markets, the El Nino disasters and other catastrophes. Like a dark spirit or a blood-sucking vampire, the Sanctum thrived on catastrophe.

They were profoundly wealthy and supremely confident. They stood alone as the most prominent rulers of the global economy. They were more powerful than any nation on earth or any international alliance.

It is the mark of hubris and unbridled arrogance that this all-powerful organization now felt threatened by some unknown individual or group of individuals operating under the name of jazzman. This was an adversary who understood that the way to fight them was not through force or finance but through information. The jazzman knew that the way to destroy them was to identify them one by one and shine a light of public scrutiny in their direction. That was a possibility the Sanctum could not allow.

The jazzman was using their own methods to get at them. By threatening their lines of communication, he threatened the very essence of their operation. It was only a matter of time before he discovered what their operation was. What he would do with that knowledge remained a mystery. If money was his motive, he would use it for personal gain. When he went too far, when he dipped into the well once too often, they would discover and end him. If his motive was political or philosophical, the threat was more dangerous. He would attempt to expose them. Like a sharpshooter under cover, he would take them down one by one. His operation had already begun.

He had to be stopped but they could not stop him until they could identify him. As yet they were only able to determine that he resided in the Great Northwest with his base of operations in the Seattle community. He was too knowledgeable, too clever and too cautious to be tracked by electronic means. They would have to draw him out.

They had a number of agents in Seattle and one who had managed to infiltrate the jazzman's organization. The jazzman trusted their spy enough to use him as a contact but not enough to reveal his identity. Not yet. It was only a matter of time.

They had learned a lot about the jazzman. They knew his plans for limited development on Olympic Peninsula. They had identified some of his connections. They knew enough to hurt him personally and financially but they could not predict how the jazzman would react. If they went after his business, he would only relocate, go into hiding and resume his operation elsewhere. They were not interested in his financial holdings. They wanted him.

They opted for another approach. They would exert the pressure of competition. They began meddling in his affairs. It was poetry in motion. Through him they had used Sara Kent to bring down Bill Miner – a colleague who had turned against them. Now they would turn Ms. Kent against the jazzman himself. They would enter the bidding for land on the Olympic Peninsula. He would suspect a leak within his ranks. He would not suspect the Sanctum.

The truth is they were intrigued. The jazzman, like themselves, spun an intricate web of deception to cover his tracks. They liked his style. They like the way he operated and the way his mind worked. Like a chess master he was methodical and relentless. They considered him a prime candidate for membership with the distinct possibility of moving up the ranks even to the Inner Sanctum. In the wake of Miner's death, they needed a man to head up the northwest sector. But before they took that next step, they needed to know who he was and what he was about. They needed to know before he knew too much.

They made a critical mistake when they recruited Bill Miner. They would take every precaution not to repeat the error with the mysterious jazzman.

Chapter 28

THE PENINSULA PROJECT

With Jake's help Sara had discovered the source of the false numbers that threatened her loyalty to the cause. They came from a real estate agency within the Miner empire, operating under the name of Puget Sound Realty.

Jake tried to explain that there were limits to what he could reveal. At this stage in the operation, he could only tell her that they were in battle and that the enemy was both powerful and cunning. He said it would often be difficult to determine which was the side of righteousness. It would require faith. They needed loyalty. All would be revealed in time but to do so now would not only endanger her but also jeopardize the cause. They would not take that risk.

Sara believed him. She had fallen in love. She felt she owed him her life. Jake had urged her to see a counselor in order to resolve the internal conflicts that haunted her in her nightmares. After several sessions the truth came bursting forth like sunlight on a dark day. With Jake's understanding and affection she was in the process of gathering the pieces that would make her whole again.

She now understood why she was wary of intimate relations. She had always wondered what was wrong with her. She had questioned her sexuality. Before Jake she had never really enjoyed sex. She had never experienced orgasm during sex. Now she understood: Her father, a pillar of community values, a man who attended church every Sunday and earned the respect of community leaders, had molested her in childhood.

It began when she was no more than four years old. It ended when she was seven. Her mother discovered what he was doing and put a stop to it. In all the years since, no one in the family said anything about it. It was as if an unwanted baby was buried in the backyard and as long as no one spoke the name, the child never existed. But it did exist with or without a name.

She made peace with her mother. She thanked her for stopping him and forgave her for withholding the truth. Confronting her father was far more difficult. It wasn't easy witnessing his breakdown as he begged her forgiveness. It wasn't easy forgiving him but she did so on the condition that he attend counseling himself. He swore to her that he had never repeated the crime and never would. He was overwhelmed with guilt. He agreed to counseling. It would be his penance. The family experienced catharsis and the healing process began.

For all this Sara was beholden to Jake Marshall. She was not yet ready to make the commitment he asked of her. That would take time. But she was prepared to give her love in exchange for his. The dark clouds that had covered her world since she was a little girl had lifted. The nightmare of unknown origins was dead. She was ready to begin life anew and she would do so with Jake.

The job was going well. In response to the unexpected competition from an unknown source for reservation lands on the Peninsula she proposed a unique approach. The company would enter into partnership with the tribes. The native communities would retain control of the land and any projects, large or small, would require their explicit consent. At any stage of development, regardless of cost, they would have the right to withdraw consent and halt the project at a moment's notice.

Fundamentally, she was proposing a series of treaties with the tribes. They would begin with those closest to the Sound – the Skokomish, Port Gamble and Squaxin – and proceed outward eventually reaching the Makah on the northwest tip of the peninsula. Word would spread from tribe to tribe that Olympic Realty was fair and honest and that word would carry them to agreements on the eastern side of the Sound.

It was an ambitious and well-calculated plan. It depended on their good will for success. They would continue to buy and sell privately owned lands as the opportunities presented themselves and they would negotiate with the Department of Interior for the use of public lands. In time they would ask the tribes to join them in these endeavors as well. It would be an opportunity to seize back control of their most sacred lands.

Sara rolled to her side on the sofa, bearing the soulful smile of a young woman who had at last discovered her calling in life. She gazed into her lover's dark brown eyes, aflame with passion and inspiration.

"Brilliant," he said upon reviewing the proposal. "It's absolutely brilliant."

The competition would never envision a partnership with the tribes nor would they be likely to pursue such a path. It would require them to sacrifice control and profit-motivated corporations would never do that.

Jake assured her the jazzman would approve the plan and set the wheels in motion. He promised to put her in touch with Jimmy Longbow, a native whose mother still lived on the Skokomish Reservation, to assist in the negotiations.

She melted into his arms and felt the flames of his desire. Was this why she loved him? Her father had always scoffed at her most creative ideas. "Come back to earth," he would chastise. It was such a rare pleasure in her life to know a man who was not jealous of her talents, who nurtured and encouraged her creativity. She never knew how much joy love could bring. Opening herself to Jake was as natural as wind through the trees. Touching him and feeling his passion, pounding like the bass of a jazz quartet, like a symphony of heartbeats, unleashed something deep within her that had been waiting most of her life.

Outside the northern wind blew a chilling breeze through the heart of Seattle. Waves of the northern Pacific pounded the rocky shore at the Point of Arches, delivering a message of strength through the Straits of Juan de Fuca and down to the southernmost tip of Puget Sound. Inside the winds of passion and desire blew hot and wild and waves of sensation rode high and low, rising and falling like tides of ecstasy, settling alas into a deep, spiritual silence.

Peace, satisfaction and silence.

In the morning while she waited by the fire, he cooked breakfast and sent her off with a loving embrace.

Chapter 29

ACCOUNT CLOSED

Edward Kramer awakened to a hypnotic Tropic of Capricorn sunrise. He rose, stretched and breathed in the fresh south Atlantic breeze from an open balcony on the third floor of his high-rise hotel. He felt better than he had in decades – more vibrant and more alive. He wondered if it was possible that after all the dirty deals that marked his life, he could finally be experiencing the process of rebirth.

He smiled at the morning gulls and acknowledged the familiar faces of those who made a habit, as he did, of walking along the beach and bathing in the glory of the sea as the sun still seemed to rise from its maritime depths. He threw on his swimsuit, grabbed a towel and rushed out to join them for a morning swim. It was the last swim he would ever take.

When he returned to his hotel room he was greeted with a .32 caliber slug to the back of his head. It was over in an instant, the smile of a new life still frozen to his face in death. He never saw, never heard and never knew what hit him.

His last mistake was one of the few sentimental acts of his life. He phoned his wife just to hear her voice and let her know he was okay. He knew better than to mention his name or where he was but he stayed on the line long enough for her to ask. He wanted to believe she cared. As it turned out, she did but not in the manner he had hoped.

The Sanctum dispatched a liquidator on the red eye. A man in a gray suit and amber shades arrived in time to watch a contented old man take an early swim. He watched from the balcony of his hotel room as he fastened a silencer to his handgun. He positioned himself behind the door just before his mark returned and took him out as the door clicked shut behind him. He unscrewed the silencer, placed it in the inside pocket of his coat, holstered his weapon, walked out and took the elevator to the lobby.

He hailed a cab and rode down the beach to another high-rise hotel. There he drove his rental to a connection in Buenos Aires where he deposited the gun and silencer for disposal, drove to the airport and caught the next flight to Miami. It was all so quick and easy.

Mr. Kramer would make no more phone calls. What remained of his wealth would go to his attractive young wife. The authorities in Buenos Aires would be unable to contact his relations and no one would mourn or even notice his passing. No one except the jazzman.

He had monitored Joshua Logan's line with a new cover and detection scheme that would alert him to the presence of a trace device. He was online when Logan received a cryptic message: *E.K. account closed. Miami.*

Chapter 30

A PRIVATE SUMMONS

The Christmas season always reminded Cheryl Miner that she was alone in an unkind world. It was a time of remembrance. Her childhood had been one of a modern American gypsy. Raised in perpetual motion by a single mother who migrated from town to town in search of a better life, she had always felt apart from the world.

At seventeen she struck out on her own, as much to relieve her mother of the burden as to seek her own life. The last she'd heard, her mother was living in Golden, Colorado. She was married and doing fine. That was more than a decade past and they'd lost touch.

She often wanted to call her mother, especially during the holidays, if only to thank her for doing her best and giving what she had to give. She wanted to tell her she loved her and that she always had.

The Sanctum forbade contact with her family. It was her lack of ties as well as her appearance that made her an ideal employee. Cheryl understood. If she contacted her mother now it would place them both in danger.

She was enjoying a brief respite from her obligations of employment. It didn't happen often. At one time she thought her association with the unseen hands that controlled her like a puppet on a string, would eventually come to an end. She would live out her life in relative comfort and prosperity. Now she knew better. Her association would end only when her usefulness ended: when she was no longer a sufficiently attractive lair. She figured she had eight to ten good years before she would no longer be young enough to satisfy their needs. With cosmetic surgery, a strict diet and a daily regimen of exercise she could prolong the inevitable. She could develop her charm so that her appeal was not so dependent on physical appearance. In the pall surrounding her and pressing her spirit downward, it seemed unlikely. After Big Bill got his pink slip she understood too well that there was only one way out and it was not a pretty picture.

Her best hope was that her next conquest would remain loyal to the organization and rise within its ranks. She would serve as a good wife, a loyal wife and a wife that provided more than sexual fulfillment. She would have to win his love and devotion. It was easy for a woman with her attributes to claim a man's desire. Passion was her trade. But winning his affection, the passion of the soul, a love that would outlast her fading, illusive physical beauty in the rushing river of time, was as mysterious to her as the alignment of planets or the kindness of strangers. To be loved she must learn to love. It was a road she had never ventured. It was the season of miracles and all things were possible.

This Christmas was different. It was the first she could recall when more than a husband or lover remembered her. Even Joe Thomas affirmed their friendship though their affair had ended. He almost seemed relieved. Though Cheryl was certain Maggie knew what had transpired between her father and her, she remained warm and caring as always – maybe even more so. Even Jake remembered her with a turquoise necklace and a smile. He asked her to stay in touch.

The move to New Orleans was coming. She was no longer under suspicion. Soon she would meet the mysterious man whom she would claim as lover and husband. It would occur at a small gathering of elites in the Thomas household.

The guest list included Roger Thomason, Big Bill's successor as CEO of the Miner Corporation, and his beautiful young wife. It also included Roman Mason, the consultant and entrepreneur, as the guest of Maggie Thomas. Finally, it included the guest of honor, Marcel La Conte, from the Louisiana bayou country. His enormous wealth was in oil and plutonium but he was looking to expand into real estate and development. His associates put him in touch with Joe Thomas, who in turn arranged this gathering.

Cheryl did not know why or how but the Sanctum was behind it. There was much, much more on the table than real estate advice or matchmaking. She could not help but wonder who the connection was. She was certain that Thomason was little more than a front man for the Sanctum. Joe always sheltered himself from direct involvement and knowledge. He had no desire to move up in the organization so it certainly wasn't him. She hoped for Maggie's sake it wasn't Rome Mason. He'd been around and he had high-powered connections. If not for Maggie's implicit trust in him, he would be a prime suspect.

She could only wonder. La Conte might be the only player in the room. The arrangements might have been made by anyone – with or without knowledge of its greater purpose. Joe might be acting as a businessman, eager to make powerful contacts for the firm. As always Jake only told her what she needed to know. She had her mark and it was up to her to make it stick.

If not for Maggie and the spirit of Christmas she would have thought no more of the matter. But she was finding it difficult not to confide in Maggie. It was a dilemma: If she told her everything she knew, that knowledge would place Maggie in the same predicament that she was in. If the organization found out, it could end them both. If she did not tell Maggie, her persistence could lead her into a world of trouble.

Cheryl sipped her cappuccino and looked out the window at the bustling shoppers in the street below. Someone was watching her. She could feel it.

"What's wrong?" said Maggie softly from across the table at a waterfront bar.

"Nothing," she replied. But a tear rolled down her rose colored cheek, flush from the chill of winter. She wiped it away with Maggie's handkerchief and resumed a cheerful pose. "It's just Christmas, Maggie."

Maggie nodded and smiled. She sensed there was more to it than Christmas but she held back. Cheryl would tell her when she was ready – in her own time and way.

Cheryl knew what Maggie was thinking but she could only smile: *If you only knew!*

Maggie took leave reluctantly. Cheryl had become a good friend but she needed to keep an appointment with Rome at a place just down the waterfront. They had spoken only briefly on the phone – just long enough to invite him to a social gathering.

The following day Jimmy delivered a message to her outside the office building where she worked. Rome wanted a meeting. She was to indicate where and when. No one else would know.

The level of secrecy baffled her. They were business associates. They ran in the same circles. Why would anyone think twice if they chose to meet publicly or privately?

Maggie stayed long enough to make sure Cheryl was okay. She gave her a warm hug, admired her innocent beauty and obvious underlying strength. She was like a delicate flower with the heart of an oak. They exchanged good cheer before Maggie walked out in the mist. Within half a block she became aware of someone edging up to her side.

"You're being followed," said Jimmy. He spoke without turning his head and instructed Maggie to do the same. He told her to delay at the next window and then walk into the shop. She did so while Jimmy continued down the street.

A man in a gray suit with amber shades hesitated at the shop where Maggie had gone inside. Jimmy turned the corner and waited before turning back to confront the man. He stood shuffling his feet in the uncomfortable position of being out in the open with nothing to do and no apparent reason for being there.

"What's the story?" said Jimmy.

The man stood a good four inches taller than him and did his best to remain stoic, like a bobby outside the royal palace in London. Jimmy continued.

"It's bad style to let a lady know she's being followed."

The man bolted as if a cloud had lifted and he realized he'd been outfoxed. He shoved Jimmy aside, sending his shades flying to the sidewalk, and dashed into the shop. Maggie was no longer there.

"Too late, Mack," smiled Jimmy. He picked up the man's shades and walked calmly down the street. By the time the man gave up, Jimmy was long gone.

"That'll teach 'em," Jimmy thought. "Sending a white man to do a red man's job."

Chapter 31

THE VISION

Detective Jones had an extensive collection of books and he'd read every one of them, from Nietzsche's *Thus Spake Zarathustra* and *Black Elk Speaks* to an odd assortment of dime store detective fiction and true-crime stories, from reference books in virtually every scientific discipline to the most esoteric sources of magic and mysticism. His books, he told his wife, were a winding road to his undiscovered self. The reference was to Carl Jung, the untamed colleague of Sigmund Freud with whom he shared a philosophy and who he admired more than any other being within his universe.

He gazed blankly at the ever-expanding chart in multi-colored pens on white butcher paper covering most of the north wall in his cluttered study. He did not know how long he had been fixed in this position, entranced by his latest graphic additions to his representation of an evil and as yet unknown organization – an organization without a name. He decided to call it "the organization" until a better name came to light.

Off center to the left was the deceased William Miner, connected to a circle of Seattle's financial leaders. He recorded names in red to signify their allegiance to the organization. In a maze of interconnected circles, the still anonymous jazzman was at the center of those opposed to the malevolent organization. He knew that the jazzman could be anyone within or without the organization's power structure but figured he or she was most likely within.

The detective made a leap of faith deciding that this

unknown jazzman without motive or identity was the good guy among good guys. He wrote good guys in blue.

It was not simply a leap of faith. It was the knowledge he gained through dreams, meditations and waking visions that were happening more frequently now.

He wrote possible candidates for the jazzman as well as the organization's connections, members and associates, in pencil until the nature of their associations became clearer.

At the center of his graph was a large circle representing the organization's control center, its Board of Directors and executive officers, with a short list of candidates. Through his associations in the investigative community, by following the money trail and communication networks, he had identified connections from the Seattle branch to virtually every major city across the nation.

"The magnitude," he said to himself. "The sheer magnitude" boggled his mind and left him in an altered state. He could not grasp the magnitude of the organization or the task at hand. To his knowledge the only crime they had committed had already been dismissed as a suicide. To bring the case to justice he would have to identify both the criminals and the crime.

But he was not considering the facts of the case now. Though his eyes remained fixed at the center of the chart, he did not see the carefully drawn circles and lines. He did not see and could not read the multi-colored names and sprawling notations. He could not see what was directly before him because his mind, his spirit, the soul of his being and his undiscovered self were transported somewhere else.

He was himself yet he was not. He was his dream self. He was dreaming yet he was aware of dreaming. He could control his movements. He could direct his vision and his thoughts.

Standing beside him was a medicine man, a spirit guide, with deep powerful eyes. He did not say he was a spirit being but the detective understood, just as he understood that this old Indian was his friend and advisor.

"I am Song of the Wind," the old one said. He spoke in his native tongue but the detective understood without need of translation.

He gestured to a circle of chanting natives that appeared before them. "Here the people dance. It is the dance of the ancestors. It is the dance that makes the earth tremble and signals the coming of floods, powerful winds and pestilence. They sing that the spirit of the old ones not be forgotten by their children. They pray that the ancestors take their place upon the earth once more. They ask that the great mother remember and aid those who are her friends, that she obstruct those who are her enemies."

He looked deeply into the detective's eyes. "It is the dance the white eyes call the Ghost Dance. It is the dance of Big Foot and Black Elk, of Crazy Horse and Sitting Bull, of Kicking Bear and High Hawk. It is the dance of the Paiute and Shoshone, the Cherokee and Cheyenne, the Kiowa and Crow, the Apache and Arapaho, the Navaho and Comanche. It was the dance of the Hunkpapa and Minneconjou Sioux at Wounded Knee."

The old man's piercing gaze was relentless now as he reached into the detective's inner thoughts. "I have thought long, white eyes, before inviting you to see this – no less to participate. But there is no other way. I have decided that an Indian is here." He pressed his long, leathered hand to his chest. "I have decided you are one with the people."

Not knowing why the detective pressed both hands held in fists to his chest and extended them outward to Song of the Wind. He knew without knowing it meant: "I am honored and I give myself to your cause."

The circle of dancers immediately opened to them. They linked arms with the others and began to move in harmony with the whole of the circle. When it was time for him to sing the words came to him without thought. They danced and sang for hours and hours until time ceased to function.

There was only movement and sound and spirit. There was only emotion and reverence and joy in being. It was easily the most invigorating experience in his life.

When he awakened he was back in his study gazing in the direction of the expansive chart, vaguely aware that his wife was yelling something from another room. It might have been another world. He responded to her without knowing what she had said. He felt uplifted, enchanted and alive yet there was something uneasy, something wrong or something missing.

He realized that he had learned nothing that was even remotely useful – at least in the usual sense. He had gathered no clues, no leads and no suspects. Yet he had affirmed the cause and he felt confident that everything would work out. He would know exactly what to do at exactly the right moment. He was not naturally a creature of faith but faith was required of him now.

He smiled at the revelation and accepted the challenge. He took a deep breath and went to investigate whatever had transpired between him and his wife.

Chapter 32

JAZZMAN UNMASKED

Rome was waiting when Maggie stepped inside the shop. They slipped out the back, jumped into his jeep and got lost in the flow of Seattle traffic by the time Jimmy made his move. They were headed north on the interstate when Maggie caught her breath. Rome was looking her over as he drove, trying to judge by her reaction how much she had pieced together.

"You want to meet the jazzman?" he asked.

His tone heavy and ominous, it sent a chill up Maggie's spine. Until this moment she had discounted any notion that Rome was somehow affiliated with the jazzman. She had fallen into the trap of thinking of the jazzman's group as a radical fringe organization, a misguided leftover of the late sixties that progressed from psychedelics to advanced technology. She would have to rethink that assessment. Clearly, they were not a hacker brain trust sitting in a circle of computer terminals. Rome's involvement meant they had powerful connections in the business world. They were a force that could not readily be dismissed.

Stunned, she nodded but she could find no words.

"What if I told you, you already have?"

Her mind was a spinning circle of thought, searching for clues missed and leads not followed. Jimmy had tried to prepare her. He concocted a story about sending out feelers. He told her he had received a message that seemed credible. He advised her that, from what he could decipher, the jazzman was on her side. They were both pursuing the truth regarding Bill Miner's death.

But Miner was only the tip of the iceberg. She knew that now. There were others involved: a powerful organization of business associates, well connected and almost impossible to track down by traditional means. Maggie had shared with Jimmy her theory concerning the Makah endowment. She was certain it was an important lead.

Her thinking had progressed. She now believed Miner left something tangible on the reservation itself. He would have known that his papers and files would be scrutinized. If he wanted to leave incriminating evidence, he would leave it someplace else, somewhere the organization would never think to look. What better place than an Indian reservation far off on the northwestern tip of the Olympic Peninsula? Jimmy had advised her to keep it to herself until he could check it out. When she inquired about Roman Mason he advised her to put it on hold.

"Don't keep me in suspense," she said.

"The stakes are high, Maggie. I have to be certain," he replied.

He squirmed in his seat. He knew she knew too much already. The Makah revelation was a gold mine. The Sanctum had been searching for something, something they had lost track of in the Santa Anna fires. Why someone like Edward Kramer had been entrusted with it – if in fact he had – was a mystery. Rome theorized that it circulated within the organization, too hot and too important to keep in one location. Maybe they all felt safer if it was kept in neutral hands. Alternatively, Kramer might have stolen or copied the materials as a measure of security.

Why such incriminating evidence was allowed to exist at all was another, even greater mystery. It could only be answered by invoking vanity. The Sanctum and its illustrious inner circle wanted to be remembered to the end of time. They wanted a written account of their history and they wanted to write that history as well.

Whatever their motives, the files did exist and Bill Miner knew about them. The fires provided a cover and the files came into his hands. His relationship with the Sanctum was already strained. He was a natural suspect. He was sure they were the source of his legal problems and they were right. They used the jazzman as the hammer but they were the force behind the blow.

Miner recognized that he and the jazzman were allies in this fight. He hoped his friends would figure out the Makah connection before the Sanctum did. With Maggie's help, they had. He took his own life before the organization could put the squeeze on him. He had sacrificed himself for the knowledge and the evidence they now possessed.

"I want to level with you," he said. "That's why you're here. Before I do, you have to know what we're up against. You have to know the risks."

"I'm a grown woman," she replied. "Explain it to me."

Rome cleared his throat and chose his words carefully. He did not want to get ahead of himself. He wanted to be sure not to say too much too soon. He wanted to leave room for Maggie to back out.

"You were right. Miner did leave something at the Makah Reservation. He left written instructions at tribal headquarters to hold it for someone operating under the name of jazzman. We now have it in our possession."

"Don't hold out on me now. What is it?"

He was right when he implied there was a lot more involved than she imagined. She sensed by his tone that she had no concept of the magnitude the case now encompassed. It went well beyond a simple murder.

"Okay," he said. "You won't believe it but: It's a history book."

"History?" she replied. She was incredulous. What did history have to do with Bill Miner? Why would these people, whoever they were, be willing to kill over a book of history? It seemed absurd.

"I know," he said quietly. "But this particular history chronicles the major accomplishments of a group of men known as the Sanctum."

He let it settle and watched Maggie squirm. She was becoming angry and he wanted to calm her. He wanted to tell her everything but he held back. One step at a time.

"That's what this whole mess is about? History?"

"I want you to read it. Then decide."

"Decide what?"

He took a breath and spoke the simple truth.

"You'll have to decide if you're with us or not."

"And if I'm not?"

He knew what she was thinking. The Sanctum would not allow her to live with the knowledge she was about to acquire. But they were not the Sanctum.

"We're not like them, Maggie. I'm taking a big chance letting you in on this. You've earned it. If you want out I'll understand. You're free to do as you see fit. You can go back to the firm, turn your back on all this and pretend it never happened. Believe me, I almost hope that's what you'll decide."

"Not likely."

"I realize that."

He tried to give her a reassuring smile as he turned off the interstate and drove onto the Tulalip Reservation where a chopper was waiting. They boarded and Rome started up the engine.

"We'll be there in thirty minutes," he said. "Enjoy the view."

It was a magnificent view. They crossed over the long, evergreen islands of the northern part of Puget Sound and headed up the Straight of Juan de Fuca. Down below, through a layer of gray mist, the pulsing, billowing waves vacillated between sea green and ocean blue.

They veered south and traced the northern peninsula, the lower view now changing to the dense, moist green of rich forestland with Mount Olympus piercing snow white clouds in the distance. They skirted the mountains and broke through the mist to the open sea.

It took her breath away.

Rome pointed out the Makah Reservation before heading south to the Point of Arches where he set the aircraft down. They had arrived.

Chapter 33

COMPLEX MANEUVERS

Sara was enraged. She practically flew into Jake's office, tossed a file on his desk and demanded: "Who are these people? They're putting out bids on everything as if they knew our plan!"

Jake opened the file and carefully scanned the printout. There were more than a dozen bids and all of them originated with Puget Sound Realty.

"Calm down," he said. "Let's take a look at it."

He did so but only for a moment. He closed the file and handed it back to her wearing an expression of grave concern.

"Of course they know our plan," he said. "I gave it to them."

Once again she was stunned and she wondered how many more of these surprises she could take. He motioned for her to sit and she complied.

"What's going on, Jake?"

"Look, they'd have found out anyway. They're in the business and their eyes are wide open."

"Is that any reason to help them along?"

"Think about it, Sara. They're buying, right?"

He waited for her agreement. She felt like she was being sold and she didn't like it. Still, it was Jake and she wanted to believe him.

"They'll keep buying at almost any price. We have holdings. We sell. Let them finance the project. As long as we make the agreements with the tribes, our competitors will be out in the cold. Unless they have connections we don't know about, they won't get any government concessions on the peninsula. That leaves the reservations. By the time they figure out what's going down, they'll be selling back to us at a loss."

Sara was not quite convinced. There were too many loose ends and too much secrecy.

"What if they do have the connections? What if they get the government concessions?"

"Then we'll know more than we know now."

"Where would that leave the tribes?"

"We'll cross that bridge when we get there."

"What if they get there first? What if they sign the agreements with the tribes?"

Jake was a little exasperated and it showed but this was why he valued her services. Nothing got past her and everything was subject to inquiry.

"In the first place, they don't know what the endgame is. They're not interested in doing the groundwork. They'll let someone else do it and take a profit. That's how they work. In the second place, the tribes will never deal with these people. You have to take my word on that."

She didn't like taking his word. One of her cardinal lessons in life was never to trust anyone who said trust me. She felt Jake was putting her off again. She was on the outside looking in. It had to stop. There was so much she didn't know. What did she have to do to earn their trust? How much longer was she expected to go along in the dark before they finally came clear?

"I've got to tell you it's getting harder, Jake. Why didn't you tell me?"

"Because I didn't want you to know."

"You knew I'd find out."

"Did I? It's not your job to review outside bids."

She felt her face go flush. He was right. It wasn't her job. She had done so out of mistrust and Jake knew it.

"Sara, please," he implored. "You have to trust someone. Let it be me. If I don't tell you something it's because I care and want to protect you. Knowledge is power and power is dangerous."

She understood but it did not make it easier.

"I love you, Jake. You know I do. If you're in danger I want to know it. If knowledge is dangerous I want to share it. Don't cut me out. I can live with danger. Haven't I proven as much? But I can't go on this way. I can't be on the outside. You can't shelter me. I can't live without you."

He couldn't help but smile. Outside a moment of intimacy she had never given voice to the word love. It warmed his heart and filled him with the spirit of Christmas. He looked at her like a smiling, teenage fool and counted his blessings. How could he be so lucky?

"You want it all?" he asked.

She could not at this moment distinguish between the folly of love and the uneasy feeling that he could so easily manipulate her. It was a feeling of helplessness. Never before had she allowed a man to have so much power over her. Never had she so desired to give in.

"Yes," she replied in a tone of exasperation.

"Then marry me," he said.

He disarmed her. How strange life could be. She had entered his office in anger with a sense of distrust and accusation in her mind. Now she was powerless to resist his charm. She walked around his desk, lifted her business style skirt above her hips, removed her silk white panties and straddled him with a long wet kiss.

"I will," she whispered as she unleashed his burgeoning desire and rode the cresting waves of renewed passion. A moment of unbridled pleasure stolen from the daylight hours to dwell in the memories of the heart until their hearts beat no more.

Later, in the still of the night, beneath a rare Seattle sky of a million stars, clear and shining like hope reborn, he would tell her everything and she would pledge her life, her love and all of her being…forever and always.

Chapter 34

GERONIMO'S REVENGE

Jimmy slept restlessly in the confines of a cave in the forest – his refuge for the day. His vision was clouded with the images of the fox and the raven. The old one's voice was distant and faint. He sensed another presence, darker and closer. He strained to hear a voice in the wind through the tall trees. A single word suddenly came clear: Geronimo!

He awoke at once and knew the meaning of this sudden appearance. Someone was on his track and it was not the shape shifting fox, the crow or the raven. It was not Song of the Wind nor was it the men in gray suits and amber shades. They were not capable of tracking in this terrain. He was being followed by his own brothers in the Skokomish tribe. The cry of Geronimo was not a war cry but a warning. He had been betrayed. It was a reminder that the great Apache warrior and spirit guide was tracked down and imprisoned not by the blue coats and not by the whites but by his own Apache brothers: Chato, Martine and Kayeeta. Their names deserve to be remembered in infamy.

Jimmy thought through his options. He could feel their presence. He even sensed their eyes upon him. He counted their number and he knew that by detecting their presence he had defeated their purpose. He would no longer be meeting the jazzman at the Point of Arches and they would learn nothing.

He grabbed a handful of dirt with one hand, a leather pouch with the other and rose up from his cover. Standing proudly, defiantly, on the overhang, he raised his fist to the heavens like a celestial warrior.

"Brothers!" he declared. "I hold in my hand the earth and know it is my mother! I look to the heavens and know it is my father! I have heard the voice of the raven! It cries with the shame of my brothers! It cries the shame of the ancestors and the shame of my blood! To me it cries Geronimo! Remember! Remember the glory of that great Apache warrior who defied the eyes of darkness! Remember the shame of those who tracked their brother like a rabid dog! As Geronimo lives in greatness so they must live in shame!

"You have looked into the eyes of those who sent you! You know the evil that lives behind them! Turn back, my brothers, and tell them the one you follow seeks only peace and solitude. Tell them he cries for a vision! It is the Indian way. Turn back and carry this shame to the grave!"

He sat and spread the earth before him. From his pouch he pulled a long wooden pipe adorned with beads. He filled it with tobacco, lit a match and smoked. He then held it outward as an offering to his brothers.

He heard a rustling in the brush before they emerged from hiding and joined him, their heads bowed in humility. Jimmy nodded and they sat. He knew them. They were the new breed of Indians. They wore blue jeans and hiking boots. They were a lot like him, educated in the white man's schools and aware of the value of money in the white man's world.

They passed the pipe and smoked in silence before speaking. They told him about the gray suits who came to their village inquiring after Jimmy.

"We told him nothing but they knew the house of your mother."

Jimmy listened and nodded but still remained silent.

"We refused their money but they left their card. We needed the money so we called. They told us they meant you no harm. They only wanted us to track you and tell them where you went. We thought: What harm is there? So we took their money."

Jimmy knew their words were shallow. They took the money not out of need but want. He also sensed their hearts were good. They would not act now as they had then.

"Would the gray suits offer their money if there were no harm? Do their amber glasses hide their purpose so well that you cannot see through them?"

Again they bowed their heads in shame.

"We have done wrong," said one. "What can we do to help?"

Jimmy waited before deciding to trust them. He let the guilt sink into their souls and seal their desire for redemption.

"Retrace your steps and cover them. Go to the Heart of the Hills and camp there this night. Return to your village tomorrow and tell them you have seen me there. Tell them I seek no company and receive none. Tell them I seek only communion with the Great Spirit. This they will believe. They are white men and know nothing of our ways. Take their money and ask no more. When they come to you again, refuse them. Tell them the Great Spirit came to you in a dream and warned you against them. The Skokomish will deal with them no more."

The men smiled and nodded in agreement. They rose and embraced their wiser brother with good will. They swore never again to forget that they were Indians. They had learned the lesson of Geronimo. As they took their leave they turned to the mestizo and said: We think you are more Skokomish than white man.

Jimmy nodded and watched them closely until they vanished in the trees below. From behind him the caw of a crow sounded with a fluttering of wings. He turned and saw it trace the sky toward the Point of Arches. His way was clear.

Chapter 35

THE SANCTUM CHRONICLE

"Merry Christmas," said Rome as he lowered the book to the table before her. "This is what it's all about."

Maggie gazed at it in wonder: a leather-bound volume of three hundred and sixty pages labeled, "History of The Sanctum." The authors were not given credit. A quick glance revealed it chronicled events in American history from the 1920's through the eighties. The only names included in the account were those of its founding fathers, whose facsimile signatures were affixed in gold to the dedication page of the manuscript like a perverse version of the Declaration of Independence.

The list represented the grand champions of the American dream, a capitalist hall of fame:

Irenee du Pont: Chemist-Industrialist 1771-1834.
Cornelius Vanderbilt: Financier 1794-1877.
Jay Gould: Financier 1836-1892.
Marcus Alonzo Hanna: Industrialist 1837-1904.
John Pierpont Morgan: Financier 1837-1913.
Andrew Carnegie: Industrialist 1835-1919.
Henry Clay Frick: Industrialist 1849-1919.
Daniel Guggenheim: Industrialist 1856-1930.
John D. Rockefeller: Industrialist 1839-1937.
John Pierpont Morgan Jr.: Financier 1867-1943.
Andrew William Mellon: Industrialist 1872-1953.
Bernard Baruch: Financier 1870-1965.
Joseph Patrick Kennedy: Financier 1888-1969.

The list itself was fascinating. Thirteen obscenely wealthy men, the titans of the capitalist machine, they were arguably the richest individuals the planet had ever witnessed. With the exception of JP Morgan, most would be remembered almost as well for their philanthropy as for their business acumen. To a man they profited from the misery of humankind. They were war profiteers. While paying off governments, regulators and politicians, they built empires. To a man they were obsessed with leaving a living legacy.

The account did not draw a clear connection between the founders and the organization that became the Sanctum. It seemed they were the epitome of the organization's ideals. They represented the last public defenders of what was known as Social Darwinism. The Sanctum believed that they and those who succeeded them were superior beings, exemplary models of the American ideal and more qualified to rule than elected officials. To the Sanctum, as to its founders, democratic government was a mere inconvenience to be overcome.

Their motto: *Leadership Through Strength.*

Maggie skimmed through the first part of the book, a series of historically based novellas featuring each of the founder's accomplishments. She stopped to consider the cumulative effect or the composite character drawn from these accounts.

They were all brilliant financial minds. Each of them accumulated vast fortunes from modest beginnings. Each took great care to portray himself as a socially conscious and responsible citizen yet in their day-to-day practices each was notoriously devious and, by any standard of decency, grossly immoral. Their collective ambitions and wealth were surpassed only by their incredible vanity.

Du Pont, Baruch and the younger Morgan were major suppliers of gunpowder, munitions and war supplies. They controlled the pipeline that connected industry to the military. Baruch served as a key advisor to presidents from

Woodrow Wilson to Harry Truman. Mellon was the aluminum baron. As Secretary of the Treasury to Warren Harding, he orchestrated the repeal of Wilson's taxes on the very wealthy. Morgan served as a government agent for a period encompassing both world wars. It could be said that these men were the fathers of the military-industrial complex.

Assisted by his good buddies at Tammany Hall, including Boss Tweed and James Fisk, Gould was the most notorious stock manipulator of his time. His work triggered the first major market crash in the 1860's. Hanna bought politicians wholesale, including President William McKinley. He gave birth to the concept of an inner circle governing the nation. Carnegie was the leading proponent of Social Darwinism though he was himself bettered by the senior Morgan. Frick was noted for his brutal strike breaking.

Rockefeller and Kennedy developed more sophisticated political connections and devoted much of their efforts to public service and philanthropy. Despite their Machiavellian business tactics, Guggenheim and Vanderbilt are also remembered for their philanthropic endeavors.

These men formed the Sanctum's foundation. They were intended to provide a mode of behavior, a code of conduct and an historical justification for what the organization would become.

The second part of the book was infinitely more interesting. Labeled *The Modern Era* it chronicled the birth and evolution of an organization whose inner circle was the ruling class of a contemporary American Dynasty. The language was pointedly bland and laborious.

It began with a gathering of elites on the sixth of June 1959. Those attending were the nation's most powerful corporations. Their purpose was to form a permanent alliance with common goals, principles and a defined code of conduct. The natural descendants of the founders, they were the wealthiest and most influential Americans: financiers, industrialists and masters of the market place from Wall

Street to Main Street. They were the barons of steel, oil, coal, uranium, gold and silver. They were the suppliers and manufacturers that fed the American economy and the military machine.

It was the age of the red terror. The nation was still reeling from the McCarthy hearings on un-American activities in the early part of the decade. In the wake of Korea the Cold War raged on with a policy of strategic military interventions. The Sanctum was still in an era of direct control, buying, bribing and breeding politicians and judges. Even those who could not be bought – war heroes, independently wealthy individuals and grass roots leaders – were surrounded by Sanctum people. They were invariably best qualified for the job.

The economy was healthy and growing but it needed constant impetus to sustain it. By far the largest and fastest growing government expenditure was the military. The Cold War assured that the trend would continue indefinitely but as the stockpile of advanced weaponry and munitions grew, large-scaled interventions were required to sustain and optimize the profits. A policy of small interventions provided a constant source of funding but what the country really needed was a major war – something that would make Korea look like the Dominican Republic. They needed a protracted and escalating conflict that would catapult the Sanctum to a level of dominance unseen since the days of Rockefeller and Morgan.

The Sanctum pushed hard for an invasion of Cuba. It was a natural choice. The elements were in place: All the president's men, the Pentagon, the intelligence community, congressional advisors and political consultants. The stage was set for what came to be known as the Bay of Pigs invasion. Unfortunately, the CIA bungled the operation and the young commander-in-chief, who had forgotten his privileged roots and somehow saw himself as a Knight of the Round Table, pulled out before the war mentality could set in. To make matters worse, the president and his brother lost faith in the intelligence community as well as the advisors who had pushed the ill-fated invasion.

The stage was reset with the Cuban Missile Crisis. This time the president could not back down. The Russians were attempting to establish a nuclear weapon facility in the nation's back yard. A missile launched from Cuba could reach Washington before a hand could be raised to stop it or even to retaliate in kind.

Tragically, the president found a way to disarm the most explosive crisis the nation had confronted since its founding without firing a shot. The missiles were withdrawn. The young president had thwarted the Sanctum's most important plans for a prosperous future. It was a significant failing and one that would clear the path to the liquidation of a president. Until then, the son of an illustrious founder was considered sacrosanct.

Cuba was history. Castro was off the hook. The window of opportunity slammed shut and the Sanctum was in search of an alternative. Their next target was a harder sell. Cuba is in our neighborhood; operations would be much easier. Viet Nam is three thousand miles away and its neighbor to the north is the most populous nation on the planet. Defending the hemisphere had a more logical appeal than the abstract Domino Theory.

Given his experience in Cuba, the young president was resistant to any new plans for military engagement. He announced to his inner circle that he would oppose any attempt to escalate the involvement in Southeast Asia. Rumors circulated that he had yielded to the persuasive power of his brother, the Attorney General, who clearly had presidential ambitions of his own. Together, the brothers of Camelot forged a formidable force of opposition to the future wellbeing and prosperity of the Sanctum.

They were surrounded by Sanctum agents both within and without the government. It became clear that their vision did not include the ruling class. They wanted to dismantle the established order and replace it with something resembling a working democracy. They had alienated the military, the intelligence agencies and many of their colleagues in congress. The Attorney General was gearing up for a war on organized crime. It was not the war the Sanctum had in mind. For the good of the nation and its people the Kennedy's had to be stopped.

The account evaded the question of accountability, insisting it was impossible to tell which of the involved parties first conceived the notion or who gave the order – as if it mattered. It was a consensus. They all gave their respective consent. They played their parts. They spread suspicion in all directions so that, in the end, no one would be held responsible. It would be decades before anyone could begin to untangle the web of deception and even then its scope and complexity would defy credibility.

Intelligence agents prepared the area, provided the fall guy and controlled the investigation. Organized crime provided a hit squad and a sacrificial lamb. The Sanctum acted as coordinator for both the assassination and its cover-up.

The president never knew what hit him. His successor was a Sanctum man, tried and true, who knew firsthand the consequences of defying them. The Attorney General was effectively disempowered. He would have to be dealt with again years later when he attempted to recapture the White House. He should have known better.

The war in Viet Nam guaranteed the Sanctum's wealth and secured its position on the highest rung of power. They ruled with an iron fist for twenty years. Through the Johnson, Nixon and Ford administrations no significant decisions were made without the Sanctum's informed consent. The Carter administration was a temporary but insignificant setback. More than any president since Warren Harding, Carter learned the limitations of executive power.

With the election of Ronald Reagan the Sanctum was back with a vengeance. By the end of Reagan's second term the concept of a Shadow Government was fully secure, reducing the presidency to one of many branches of power. The Sanctum remained the key economic, strategic and military force of the nation and the backbone of the new order.

The book went on to chronicle the organization's transition from military-industrial to technology and pure finance. It described the instruments and ingenuity used to control the major markets and explained how fortunes were made from the collapse of the gold and silver markets, the creation of the oil crisis and the ongoing manipulation of the stock and commodities markets.

They managed to gain control of the flow of information through the computerized market systems, a control that enabled them to halt trading at any given time while they made their play. In a single day during the most recent market crash, when trading was inexplicably halted for over an hour, the Sanctum and their shadow government associates made billions in the space of a few hours.

It was officially written off as a computer glitch, the unfortunate result of information overload. It was anything but accidental.

Little wonder "playing the markets" had become the method of choice for the modern Sanctum. It marked an end to the old and more laborious ways. No longer was it necessary to orchestrate takeovers and create shortages. No longer was it necessary to maintain a worldwide intelligence apparatus to engage in espionage. No longer was it necessary to bribe public officials. Connections to organized crime could safely be severed.

The Sanctum maintained its ties with government, particularly the Securities and Exchange Commission, but they rarely asked for favors and exerted no direct control. They dealt in information and that's all they demanded in exchange for their substantial contributions. It was a new and benevolent organization. Its members engaged in philanthropic enterprises but always avoided public recognition.

The account ended with a summation of the Sanctum's achievements: They secured the nation's position as the dominant world power both economically and militarily. They elevated and defended capitalism as the dominant global economic system, dealing a deathblow to socialism. They secured representative democracy over communism as the political system of choice by demonstrating that the ruling class could assert control over democratic institutions. They assured constancy across administrations in American policy. They protected the nation from subversive elements within and without. They assured survival of the planet and finally, they provided what Presidents Bush and Reagan called "a thousand points of light." A list of philanthropic programs was attached in appendix.

At long length, Maggie closed the book and sat staring at the wall. This was by far the most vain, presumptuous, self-aggrandizing account of any group of individuals she had ever encountered. It left her feeling sick. But the sensation of numbness from the sheer breadth of the account gradually gave way to indignant rage.

Who were these men to justify the killing of a beloved president with rationalizations of capitalism? Who were they to proclaim themselves heirs to an imagined ruling class? Who were they to paint the flagrant extortion of billions upon trillions of dollars from the American economy in the colors of patriotism?

"It's incredible," she said.

Rome had been waiting patiently in the next room. He now came in with two snifters and a bottle of brandy, pouring one for each of them.

"Isn't it?" he answered. He sat on the sofa across from her, prepared for a battery of questions. Maggie was not one to accept anything at face value without substantial proof.

"Why would these people leave a written account? It makes no sense. In every other way they value secrecy. They hide their philanthropy. They cover their tracks. They're even willing to kill anyone who might expose them. But they leave this for anyone to find?"

"Why did Nixon make the tapes? Like LBJ before him, he was obsessed with history. These people actually believe in what they're doing. They believe that history will vindicate them. They believe they can justify killing the Kennedy's and whoever else stands in their way because the end justifies the means."

Maggie thought it over and rejected it.

"These are rational people but this is not! You can't rationally believe Americans will forgive the killing of the president!"

Rome had already gone through the process and arrived at the place where Maggie was destined to join him.

"Is it really that hard to believe? After all, the great majority of us have accepted the extermination of Native Americans, haven't we? Already we're beginning to accept rationalizations of Viet Nam. In time people can accept almost anything. The government lies? So what? Who doesn't? It all comes down to who is telling the story."

"They want to tell the story," replied Maggie, her head still reeling from the onslaught of information.

"That's right. When it all comes down, the individuals in this circle do not want to be forgotten. They want the world to know what they've done. They're proud of their legacy. They want their names to be entered in the capitalist hall of fame, right beside Du Pont and Rockefeller and Morgan."

She sifted once again through the facts, searching for alternative explanations but found none. Finally, she came to the conclusion Rome had.

"They want it known only after they're dead."

"It's the only explanation that makes sense," he nodded.

Again Maggie took a moment. She drank her brandy and

poured some more. It was her way. She had to make sure she considered all angles and possibilities. It was this quality that made her invaluable as an attorney. Deep in thought, she tapped her finger on the leather bound book.

"Where exactly does this leave us?" she challenged. "It's fascinating. It would make a great study on the nature of greed and arrogance but it's otherwise useless. There are no names beyond the so-called founders. We don't even have an author. You need collaboration."

"We'll get it."

"Persons, places, dates and witnesses with impeccable reputations."

Rome took a moment to take a measure of where they stood and how far she was willing to go.

"We're not planning to take them to court," he said.

"What are you planning?"

"Are you ready to hear that?"

It was not an easy question. She had to understand by now that the stakes were high – as high as they could be. He watched as she rose and drifted to the windows where she sought the wisdom of the sea. She allowed her mind to ride the rolling waves that pulsed to the heartbeat of nature. It was a calm day and it eased her psyche.

"It's a good question," she replied. "Who knows that I'm here?"

"Only Jimmy and me."

"Jazzman?"

He could not help but smile though he recognized the importance of the question and the gravity of its answer.

"I thought you'd figured it out by now."

"I like things straight up," she replied as she turned to look him straight in the eyes. "Are you the jazzman?"

He held her gaze for more than a few moments. He wanted her to know he trusted her completely. He wanted her to know there would be no more secrets. He nodded and that was it. She understood.

"Then I already know too much, don't I?"

"That all depends on where we go from here. You know enough to be dangerous but not enough to be useful."

"Haven't I already been useful?"

He perceived a hint of resentment in her tone and he understood. She had become involved in something far greater in scope than she could have imagined. He had known the implications and deliberately withheld that knowledge. Now she was more deeply involved than ever. She had a right to some degree of resentment. Still, she had wanted full disclosure, hadn't she?

"Would it have made a difference?" he asked. "You'd already made me a suspect. If I'd have told you everything would you have backed off?"

She broke from the windows and began to pace the length of the room.

"Of course not but I prefer to operate from a well informed position."

He watched and waited until he could re-establish eye contact. He wanted her to know that he was speaking from the heart. He wanted her to have no doubt.

"Maggie, please sit down."

She did. She did not know why but she knew she could not maintain her businesslike persona with this man. She instinctively recognized the wall of resentment she was attempting to build between them. Maybe it was habit. She was accustomed to building walls, shielding herself from personal involvement, protecting her objectivity. But something about him – his tone of voice, his calm demeanor or the depth in his eyes – disarmed and settled her. She let go of her defenses and listened.

"There's no one in this world I value more than I do you. If I could have left you out of it, I would have. But now you are involved and you're about to become more involved. You wouldn't be here otherwise."

"That requires some explanation, doesn't it?"

"Yes, it does."

For the first time he realized he would have to tell her everything he knew. He had hoped the book would be enough to bring her on board. But the book only painted a picture of the monster, much like the American press painted the Japanese during the Second World War, the Native Americans during westward migration or African Americans in the age of slavery. She would have to know the enemy of the enemy lest the cure be worse than the disease.

"It may take some time," he began.

"I've got time."

"Is there anyone you need to call?"

"No. I've got the day off. Christmas shopping."

"That's unusual, isn't it?"

"It is," she reflected. Her father seemed almost anxious to get her out of the office. She thought he was concerned about her working too much but now she wondered.

Rome refilled her brandy and his own. He sat beside her and took a deep breath.

"I don't know how else to say it but flat out. Your father's firm belongs to the Sanctum."

Anger flared in her deep brown eyes. She was not ready to hear this.

"The hell it does! The firm belongs to the partners and I'm one of them."

Rome gave her time but it was too late to back down. She had to know and she had to know now.

"Maybe that's the wrong term," he conceded. "The Sanctum provides the firm with a very large retainer. It was under the name of Bill Miner. Now it's a man named Roger Thomason. He transferred from Chicago about a month before Miner died. He worked for a man named Bates, Robert Bates. He's another Sanctum man. I'm sorry, Maggie, but there's no doubt."

She fought back the urge to stand and resume pacing. She downed her brandy and he poured another.

"How do you know all this?"

"I've monitored certain communications. I've gained access to their files. Miner led to a man named Kramer in Los Angeles. Kramer was the holder of the book. Before Kramer died he led us to Robert Bates."

Her brow furrowed as she scanned the collection of devices connected to his monitor in the corner of the room.

"Who else have you monitored?"

"Anyone and everyone I suspected as an associate of the Sanctum." He saw what she was thinking: Had he monitored her? Was she a suspect? "It's a dangerous game against a powerful enemy. If you have any doubts about my methods, consider what you've just read. These are people who would stop at nothing to protect their interests. They have virtually unlimited resources. They are connected to the intelligence community and the Shadow Government. They have eyes and ears everywhere. We can't touch them if we're not willing to break the rules."

She knew he was right. Given the scale of the unfolding drama, unauthorized eavesdropping was a small matter – something akin to a lie that saves the innocent from pain or suffering. In his position, would she have done the same? She had engaged Jimmy on assignments that required just that. But she could not help but wonder if he had monitored her own communications. She recoiled at the thought. It was a personal misgiving – a gut reaction to an invasion of privacy. Once recognized, she was able to let it go. Her thoughts turned to her father and once again she recoiled instinctively. She sprang to her feet and spoke without restraint.

"No! My father is a good man. He would never consent to being a part of this criminal enterprise. He despises corruption! He hates dirty politicians! He's fought against them his whole life!"

Once again, he gave her time to settle her emotions. She would accept the truth but it would not be easy. She would have to realign her understanding of the world.

"Bill Miner was a good man," he said. "You knew him. That's why he gave his life. So that we might be able to do something to stop them. He was not alone. That's why we've uncovered the book. We'll find others like him. Miner didn't know what he was getting into any more than your father did. That's how they operate. Once you know, you're in and once you're in you're in for good."

He observed her pacing the room as he spoke. She was working it through. She stopped with her back to him and he sensed that she had arrived at the same conclusion he had come to so many moons ago: There were no options. There was no choice. It was the opportunity of a lifetime. This was their shot. If they failed, like Bill Miner had, there would be no second chance. It was do or die. It was stand up now or be swept away by the winds of time.

With a swipe of her hand, she wiped away her silent tears and turned to him with resolve.

"I'm sold," she said with a grim determination that rivaled his own. "I'm in. But there's one more thing I need to know."

He nodded and his eyes drilled into her soul. It was as if he knew her thoughts before she spoke them. It was as if he felt what she felt and understood what she understood.

"The rest of us – my father, Bill Miner, Jimmy, whoever else – have been drafted for this war. One way or another, we've been drawn in, if not by the Sanctum, then by you. But you went after it. Why? What motivates you? What do you want?"

Now he knew they were born to be together. He sat calmly, poured brandy and drank.

"It's a question I've asked myself many times. Was it any one thing? Was it the whole of the sixties? Was it Kent State? Was it Chicago, JFK or Bobby's assassination? Was it the fact that my best friend from high school died in Viet Nam? Was it the fact that Richard Nixon got credit for ending the war he prosecuted? Maybe not any one thing but all those things are a part of me and make me want to act."

Maggie listened intently. She was finally getting to know the man she felt so close to by pure instinct – as if somehow there was a bond in their souls, as if their destinies were shared. She felt her heart open to him like a rose in morning light.

"No," he reflected. "I believe it was my grandfather. He was a great man. Like so many others of his generation, he believed in hard work. He believed in the fruits of one's labor. In retirement he discovered the stock market. He read everything he could get his hands on. He read the Wall Street Journal every morning, front to back, until his eyes gave out. The market was in the great surge of the eighties. He did very well. Sight unseen, he was asked to join a brokerage firm. He refused. He valued his independence but his eyes were filled with pride. Finally, after so many years of working dawn to dusk for the other guy, he was gathering a legacy – the fruit of his labor. He amassed a small fortune that he intended to pass down to his children and their children."

He fought back the urge to stare out at the dull, gray skies of the sound. He needed its power to calm the soul. All the old emotions came forward like the ghosts of Christmas past. He found it difficult to go on. He found it hard to look into Maggie's eyes where his pain was measured and mirrored.

"Then came the crash of 1987. My grandfather always said: Know when to take a loss. It was one of the keys to his success. Get out at the first sign of trouble. He knew that the big orders were always processed first. The small investor couldn't hesitate."

He took a breath and drank.

"Well, he didn't hesitate but somehow his orders never went through that day. For twenty-four hours he could only watch while everything he earned over the last seven years vanished like a puff of smoke. He never talked about it. He didn't blame anyone. But I believe in my heart his spirit died that day. They drained the life out of him. All his hopes, his dreams, his pride and enthusiasm were gone."

Her heart was breaking with his. If he intended to arouse her moral indignation and strengthen her resolve it was working. She could only say, "I'm sorry."

They sat in silence for a spell, a lapse of time that was infinite in depth and thick in substance. When Rome finally stood and walked to the balcony, Maggie followed.

They leaned side by side against the wood rail and admired the view. It was cold but the sun still shined on the horizon and the only discomfort they felt was that which rose from their souls. It was at this moment when the ocean's most miraculous property in all its magnitude and pulsing strength made itself clear: its healing powers.

"When did you put it all together?" she asked.

"Years later. My grandfather passed and I became involved in real estate. I became obsessed with wealth and the wealthy. I started studying the crash. I learned that the system had ceased to function and that trading was held up for more than an hour. I knew enough about computers at that time that it didn't make sense. I started having a dream where I was climbing a mountain, struggling to get to the top. When I finally got there I discovered a path that continued upward through a series of cloudlike circles, one after another, as far as I could see. I knew then what I had to do."

"You had to fly," she said and they laughed, breaking the cycle of sorrow.

"That's right, Maggie. I had to learn how to fly. Do you still want to join me?"

"What choice do I have?"

He opened his body to her and she moved into his arms. There is a deep feeling that comes from waiting, anticipating and imagining the warmth of another body. They felt that warmth and they held onto it. Embracing, giving up and letting go. The skin of her cheek against his neck sent a pulse of divine fulfillment coursing through their bodies. The strength of his arms and chest, pulling and pressing against her breasts, made them feel like children enraptured in the arms of eternal love. Sheltered and protected. Feeling, opening and letting in. They were magnets drawn by a force greater than themselves, closer and closer, stronger and stronger. It was more than passion. They were soul mates. Their spirits were made of the same matter.

All that they were, all that they had ever been and all that they would ever be came together. No longer would they shield themselves from the deep sea of emotions that now engulfed them. Their bodies, their souls, their thoughts, their hearts and their sacred destinies were now and forever one.

United in love by a common enemy, a malevolent force surrounding their lives and everyone they cared about, leaving nothing and no one untouched. Enthralled in waves of boundless passion, Maggie remembered an old maxim: Even from evil goodness springs.

Was Hitler an angel in disguise?

The first step toward a new world is atonement for the sins of the past. The first step is cleansing. The first step is a commitment to justice at any cost. Only then can balance be restored.

One by one the rings of power must fall.

Maggie lay in Rome's embrace, surrounded by warmth, comforted by the sea and she sensed a powerful presence. A crow cawed in the distant sky and she knew: They were not alone.

Chapter 36

DOUBLE HELIX

On the ride over, Jake had a vague sense of discomfort – that disquieting feeling that starts in the gut and spreads outward like ripples on a pond. Marcel La Conte was at the top of the chain in the organization. Everything about him, the way he operated, his supreme confidence, his smooth easy manner and his unflappable disposition, spoke of his prestige and commanded authority.

That La Conte had summoned him to a meeting was irregular to extreme. Followed by the organization's gray suits in their typical amber shades, he followed intricate directions to assure that no one could track them. Jake was reasonably certain La Conte wanted a report on the jazzman problem. They wanted to know who they were dealing with and that Jake would not tell them. He had made contacts and built trust but that was all. He didn't know who he was or where he was headquartered.

The Sanctum was not known for patience. They might suspect a double cross. If they suspected him they would not let on. They would not be able to confirm it. His status as a double agent was its own protection. Under the rules of secrecy, diversion and deceit, neither side could be certain. It was all a matter of trust.

He feared they would identify the jazzman through other means. That would render his services unnecessary. He would be reassigned or dismissed. He was fully aware of the implications of dismissal. One did not walk away from the Sanctum upright.

He sat in the study of La Conte's luxurious mansion, listening to his patter on the various works of classical art adorning the walls. Jake was impressed but to what end? La Conte was playing with him and he was beginning to squirm. Maybe that was the point. How much did this man know? What scheme had he devised to test Jake's loyalty? What was the next play?

Sensing his impatience, La Conte smiled and poured a very expensive red wine: a Chateau Margaux 1948. He offered his guest a glass. Naturally, he accepted. He knew the rules. He was powerless to refuse an offering from the organization. He appreciated the rich bouquet despite its lethal potential. Its richness would easily disguise a deadly supplement.

"You like?" La Conte inquired in a playful manner. Jake nodded and he appeared satisfied. He poured another glass, breathed in the aroma with deep appreciation and proposed a toast: *To the Sanctum!*

They drank and Jake hoped his relief did not show. La Conte settled behind his desk. His voice like his manner was disarming. There was a hint of the French-Creole of his upbringing – just enough to be charming to the ladies and intimidating to the men. His skin had a subtle tint of olive, suggesting a Latin or Mediterranean influence. He sat back and admired his surroundings.

"Fine wine, exquisite art, beautiful women and unlimited travel: What more could a man want?"

His manner of speaking made it clear he neither expected nor wanted a response even when he asked a question. He was not accustomed to these sorts of interactions. When called to a case, he was used to a more direct approach.

"Allow me to set your mind at ease, Mr. Marshall. You are wondering what I know and what it is safe for you to tell me. I can assure you I know what you know and considerably more. For example, I know that you are the point man for the organization in Seattle. I know that you are in contact with the so-called jazzman. I know that the company you work for is owned by this individual. I know that you are intimate with an attractive young attorney by the name of Sara Kent. I know that you are acquainted with a tracker by the name of Jimmy Longbow and the grieving widow Cheryl Miner. This is not all that I know but it is sufficient to my purpose."

La Conte was laying his cards on the table and they were all trump. He was establishing his credentials and putting Jake on the spot. This was the real deal and he would not be able to take it for less than it was worth. The organization was leveling with him and he was expected to reciprocate. Everything was on the line.

"I get it," he acknowledged.

La Conte sipped his wine and studied him, as if waiting for a confession that was not forthcoming.

"Very well, Mr. Marshall, I believe you are being straight with me. Why wouldn't you? I will tell you now what you will do. First, you will tell this jazzman we wish to meet with him. We wish to engage him on terms that would be most favorable. We admire his talent and his methods. We believe he would be an asset. We need a man like him and we have an opening. He would gain more wealth and influence than he could ever dream of having. He would have the resources to help whatever people he cares about. He could build hospitals, shelter the homeless, secure sacred native lands – whatever he desires."

"Why not ask him yourself?" replied Jake. "You have the codes."

"We prefer to do it this way. He does not need to know what we know."

"He'll refuse."

"Yes? Maybe. But you will tell him and when he refuses, if he refuses, you will go to Sara Kent. You will make an offer she cannot refuse. You will double, triple or quadruple her salary. She will leave her job and she will accept a position at Puget Sound Realty. Are we clear?"

"I'm afraid that will put me in an awkward position."

"You are already in an awkward position, my friend. You will follow her and the jazzman will not suspect any more than he does now."

"Am I under suspicion?"

La Conte shrugged and showed no signs that he was prepared to elaborate.

"Why?" he pressed. He was beginning to resent this man's arrogance, his seeming indifference to all matters beneath his station.

"He is a clever man. He knows far more than he reveals. How can you be certain if you cannot see into a man's heart? It is uncertainty that keeps you alive."

"If that's true, it complicates matters," reflected Jake.

"My thought exactly. And you will further complicate matters. After you have carried out your orders, the Indian will come to you. I am told he is the best there is in the business of tracking."

He was talking about Jimmy Longbow.

"He's not exactly a friend of mine."

"Friendship is unnecessary. You will ask him to join us as well."

"You can't believe he'll accept."

Once again, La Conte shrugged. He seemed to exist apart from the world. His manner was constantly aloof as if he had no care.

"Maybe he will. Maybe he will not. Either way, we learn. We gather another piece of the puzzle. And the jazzman will know what we already know: it is only a matter of time. He can run, he can hide but…"

"Something's got to give."

"That is correct." He seemed to find the phrase amusing. "And when it does, we will be ready."

Jake felt the walls closing in. He had nowhere to go. It was beginning to look like a grandmaster chess game and his status was in rapid decline. He would have considered himself a bishop or a knight. Now he felt more like a pawn. He only wanted to get out.

"Is that all?" he said rising.

"That is all."

He flicked his hand to dismiss his underling but stopped him before he reached the door.

"Mr. Marshall, I was wondering about the grieving widow: How is she in bed?"

He wondered if La Conte knew or was just guessing that he had made love with Cheryl Miner. He supposed it didn't matter. A man like La Conte gets what he wants.

"She's the best," he said truthfully.

Chapter 37

SPIRIT CIRCLE

Song of the Wind saw it all in visions, in dreams, in a state of awareness between sleep and awake, between the physical and the spiritual, between the living and the dead. He saw what many saw but unlike others he remembered. He traveled the realm of the spirits and gathered knowledge. Unlike most who traveled before him, the knowledge he gathered traveled with him.

He first saw the vision of the rings in an ancient ceremony when he was a young man, little more than a boy. With his father he traveled a great distance to meet Wavoka, the visionary shaman of the Paiute who had the vision of the Ghost Dance. Traveling on foot they were tired, hungry and weak. He fell ill and a fever took hold.

His father nursed him as he walked the path of the ancestors. He saw the endless plains of buffalo, the ancient hunting grounds alive with deer, elk, moose, antelope and black bear. He saw streams of salmon and trout, the beaver, kingfisher and the great blue heron. He ran with the wolf, swam with the seal and soared high on the wings of the eagle. He became one with all animal spirits.

It was the crow that became his guide to the spirit world. It was the crow that heard the thoughts that came from within and spoke to him as a grandfather speaks to his grandchild. It was the crow that led him to the mountaintop and lifted him through the rings of power. And as he rose through the cloudlike circles he understood that what was revealed to him was not a journey of space and time. It was not the past but a giving of the past to the future.

He saw the bearded ones with long rifles kill the last herd of buffalo. He saw the massacre at Wounded Knee. He saw his people encaged like the white man's domesticated animals. He saw towers of smoke and dead fish lining the banks of poisoned rivers. He saw the great mushroom cloud of mass destruction. He heard the cries of children and witnessed the anguish of mothers, the rage of fathers. He saw the earth wiped clean and a new breed of humankind walking the land in harmony with all beings. He saw the natives honored for their knowledge of the old ways. He saw the white man humbled by the sins of the past. He saw a new beginning, a rebirth of spirit, a transformation of the human species. He saw a golden butterfly emerging from the sun.

When he awoke he told his father all that he had seen. His father listened and nodded in silence. With eyes of sadness he said he understood. He understood that it would not come to pass in his lifetime. He would not see the great change he desired but maybe his son would.

Song of the Wind spoke of his vision many times over the years but it was not until he was an old man gazing at the sea that he fully understood its meaning. He imagined the first wave and the vast distance in time from that moment until now. He smiled remembering, for he knew now what his father had known when he was a boy. It was a vision he would not see in his lifetime. Still, unlike his father, that solemn truth gave him no sorrow. His heart danced for he understood his part in the river of time. He understood that his spirit would outlast his days upon the earth, just as the spirits of those who walked before him had.

"My friend the crow told me you were coming," the old one said as they approached.

"My friend the crow told me you were waiting," said Rome with a warm embrace. He introduced Maggie who wore the hiking outfit Rome had provided. She had misgivings about this adventure until she met the old man and gazed into his deep, soulful eyes. The warmth of his smile dismissed all doubt. They embraced as you would embrace a relative you have not seen in many years.

Jimmy trailed the two of them and completed the circle of welcoming. The old one felt like blood.

They were of one spirit, united in purpose. They would talk for hours about everything under the sun but first they listened as the old man spoke of the old ways. He spoke of his visions and spirit journeys and they gathered his wisdom and his truths.

He told them his enemy was their enemy and he knew their heart.

"To defeat them you must know the way of the coyote. When they track you your tracks must not vanish but lead them astray. They will try to circle you but you must circle them."

He smoked from his pipe and passed it to Jimmy, who acknowledged the honor with a nod, smoked and passed it to Maggie. She hesitated. She wanted to ask what the pipe contained. She had always believed in a clear mind and had no desire to alter consciousness. But she sensed that to refuse this offering would go against the old man's ways. She valued her place in the sacred circle of trust and she allowed her trust to guide her. She smoked, taking in as little as she could. She choked back tears and tried in vain to keep from coughing. She passed the pipe to Rome.

The old one's face transformed into a broad smile. They waited for her to recover enough to share in their laughter. Then Rome took his turn and passed the pipe back to its holder. He smoked again and blew smoke into a cloud that hovered above them in the still air.

"Indian tobacco," he said. He read Maggie's thoughts. "It holds you to the earth. The smoke is a prayer. It rises to the heavens and carries our voices to the spirit world of the ancestors."

He lightly placed the pipe on its buckskin binding.

"You must be as the crow to see through the eyes of the enemy. You must feel his heartbeat and climb into his mind. When you have learned to walk in the land of visions, the land beyond this land of hands and feet, then the crow will guide you and you will see the face of your enemy as I have. It is many faces, all of them pale. They are the faces of the dead on living bodies. They are old beyond their years and gray with worry. They are cunning like the fox but lack the wisdom of the wolf. Their bellies and their minds are filled but their hearts are empty. They have no passion for the earth or living things but their eyes burn with desire. It is not the want of things that feeds this fire. It is not the want of power. They collect things and power as the farmer gathers seed. It is not the thing, itself, but the fruit that will one day spring from it. The fire that burns within them is the desire to leave their mark upon the earth, to write their names in the great book for people to see when they are gone from this world. Without this, all that they have is nothing."

He waited and gazed into each of their eyes to see what they saw and know they understood.

"These things I have seen," he continued. "The vision I give to you for it will guide you. These things I tell you for the benefit of all living beings on the earth. You must always keep faith. You must hold it in your heart. In this you must never waver."

He turned to Maggie: "When times seem dark, help will come from unexpected sources. Always remember: Your friends are in your heart where your enemies can never reach. Do not doubt."

He filled his pipe and passed it once more. Maggie drew deeply this time and did not cough. The old one had affected her in such a way. His smile seemed warmer and deeper now like the smile of a grandfather.

When they finished smoking they talked. They spoke of the sacred earth, the rhythm of the heart, the drum of the rain, and the song of the wind, the infinite sea and the cause of all beings. They spoke of the crow and the wisdom of dreams. They spoke of coyote magic and the power of the animal spirits. They spoke of medicines and spirit ways beyond the reach of humans. They spoke of space and time, the Great Spirit and the nature of life.

When they finished speaking they sat in silence and listened to the forest and the sea, the breath and pulse of the sacred earth. They listened and each in his or her own way prayed for her eternal majesty.

When they rose to take their leave, they embraced and captured the moment in every detail so that each would remember as long as life belonged to them. The old man spoke in parting.

"I am Song of the Wind. That is the name my people have given me for I dream and speak of the harmony of all things. I have lived many lives and known many spirits. I am familiar with your spirits."

He looked to Maggie: "I will call you Eyes of the Owl for it is your gift to see what others may not. You are wise beyond your years. White Man Who Lives Apart and Thinks Deeply, thinks much of you. His heart goes out to you. He is a good man. He is my child and all that I have I lay at his feet. You are also my child and all that I have I share with you. Go now and do not be afraid of dreams. I go with you though I remain here."

Maggie lingered in his gaze. She felt no need to speak or give thanks. She knew he understood. The others had departed and she hurried to catch up to them. As she did a large crow appeared overhead and sounded a loud caw. They waved and exchanged understanding without words. A sense of wellness surrounded them like an aura of protection, guidance and wisdom.

All would be well.

Chapter 38

UNDYING LOVE

Jake was a walking cliché: Between a rock and hard place. The squeeze was on and he was caught in the middle. He was being asked to demonstrate his loyalty in a way that would put himself and the one he loved in grave danger.

Until now his role had been relatively easy: Keep both sides happy by providing bits of information they could not readily obtain elsewhere. Now the Sanctum was demanding more. Maybe they considered him expendable. Of course they did. Maybe they suspected him of lining up with the opposition. He knew the consequences of betraying the Sanctum and he had no desire to leave the world of the living. He did not know the consequences of betraying the jazzman. To his knowledge no one had ever done so.

Sara's involvement was a complication he would rather have done without. He had told her everything he knew and now he regretted it. If he was in danger so was she – now more than ever. He could accept the risk for himself; he volunteered for it. He could not accept placing Sara in the same position. She had been recruited to the cause without knowing all the facts.

He approached the subject with a delicate touch and a great deal of sensitivity. He tried to explain the dilemma that had him reeling. He asked her to understand that the line was not as clearly drawn as it first appeared. How much did she really know about the jazzman? What did she know about his true intentions? Was it sufficient to risk her life?

Rome had assisted the Sanctum in getting rid of Bill

Miner and was likely responsible for the death of Edward Kramer. You could argue that they brought it on themselves but the scales have to be balanced. What had they gained? The Sanctum's operations were hardly inconvenienced. What then had they to show for the loss of two lives?

"We have the book," Sara countered.

"To what end?" replied Jake.

La Conte had laughed when he reported the missing manuscript and the likelihood that the jazzman had possession of it. He said flatly that it was of no value to anyone outside the inner circle. He said it was a work of fiction that was commissioned to satisfy the unbound egos and grand delusions of an antiquated circle of old men.

"Let him have it!" he proclaimed. "It is only nostalgia, the stuff of sentiment and memories, like a scrapbook of faded photographs. Who cares but the old folks who sit on their asses and dream the dreams of youth?"

He implied that the elders would soon be replaced by younger men who would harbor no such sentiments. He made it sound like a certainty, as if the wheels were turning as he spoke. Was it confidence or arrogance? La Conte possessed both and Jake couldn't get a read on him.

His assessment of the jazzman was fascinating.

"What does he want? He wants what I want: power and wealth. Like me, he wants to claim his seat at the table of the ruling class." He laughed and shook his head in mock dismay. "He is a child in a game of masters." He was not impressed with his "petty meddling" in the affairs of his superiors. He would have to do infinitely better if he wanted to make his mark on the Sanctum. To Jake it sounded like a challenge.

Sara listened intently and silently but she could not remain seated as he delivered his account of the encounter with La Conte and all it entailed. She preferred to pace the confines of Jake's high-rise apartment, alternating her gaze between Jake and the Seattle skyline. When he finally finished, she rose to the defense of their mentor and benefactor just as he had expected.

"How do you measure loyalty?" she challenged with a glare of accusation. "You want to know what Rome Mason has accomplished? Is that it?"

He did not answer. It was rhetorical. His spirit sagged and his body followed. His plea had produced the exact opposite of its intended effect. He could only listen as she looked out toward the Sound and the Peninsula.

"He's established the Olympic Peninsula Project. If he accomplishes nothing else, that alone is enough to warrant our loyalty."

"The project is hardly off the ground," he rebutted. "Who can say where it goes from here? Who's to say he wont' sell us all out when the time comes?"

Her eyes flared and bore into him like a warrior at a council of chiefs. "Weren't you the one who assured me the project would remain true to its objectives? Weren't you the one who promised it was worth the risk? Weren't you the one who asked me to have faith?"

He nodded and all but gave in. He had not intended to make an indictment against Rome but that's exactly what he had done. What he did not say but implied was that if she could not trust Rome, she could not trust Jake either. The two were partners and longtime friends. She pressed on.

"You know as well as I he wasn't responsible for what happened to Bill Miner any more than I was. You don't actually believe that, do you?"

"No, Sara. I don't."

She looked at him, slumped in his chair like a man mourning the loss of his dog, and realized the argument was over. Whatever was bothering him, it had nothing to do with Rome. Jake didn't doubt his friend's character. He may have doubted their ability to defeat the Sanctum, however, and the dire consequences of failure.

Jake was afraid of yet another lost cause. Like Rome, he

had been a child of the sixties. He had gone to Woodstock in the Summer of Love. He was gassed by the riot cops in Berkeley. He was stoned in Chicago and mourned at Kent State. Like Rome, he was frustrated that the sum total of their cause was the re-election of Richard Nixon.

But had it failed? There were millions who shared the experience. If only thousands remembered as he did, there was still hope. As long as there were people like Rome Mason the movement was still alive. It seemed Sara knew him better than he knew himself. Rome, if not their only chance, was the best chance they had at making their mark. Though he had not seen him in years, Jake knew him as a friend and trusted him like a brother.

Sensing the change in his disposition, she brought it home, confirming what he already knew in his heart and soul.

"Look, Jake, we know what the Sanctum is. We used to call them the establishment. We know what they've done and what they intend to do. Whatever doubts you may have, we both know who the enemy is."

He nodded in agreement, letting go of any further notions of resistance. By playing it out he realized the source of his fears. His mood shifted from analytic to worrisome. He looked into her captivating eyes and he understood. He sighed and confessed the solemn truth: "I only wish I hadn't brought you into this."

She smiled as if relieved and held out her hand to his. Taking hold, he felt his burden lighten as if a dark veil between him and his love had lifted.

"So that's what's bothering you," she said. "For a moment I thought it was serious."

"It is serious. Believe me."

She held him close long enough to let him absorb her faith and affection.

"Look, you didn't drag me into this," she whispered. "Whatever you think, I volunteered. I was in it before I ever laid eyes on you. I'd be in it whether you were around or not. This is my cause as much as yours or Rome's. I was born for this."

"My little warrior," he smiled.

"Cute," she replied.

She was more relieved than he imagined. Her love belonged to Jake but her loyalty was with Rome. If he hadn't known before, he knew now: She would never betray the cause.

"The question is," she postulated, "what do we do now?"

Jake reluctantly broke from her embrace. He poured some wine, leaned back on the couch and looked around at his living room. She had made her presence felt with candles, incense and a picture of her mother, a sculpted goddess and an ashtray. Her smoking seemed at first inconsistent with her personality. It was not. She supported the causes of naturalists and environmentalists but she was not one of them. She was an activist and a revolutionary.

"It ain't good, babe," he said finally.

She lit up and took a drag, her back to the wall separating the living room from the kitchen. In faded blue jeans, braided hair and an off-white pullover sweater, she looked like the female equivalent of James Dean.

"Maybe it ain't," she replied. "But it's obvious."

He could not but admire her unflappable poise and confidence. She was beautiful, intelligent, sensitive and strong. She had the spirit of a warrior and he adored everything about her.

"You want to play?" he asked.

"Do I have a choice?"

"Barely," he confessed.

She joined him on the couch and huddled up to his shoulder. He felt that sudden urge which she encouraged with a look of wanting. He fought it back if only for a moment. The matter at hand had not been resolved.

"Are you ready for this, babe?" he inquired.

She glowed with an inner strength of resolve that would

back down a junkyard dog.

"Like I said, I was born ready."

His resistance vanished. He let himself go to where he would never wish to return. She obliged his longing by lifting her sweater over her head and leaning back on the couch, exposing her honey glazed breasts, and unsnapped the button of her jeans. He lowered himself upon her, slowly so that she could loosen his belt and free his rising passion. Jazz filled the air with a rhythm and scent of pure ecstasy.

She knew at that moment, with as much certainty as any human can endure, that he would never betray her. They were entwined, kindred souls, one spirit, one being till death do they part. They could only hope it would not be too soon.

She squeezed out of her jeans and welcomed his undying love.

Chapter 39

CALL OF DESTINY

Detective Jones pressed on with his investigation. He collected names, mapped connections, gathered background information and formulated hypotheses. He had an indelible sense that his part in this story was somehow preordained.

"Destiny is the offspring of diligence," he said aloud if only to hear his words spoken. It sounded like Shakespeare but if it was he could not recall the play. The truth was less poetic. The detective was incapable of sitting still. As long he breathed he could not do nothing. Patience is a virtue he admired but his was born of labor. If fate were to be his mistress, he would take her on his own terms.

He stuck to his routine like a fly to molasses. He followed all leads, dug up background information, traced lines of communication and followed the flow of money. He also refined and practiced his methods of meditation and active dreaming. It was by these means that he pieced together the big picture of a global conspiracy. Yes, conspiracy. Who would have guessed after all these years that he would join the army of conspiracy lunatics? Along with virtually all his colleagues in the law enforcement community, he had always scoffed at those who engaged in conspiracy theory as deluded minds attempting to explain what they could not accept: the assassination of a beloved president by a lone gunman, a volatile world economy and the necessity of poverty, the myth of life beyond earth, the spread of incurable disease and the inevitability of nuclear catastrophe.

He had always considered skepticism prerequisite to any investigation but he could not ignore the overwhelming accumulation of evidence. This was a conspiracy and one of such magnitude that it encompassed all others and made anything possible. While it seemed to center on economic institutions, it was by no means limited to the business world. The web of connections seemed to lead everywhere at once, coursing through all branches of government and all centers of power. It involved the entire intelligence community from the NSA to the Secret Service, and all leaders of technology from Microsoft and Apple to Amazon and Pay Pal. It involved financial institutions from the World Bank and the International Monetary Fund to the New York Stock Exchange. It involved every major industrial corporation from Exxon and British Petroleum to Lockheed and Walmart.

The detective concluded it would be easier to list those that were not at some level involved with the all-powerful and malicious organization than it would be to list those that were. In short, only people without enormous sums of money were exempt from suspicion.

Of course, no one entity within the web could be held accountable for any specific activity. It was the nature of the beast that accusations could be routed on an infinite loop of plausible deniability. If you could find a prosecutor willing to bring the case, it would be laughed out of court and no respectable news organization would report the accusations. At every stage in the proceedings – prosecutor, judge, jury and reporters – you would encounter individuals corrupted by the organization. Maybe that's why they were known as the Shadow Government. A shadow can be observed but it leaves no evidence. Under the cover of darkness it vanishes without a trace.

The detective realized how easy it would be to become lost in the mire, in the infinite magnitude of the web. The organization was only one part of an omnipresent whole but it was the center. The key was to maintain focus on the core.

He learned to limit his view, to direct his investigative powers and to target his dreams and meditative visions. They were coming with greater clarity and frequency now. It was by this means that he determined the central crime for which the organization could fall: The crime of the century and the granddaddy of all conspiracies – only it was two crimes or more if you considered the witnesses who were made to disappear. It was the crime of killing the Kennedy's.

But it was not the assassinations that drew his attention now. They were too far removed from the source. What was more revealing was an impressive pattern of market manipulations. He did not yet understand how it worked but he had tested his hypothesis by comparing major market moves against transactions and communications by known organization members. They fit like a tailored suit.

Members were tipped off in advance. They made their calls, placed their bets and took enormous profits without fail. How could they predict the markets with such infallibility unless they knew? No one is that good. It was mathematically impossible.

He had absolutely no doubt that the organization was guilty of market manipulation and fraud. It was a crime but there was no evidence. You could not convict them on the laws of probability. He needed verifiable facts.

He entered his evening meditation with his mind focused on these concerns when he received a visit from a familiar but as yet mysterious source. He found himself soaring high above the Seattle skyline on the wings of a large black bird. He knew without knowing that the crow carried the spirit of a man and his name was Song of the Wind. He had no fear, no anxiety of any kind – not even the exhilaration of flying. He felt no sense of anticipation. He was the crow or rather he had the eyes of the crow.

He rode the fluttering wings across Puget Sound toward Mount Olympus. They veered north and traced Highway 101 along the coast and then south on a two-lane road that came to an end at Sol Duc Hot Springs. They let down and walked as men, the old Indian and the seasoned detective, on a trail marked by a huge moss covered boulder. The trail coursed through dense vegetation and towering evergreens.

They walked in silence for maybe a half mile when the old Indian stopped and pointed upward and to their left. The detective's eyes were drawn to a crow that cawed three times and flew away. There, all but hidden in the overgrowth of fern, shrubbery and brush, was the opening to a cave that he knew by instinct held the secret that was his to discover.

The vision ended there. He rose and walked into the bedroom where he kissed his wife awake. She welcomed him with a warm embrace. He needed her love and comfort now and he would need her more than ever in the days and weeks ahead.

His time had arrived. No words were exchanged but his instructions were clear. In the morning he would pack up his hiking gear, including a fold-up spade and a flashlight, and drive out to the peninsula. He would find the trail the old man revealed to him and he would stake his claim to destiny.

Chapter 40

JAZZ IN B FLAT MAJOR

Rome Mason was acutely aware that his efforts up to now had fallen short. He had failed to make even a crack in the wall separating him from the Sanctum's power structure. That was about to change.

The rich, soulful sound of Thelonious Monk injected fresh inspiration into his core. Maggie stayed the night. They sketched out plans and discussed scenarios late into the evening. When he realized the hour, he offered to give her a ride home but she declined.

Her body was a classical work of art, her eyes ablaze with passion, her movement pure jazz. Never had any woman so completely filled his longing and his desire, his need for love and fulfillment in both the spiritual and physical sense. Even now, long after she had gone, he felt her presence within him. Her image was implanted in his heart and in his mind. He lingered on the still fresh memory of her touch. It was a heavenly bond and the angels of grace still sang her silent praise, giving rebirth to the poet that dwelled in his soul.

He pulled out the old Belltone cornet stashed away in his treasure chest of forgotten objects. He closed his eyes and played whatever came to him. He played to Maggie in her naked glory. He played to the flame that was being reborn in him. He played like a jealous lover, holding on to those notes that reverberated in his soul.

In the middle of a B flat major it hit him like an Apache ambush in a story of the Wild West. He instantly knew the answer. Up to this moment he had been gathering scattered pieces of an elaborate jigsaw puzzle without any clear point of reference. He desperately needed a break. Now it came to him like a bolt of lightning from an empathetic god.

He had monitored the financial markets' computer communications, cross-checking them against significant market movements and transaction delays – apparent computer glitches, hack attacks, data overloads, surges and other incidents of suspended trading. It eventually led him to realize that there was a go-between, a buffer, a way station between the markets and the Sanctum. Now he realized the key to their operation: They did it the old fashioned way. They communicated person to person by telephone.

He had broken into phone data banks before. It was not as difficult as it seemed. Like any other major corporation or government agency, the phone companies had codes that were decipherable to the skilled operator. Once inside, he would look for the link that connected Joshua Logan in New York, Robert Bates in Chicago and Marcel La Conte in New Orleans. He would then crosscheck those communications to dramatic market movements. His computer had worked on the problem for several hours before revealing the data.

The next step was in place. He was monitoring the way station at random intervals during market hours. He used a variety of identification numbers, including those of Bates, Logan and La Conte. With any luck the Sanctum would not even know he was there. If they detected a foreign presence they would suspect their own.

Once Rome confirmed the way station operation, he would make a killing in the marketplace. He would then turn the tables by feeding false information through the way station directly from the floor of the exchange. Jazz in B flat major.

Timing is everything. He would not get a second chance to make this move. If he could succeed, delivering a message of an impending crash when in fact the market was heading upward, he could do significant damage. The

Sanctum would be compelled to take action. He would threaten the very heart of their illicit operation. Something would have to give.

It was the move he had been waiting for. It was the move that would put them on the map. It was the blow that would start the war. And now it was about to go down. He wished that Maggie were with him to share the moment. He would have to be content with a little Thelonious Monk.

Chapter 41

A MEMORABLE GATHERING

Maggie arrived early at her father's house for a formal dinner to welcome a very important guest to the Seattle area. Her father greeted her with his trademark low-keyed sarcastic wit: "Maggie!" he exclaimed with feigned surprise. "So glad you could make it!"

She had missed work on the grounds that she needed rest. He of course understood but still, coming in the wake of an afternoon off, it was unprecedented. In place of a reply, she delivered a wry grin of the sort a father dare not question. She was amused at his modesty. He blushed and the air surrounding them immediately became lighter. The last thing he expected was a romantic interlude.

Over cocktails, her father spoke to her about the man of the hour, a Mr. Marcel La Conte of New Orleans. Maggie maintained her quiet dignity and mentioned in passing a curious incident. It seemed a man had been following her for no apparent reason. It was particularly strange because the man she was seeing was not married. When he inquired as to his identity she changed the subject.

Joe Thomas was careful to reveal as little as possible to his daughter. He acted surprised that anyone would follow her. He promised to get to the bottom of it but Maggie explained that she already had a man on the case. He smiled and went on with polite conversation.

She decided to throw her father a curve, as much out of curiosity as anything.

"I've been thinking," she reflected. "You're right about

my spending too much time on the Miner case. It's a done deal. I think I need a change."

"That's great," he replied with a look that revealed his ambiguity. This was not like his daughter.

"I understand the firm will be handling Mr. La Conte's legal issues."

"We're hopeful."

She detected a slight twitch below his left eye. It was one of her father's tells.

"I'd like the assignment."

He gulped down what remained of his cocktail and signaled for another. It provided time to consider his daughter's most unusual request.

"We don't have the account yet, Maggie. Let's not get ahead of ourselves."

She knew of course that a team had already been assigned. They were specialists in real estate.

"Well, as we both know, I need a change."

With that she let it drop. She wondered how he could have fooled her for so long. He was as transparent as a manufactured diamond. Her mother had known all along what she was only beginning to learn: That love can blind you to even the most obvious truths. We believe what we want to believe and arrange our perceptions to conform to those beliefs.

Like Bill Miner before him, Joe Thomas was a good man – flawed to be sure but decent and honorable. If the Sanctum had been able to recruit them both to their immoral cause, what chance did the average business owner have? Who was immune? Of course, the Sanctum was not interested in the average anything. In their twisted world, excellence made you vulnerable – like the black widow's amorous affection for her short-lived mate.

She saw it all clearly now. Maybe she had changed. Maybe her encounter with the old Indian shaman had opened her eyes. She truly felt different, renewed, transformed.

Maybe it was love and passion that changed her. She was undeniably radiant. As her thoughts turned to Rome, a warm sensation rose up from deep within.

The guests began to file in. Cheryl Miner arrived in a most appealing black silk formal, wrapped in a full-length gray fox coat that she discarded at the door. Rome walked in looking mysteriously like an eastern European prince, his eyes ablaze with love's inspiration. Then Roger Thomason made his entrance, looking typically out of place despite his tailored black tuxedo and his young, blonde wife who was bursting with excitement in an elegant silver designer gown. Finally, the guest of honor arrived in a glowing white suit with a red rose on his lapel.

Maggie felt relatively plain in her blue chiffon dress of simple lines. The reluctant glances of all the men with the exception of her father, attested that she was anything but plain.

Cheryl Miner appeared at her seductive best. Unlike Thomason's wife, who was younger but new to the trade, she had mastered the subtleties of the social elite. La Conte took notice and approved. Before the evening reached its end, they would make arrangements for a future tryst. Cheryl assumed things were going according to plan. They were but she was not yet aware that the plan was his.

They settled in the sitting room for polite conversation with La Conte taking center stage. To his left sat Cheryl, seemingly engrossed in casual observations. Beyond her sat Rome and Maggie in a love seat, moderately amused with the proceedings. Thomason and his wife sat to La Conte's right, struggling for appropriate comments to contribute. Joe Thomas, from his place opposite La Conte, stood to propose a toast.

"Here, here! For those of you who have not had the honor, I would like to introduce our distinguished guest from the bayou state of Louisiana, Mr. Marcel La Conte. Rumor has it he is considering a second home in our community.

We welcome him and humbly offer our services."

They drank and La Conte milked the attention before responding. He spoke in a studied fashion that emphasized his accent, giving him a mysterious quality that generally appealed to women.

"My most gracious host does me a great honor. With apologies, I must correct a slight misstatement he has made in my behalf. It is quite true that I am considering purchasing a home in your fair city. However, it would hardly be my second."

Polite laughter emerged from all except Rome and Maggie who were content to smile.

"It is my intention," he continued, "to become better acquainted with all of you as you would naturally be my close associates here."

He glanced around the room as if deciding who would be chosen to speak first. If it seemed demeaning it was not without intent. He had assumed the position of counselor in a group session.

"Mr. Thomason," he began. Thomason cleared his throat and said, "Roger, please."

"Yes, of course," said La Conte. "I know these must be difficult times for you. You have replaced your company's founder. We all know Mr. Miner was a brilliant business leader who is greatly missed. How is the Miner Corporation?"

Thomason cleared his throat once again. Whether it was the presence of Joe Thomas or the widow was unclear but he was clearly uncomfortable with the question. It did not of course prevent him from addressing it.

"I'm pleased to say the corporation is thriving. Of course we all miss Bill. I could never hope to fill his shoes. But we do have some very capable people. If you'd care to visit me at the office, Mr. La Conte, I'd be pleased to give you a more detailed account."

"Thank you. It will be my pleasure."

Mr. Thomason was dismissed and La Conte turned to his wife with a slightly sinister grin.

"I understand you have been in Seattle…what? Six months? Do you find it to your liking?"

"Oh yes!" she smiled with a little too much exuberance. "It's a wonderful place! The arts, the theatre, the music! It's a wonderful place!"

"The rain does not bother you?"

"Not at all. I love the rain."

"Perhaps you are exaggerating?"

Again, polite laughter made the round. Maggie wondered how he could stand it – the blatant patronization. That La Conte seemed to enjoy it spoke of his character.

"Mr. Mason," said La Conte.

"Mr. La Conte," replied Rome.

"With you I am only vaguely familiar. I am told you are quite talented in the field of negotiations."

"I have a very limited specialty."

La Conte smiled. "Indeed. Damage control is a limited but essential area of expertise. Sadly, I do not anticipate a need for your services."

"One never knows," replied Rome.

"Indeed. You are most fortunate in one respect. You have attracted the obvious affection of Seattle's most beautiful and, if I may say so, most brilliant legal mind. How is he treating you, Ms. Thomas?"

Maggie resisted the impulse to put him in his self-righteous place. She told herself it was only business.

"That, Mr. La Conte, is my affair. I thank you for the compliment and look forward to working with you should you decide to become our client."

La Conte glanced at Joe Thomas who tried to hide his discomfort.

"I shall look forward to it with impunity."

He concluded his round of discussion by turning to the beautiful widow.

"And now, though I am reluctant to mention a most unfortunate matter on such a memorable occasion, may I say I find it impossible that such a beautiful, charming and intelligent woman should be compelled to wear black during the holiday season."

It was a departure from the decorum of polite society, even for La Conte, but Cheryl's gracious reaction and the festive mood of Christmas allowed for such aberrations.

"Could we have our glasses filled?"

He waited until his wish was fulfilled.

"I propose a toast to you all, my gracious host, charming ladies and distinguished gentlemen, my new and very dear friends in the great city of Seattle!"

They drank and settled in. The rest of the evening was unremarkable. Marcel La Conte was exceptionally forward. In the space of fifteen minutes all that was important had already been established. Thomason was a Sanctum underling, a pawn in the power game, and La Conte was a man of great standing. Cheryl would become Miner's mistress – if not his wife. Joe Thomas was without power and the firm was under the Sanctum's control.

All and all it was a most interesting gathering. Against a backdrop of murder, intrigue and astonishing revelation, they had finally come face to face with a major player. La Conte was an intriguing character. He gave the impression he knew far more than he would reveal. What was his true purpose in Seattle? Was he here to replace Bill Miner or would he name Miner's replacement? Was he here to solve the jazzman problem? The one thing certain: It was not a matter of real estate.

Chapter 42

A DELICATE BUSINESS

The old Chicago jazzman was at his finest. His chops were polished smooth and clean like a finely tuned Cadillac. His tone found new levels of depth and reverberation. Maybe it wasn't Charlie Parker but it was as close as anyone had a right to expect at The Monastery on a Thursday night.

There were no beat poets or funk bands to alter or obstruct his free flow of expression. Jazz is an artform that requires freedom and his was exploring both the outer and inner limits tonight. The other pieces of his trio, the standup bass and piano players, grabbed hold and hung on for the ride. The sax man was taking no prisoners. He soared to other realms and foreign dominions, dove to the lower depths of soul, only to ease back down to the confines of a hip Seattle jazz joint.

Jake sat at a corner table, back to the wall, consuming ale and waiting for Jimmy's arrival. Soon after his discussion with Sara, he contacted him. Acutely aware that Jimmy did not trust him, he thought might regain some measure of trust by coming clean before the fact. Things were getting tight and promised to get tighter. He needed Jimmy – if not for his own protection, then for Sara's. For his part, he knew no one he could trust more than the Indian tracker. Maybe it was his mystique or maybe it was just instinct. It didn't matter. He had to confide in someone and Jimmy was the man of the hour.

Deep in thought, he allowed the smooth, mellow tones of the saxophone to sweep him away to distant places where danger did not exist, where there was only harmony and everyone was what they seemed. He almost didn't notice when Jimmy slipped in and sat beside him. He didn't recognize him until he saw him close up. He was wearing a graying beard and a long dark wig of hair pulled back into a ponytail.

"What have you got, white man?"

Jake sized him up with an amused smile and turned his gaze back to the stage.

"Look, Jimmy, I know you don't trust me. I want you to know straight up: the boss knows I work both sides. He set it up himself. That's the way he wanted it. He needed someone on the inside – at least until we got closer. Well, we're close enough now. If you don't believe me, ask him yourself."

It took a lot to surprise Jimmy but this revelation had an impact. Of all the things he might have said, this was the last he expected. He was certain Jake was on the other side. He was counting on it. Rome had been vague on the subject, cautioning him not to put too much weight on either side. Now he understood why. Jake was a double agent. He played both ways. Rome had warned him there were things he would not reveal as a matter of policy until all the cards were on the table. He understood. Still, it was a rare occasion and it stung like the first wind of a winter storm.

"I didn't know," he said. He wondered how this could have happened. He didn't need to be told. He had the vision. He should have been aware by second sight. He realized now that he had been blinded by his own peculiar prejudice. Jake had always been a little too self-assured. Jimmy almost wanted to take him down a notch.

"It's time to level with you," Jake continued.

Jimmy pointed to the stage as a reminder to maintain decorum. Traitor or not, it was not time to get careless. The gray suits were everywhere. There was more at risk now. The stakes were higher. Jake directed his eyes dead ahead before he continued.

"You know about La Conte?"

Jimmy nodded.

"He's the real thing, a top of the line organization man. I don't know if he's Inner Sanctum but he's way up the ladder."

Jimmy nodded.

"He called me in to give me my orders. They want new members and he wants me to recruit them, beginning with Sara."

"Why tell me?" Jimmy asked. Jake had never confided in him before. How was this time different?

"The jazzman isn't out here, Jimmy. He can't protect her."

"You think I can?"

Jake nodded and glanced around before he continued. Several men caught his attention.

"I do," he replied. "They want you too, Jimmy, and they want the jazzman. They still don't know who he is but they want him. They're offering a lot of money and power. They think that's what he's after."

"Have you talked to the jazzman?"

"No. I can't trust the lines. They're closing in, Jimmy. I can't say how I know that. It's just a feeling. Something I picked up from La Conte."

"Okay then. I'll deliver the message."

Jake took a moment to appreciate the jazz and take a drink of beer.

"Sara is handing in her resignation tomorrow. In a couple of days she'll report to Puget Sound Realty. It's a front for the organization."

Jimmy nodded and began tapping his fingers on the table as a signal it was time to wrap things up. The conversation had gone on a little too long. An attractive woman at the bar took note. Maybe it was nothing. Maybe it was paranoia. Or maybe she just liked the look of him. However it was, he was not in the mood to take chances.

"It's coming down, my man," said Jake. "The squeeze is on. If Rome has got a move it's time to play it." He let it sink in. "That's right. I know who the jazzman is. I've known all along. The Sanctum doesn't know I know and that's the way we want it."

It dropped like a dead weight from a tall building. He had misjudged this man. He had allowed his vision to be clouded by appearances and circumstance. Both were easily manipulated. Jake's concern for Sara was genuine and Jimmy's heart reached out to them both.

The jazz trio was concluding its set. They applauded with the crowd and waited for the barroom buzz to take over, covering their conversation.

"You see that man at the end of the bar?" asked Jimmy. Jake gave it a glance. "FBI. He flashed the bartender his ID. What do you make of that?"

"Whatever it is, it ain't good."

Jimmy took a breath and agreed. It wasn't good. Nothing about it was good.

"I'll do what I can for Sara," he said. "I can't make any promises but I'll do what I can."

He made his move but Jake stopped him with a tug on his sleeve. He sat back down.

"Don't trust the phones. The matchbook has a number. You can reach me there. If you need to contact Sara, tell her to read your mind. She'll know what it means."

Jimmy palmed the matchbook.

"One more thing," said Jake. "I'm warning Cheryl Miner about La Conte. If she turns me in, I'm a dead man."

"Do me a favor: Don't."

"She's a good kid and she could be useful. Besides, she can't tell them anything they don't already know. It's worth a shot. If I'm still alive for Christmas, you'll know she's with us."

Against his better judgment, Jimmy looked at Jake with

fresh eyes before returning his gaze to the bar scene.

"I misjudged you, white man."

"Thanks, I think. If they take me out, Jimmy, I'd like to know someone will look after Sara."

"You have my word."

Jake breathed in and glanced around the bar as they finished up their beers. He noticed two men in gray suits, one with a black shirt and red tie standing at the end of the bar. He wondered if Jimmy noticed.

"Bouncer," said Jimmy without looking.

Jake finished his drink and hustled out the door with a worried glance over his shoulder. Paranoia was a part of him now.

Jimmy stayed behind with a purpose. He spotted Detective Jones at the bar. That alone was not unusual. The detective liked jazz. He regularly frequented all the downtown jazz clubs. But he was watching Jimmy and Jimmy knew it. He also knew that the detective was too good at his job to let him know he was watching unless he wanted him to know. As if on cue, the detective ambled to the beat over to Jimmy's table and motioned for permission to sit. Jimmy nodded and the detective sat.

"Old Willie's on tonight," he said.

"Yeah," Jimmy replied.

"Do you trust that guy?"

"Jake? With my life."

"That's a good one," the detective smiled. "Because we both know that's exactly what it takes."

"Are you on duty, Detective Jones?"

"No, sir, I'm on leave."

Jimmy hadn't heard. He'd worked with the detective and appreciated his professionalism. It seems he was out of the loop – a situation he would have to rectify.

"What's this about, detective?"

"I thought you'd never ask." He snapped his fingers to the beat of the trio's riff and took a drink of ale. "I've got something. I think your boss will definitely be interested."

"My boss?"

"That's right, Jimmy. Never give an inch. I'm talking about the jazzman and don't kid yourself: I know who he is. And if I know who he is, you can be sure the other guys are not far behind."

Jimmy took it all in and sipped his beer.

"Okay, detective, you've got my attention. Give it to me straight so I can understand exactly what you want."

"I'll do you one better. I'll tell you what I've got. Collaboration. I've got the original notes. Names, places, dates. What's more, I've got tapes. I've got *the* tape. I've got the killing of the century and a hell of a lot more."

"My God," said Jimmy. Only moments ago he had been touched by the affections of one man for one woman. Now the full scope of the case came crashing down on him. It was almost too much to take.

"Why me?" he wondered.

"My connection is too hot," said the detective. "She's under fulltime surveillance. If that's not enough, I happen to like Maggie and I know your man does too. I wouldn't want her to take the risk. What I have they wouldn't hesitate to kill for. That's a fact."

"Is that why the FBI is here?"

"The FBI?"

Jimmy glanced toward the man in question and Detective Jones looked him over.

"Looks like someone I should have a conversation with. In the meantime, the matter at hand is something that can't wait."

Jimmy took a moment and decided he had no choice. He had to trust him. He had known the detective for years. He was probably the last man in Seattle he would suspect of corruption.

"You want a meeting?"

The detective nodded and assumed a solemn pose.

"It has to be absolutely confidential."

"Understood."

"By the way," the detective smiled. "The old Indian says hello."

Now Jimmy was shocked. How this old detective knew about Song of the Wind was beyond imagining. He turned to the detective and realized he too was not what he seemed. He was much more. He walked in dreams.

"You always save the best for last."

The detective winked and stood in a nonchalant manner. He wore the smile of a lifetime, the kind of smile that's worn by a man who has found his core content, who has discovered his undiscovered self and grasped some secret key to the meaning of life.

"These eyes," he said, summoning the bard to the moment's truth, "have been as piercing as the midday sun to search the secret treasons of the world."

He paused in silent reflection, then walked to the bar, ordered a beer and settled beside the man with a gray suit.

"Yes, sir, old Willie is hot tonight!"

"He sure is," the suit replied. He tapped his fingers on the bar. The detective knew he was a fraud. He had no rhythm for jazz.

Jimmy gave the room one last scan and vanished into the darkened streets of Seattle.

Chapter 43

A PRIVATE RECKONING

Maggie was wary of coming to the office this morning. She had deliberately left the gathering too early to allow a private discussion with her father. A confrontation was inevitable. She was anxious about the information her father could provide but wary of his confessional.

Rome had given a complete account of the status of all known Sanctum members and associates. He broke them down into several categories: At the top of his list were the Elders, their names and number as yet unknown. They were the core and center, the ruling elite, the sanctum within the Sanctum and the almighty lords at the top rung of power. He believed they dated to the Kennedy assassination, when they formed their current power structure.

He believed the Sanctum was once again in the midst of a transitional period. The Elders were fast becoming too old to carry on as active leaders of an empire. He believed they were in the process of selecting their successors from the second tier of leaders just as the Elders had selected them. He called them the Administrators. As the name suggested, they administered daily business operations. They included Marcel La Conte, Robert Bates and Joshua Logan. Bill Miner had been groomed for such a position prior to his demise. Rome estimated there were more than a dozen of them strategically placed across the country. He expected to discover all of their identities within weeks.

The third tier consisted of the Members. He believed there were hundreds of them, including Roger Thomason of

Seattle. These individuals were the Chief Executive Officers of legitimate businesses. They provided a front for Sanctum finances and shared in the profits.

He postulated several more distinctions, including agents, associates and employees. Rome had pointed to the name of Jake Marshall as a possible agent. His clientele included Cheryl Miner who he classified as an employee. They received salaries from Sanctum fronts, including Puget Sound Realty and a variety of investment firms. They also capitalized on business opportunities the Sanctum provided.

Joe Thomas headed the list of known associates. They believed he was an unwilling accomplice whose services were contracted. He profited only by his association with the organization. In essence, he had welcomed the proverbial vampire into his house. Having done so it was no longer in his power to refuse them. There was no way out but the way of Bill Miner as long as the Sanctum existed.

Maggie was relieved that her father's involvement apparently went no deeper. What she had learned in twenty-four hours was more than her father could have imagined in a lifetime. Still she was not surprised at the first words out of his mouth when she closed the door to his office behind her.

"You have no idea what you're up against."

She was direct as she had always been in confronting her father with an unpleasant reality. She told him everything in broad terms, outlining the organization's history, its structure and operations. She told him its purpose was nothing short of worldwide economic dominance.

She told him there was a plan to stop them and she was a part of it. When he inquired what the plan was, who was involved and whether she believed it had any chance of success, Maggie deferred. Now it was her turn to withhold information. He was better off not knowing any of the details. As for their chances of success, she said it was the only chance anyone was likely to get and she believed they would succeed.

For the first time in memory, her father was speechless. The silence was thick and heavy, placing a stranglehold on their hearts and tongues as if a tranquilizing fog had enveloped them both. With shoulders hunched and drooping eyes, he looked like a child who had committed some unspeakable act. In the end he could only say: I'm sorry.

She was devastated seeing her father, a strong and proud man, reduced to shame and pity before the eyes of his only daughter. She explained that she understood. He was a victim and not a willing participant. She understood how the Sanctum had laid its bait and tempted him. Many a good man had yielded, including Bill Miner.

He protested that she was only partly correct. Having come this far he wanted her to know the whole truth even if it cost him what was left of his pride.

"There was a time," he said, "when I could have stayed out of it. Bill tried to warn me. He said there was a lot more involved than what was on the surface. He said it was a bad gamble but my eyes were glazed with dollar signs. One corporate client and we'd be fixed for life. Every man dreams of leaving a legacy and this was mine."

He paused in reflection to let the guilt settle in both their souls. He was not an innocent man.

"My sin was greed," he confessed. "I wanted too much too easy. For that I sold out."

Maggie tried to comfort him. After all, he was looking out for her interests as well — at least he thought he was. He could not have known the depth and scope of the Sanctum's malevolence. No one could have. It went beyond all reason and belief.

"I tried to keep you out of it, Maggie," he said. He was a broken man trying not to cry.

She went to him, drooped over in his chair, and knelt to take his hand.

"I know you did, dad."

She waited for him to raise his head, for his eyes to meet

hers. She wanted him to see her determination and the fire that burned within. She was not afraid.

"I know you did," she repeated. "But now I'm in it and I'm in it to the end. I have no regrets. Someone has got to stop these monsters. It might as well be us."

Her courage gave him strength and filled him with both pride and shame. He gave up any notion of talking her out of it. They were in it for the duration.

"Tell me what to do, Maggie. I'm with you."

"Just hold tight, papa, and let it unfold."

Chapter 44

SWITCHING SIDES

Jake took the usual precautions in signaling Cheryl to meet him at the cabin. A wrong number in the name of a saint – Joan or Francis or Bernard – meant: Meet me at the cabin tomorrow. The time was always sunset. If she couldn't make it she would leave a message from a public phone. It was the week before Christmas and her normal routine included shopping to the early evening hours. She was not under suspicion and would not be followed.

He arrived early, started a fire, made some coffee, spiked it with Irish whiskey and settled back in thought. He had long been in need of time and space away from the crowd, away from business and intrigue, away from orders and demands and pressure. It did not come easy. Rome recruited him with the simple explanation that he needed someone he could trust, someone whose loyalty was beyond question and someone who could get inside the enemy camp.

Rome put him in touch with Bill Miner who in turn put him in touch with others within the Sanctum power structure. He became an agent within six months. He ran background checks on prospective members, associates and adversaries. He became a link in the chain of command and hired a handful of employees, including Cheryl Miner.

Life was moving at a much too rapid pace. Now that everything was coming to a head, he had to remain alert and clear minded. All that he had worked for and everything he valued was at stake. He needed to be prepared for all contingencies.

By the time Cheryl drove up the dirt road to the cabin he had drifted into a subconscious state. He had a vision of a large crow or a raven and heard it caw just as Cheryl knocked and opened the cabin door. Instinctively, he went for his gun. She froze, mouth agape, and for an instant thought the unthinkable and watched her all too short life flash before her in stuttered, disparate images.

He came to his senses before he could pull the trigger and breathed a sigh of relief. He apologized with a shake of his unbelieving head and returned his pistol to its holster.

"I'm a little on edge," he said.

"Just a little?" she replied.

"Come on in. Let me pour you some coffee."

Dressed in tight designer jeans and a revealing white silk blouse beneath a black leather jacket, she closed the door behind her, removed her jacket and reclined on the bearskin rug by the fire. All the while her eyes were trained to Jake's expression that lingered between amusement and sexual excitation. He could not help but notice her thinly covered breasts, her nipples pointing through the delicate fabric. He was just a man and she was an exceptionally enticing woman. He stiffened his resolve and poured her coffee, pulling his chair up and sitting at a safe distance.

"I thought you might have changed your mind but you don't look in the mood for play," she said.

"I like you too much for that, sweetheart."

"That's touching."

She pulled her feet under her and batted her eyelashes, clutching her hands to her chest ingénue fashion. She dropped it as quickly as she affected it, resuming her normal attitude of hardened indifference. Say what you will, he thought, Cheryl Miner is an actress of the first order.

"What's up, Jake?"

"I wanted to warn you about La Conte."

"My future husband?"

"I doubt it, sweetheart. He's no mark. He chose you."

She thought back on how easy La Conte made it for her to reel him in. He wasn't the first mark to make the first move but he set a record. It aroused her curiosity.

"I thought he was a little too easy for a man of his standing."

"He likes younger women and you're his type. He'll keep you around a while but you can forget about marriage. He'll find someone new before the first wrinkle appears."

Cheryl cocked her head and examined the man she took her orders from. He was breaking new ground. It was as if he actually cared. Who knows? Maybe he did.

"So what is this? The day of the nice guy? Why are you telling me this, Jake? You know as well as I do, I don't have any options."

"Maybe you do."

He had her full attention now and her interest intensified. Jake was staring at her, trying to read her mind behind her enchanting aqua marine eyes. She didn't like it. She reads men; they don't read her.

"Are you sure you want to hear this?" he inquired.

"Why wouldn't I? You don't think I like this business? If I thought I had a shot at getting out, I'd take it."

Jake breathed a little easier. He felt responsible for her. He had taken her in. At the time, they both thought it was a step up but things had changed. He had hoped she would respond this way. Of course, she would know that as well and with her acting skills she could be playing him. He had seen her work her charms on many a man. If she wanted to fool him, she could. But then, why would she want to? Score a few points with the organization? Pull down a bonus check? Or maybe she could convince his superiors that she had value beyond her physical appeal.

All these things were possible and Jake had chased down every possibility. He knew it all came down to trust. It was a matter of instinct. He had made a conscious choice to trust her and he was asking her to do the same.

"Cut to the chase, Jake. You're no good at slinging the shit."

He took a hit of whiskey and dove in.

"Something's coming down, Cheryl. The stakes are high. We won't get another chance like this. Either we stop them or they drop us. If we win, the Sanctum is history. If we fail, we're most likely dead."

Her expression graduated from cynical disbelief to cautious admiration. She thought she knew this man but she never guessed he was one of *them*. She knew he was not entirely pleased with the circumstances of his employment. Who was? But she always felt he was realistic about it and resigned to make the best of an unfortunate situation. She thought he was like her. After all, what could they do? She had failed to see the rebel in him and that hurt. Frankly, she didn't think he had the balls.

"Come on, Jake!"

She half expected him to explode in laughter and admit it was all a joke. Another test of her loyalty. But she could see he was serious and he was standing his ground.

"You know them," she said. "Maybe you can hustle them. Maybe you can fool them. If you're the luckiest man on earth, maybe you can get out, change your identity and figure out a way to make them think you're dead. But you can't stop these people. They're bigger than the CIA, the FBI, IBM or any of those initials. Hell, they're bigger than the fucking government!"

Jake listened and nodded and let her get it all out. He'd been through the same process.

"Have you heard of the jazzman?" he asked.

"Who hasn't? He's the talk of the town."

What she heard was that he was a radical lunatic. What she knew was that the Sanctum wanted him and wanted him badly. They told her he was connected to Joe and Maggie Thomas. She had orders to find out anything she could. Up to now she hadn't been able to report anything.

"There's a reason they want him," said Jake. "He's not some wild-eyed radical. He's got connections, financing and an organization. Right now he's got them on the run. When's the last time the Sanctum ran scared? We've got a chance, Cheryl, and we won't get another."

The first step to believing is wanting to believe and she was almost there. She liked Jake. She always had. Unlike others in the organization he was always straight with her. She had a hunch he was up to something – nothing of this magnitude but something. Now she knew and she was flattered he wanted her involvement. But she was not the heroic type.

"So now I'm supposed to trade one master for another? Give me the hook, Jake. Give me a reason."

"Freedom," he said and allowed it to settle. "If we win, you're free, wealthy and protected. How's that?"

She smiled in her typical off center manner.

"It's good, baby. The problem is: It's too good. A woman in my position has to have assurances."

His expression became deadly serious. He hoped he had not miscalculated.

"I'm putting it all on the line, Cheryl. I can only give you my word and it won't be worth much if you turn on me."

She finished her coffee, grabbed her jacket and braced herself for the cold outside. Looking deeply into his dark eyes, alive with passion, burning with faith, she tried to remember what it was like to believe in a cause, to have hope and the courage of conviction. She shook her head and walked away. Reaching the door she felt a tug from within. It seemed her long dormant conscience was awakening. She turned back and was relieved to find him standing there, coffee still in hand.

"A part of me thought you'd have your gun out."

"We're not like them, Cheryl. We're a group of people who believe in a cause. We won't stoop to their methods."

"You'll die with honor."

She waited but his expression never wavered. She could see her morose sense of humor was lost with the tension of the moment. She mirrored his solemnity and laid down her cards.

"I'm going to level with you, Jake. I got an anonymous call from someone in the organization. He said you're holding out on them. He figured I could use my charms to find out what you know."

Stunned, he walked directly to the window and glanced between the curtains.

"Do they know about this meeting?"

"Yeah," she said plainly. "Who, when and where."

He pulled back the curtain for a wider view and scanned the cabin for signs of electronic surveillance.

"Look," she said, "if they want us dead, we're dead."

"Are you wired?" he demanded.

"Would you like to search me?" she said playfully.

"Please. Just give me a straight answer."

His intensity surprised her and brought her back to the solid earth. This was serious business. Life and death.

"No, I'm not wired. They trust me. I've never let them down. You know that."

"Neither have I," he countered.

He knew it was wrong to doubt her at this point. She could have walked out without saying a thing. He'd have been dead by morning. He was allowing his fear to interfere with his reasoning.

"I'm sorry. I know you're trying to help. But I have to ask you: Why are you doing this?"

She sighed and almost regretted her decision.

"Because I like you, Jake, and I don't like them. I know it's stupid but there it is. Life is short and it's time I took a stand."

Jake tried to reassure her with a confident smile.

"Welcome to the cause!"

She shook her head in mock despair.

"I hope your guy knows what he's doing."

"You've got to believe. You've got to have faith."

"You want to know the last guy who said that to me? Bill Miner."

They both shrugged at the irony and Cheryl opened the door.

"I won't promise anything," she said. "But I'll see what I can do."

As she closed the door behind her, he could not help wondering if she had played him after all. It was possible. Of course it was. If she intended to cut his throat she could not have played it better. Still, he believed in her. He believed he had done the right thing. No. Not the right thing. It was more than that. Someone had once said: Between the good and the right, choose the good. He had chosen the good.

He believed in her. Now he would have to believe in her. His life was in her hands.

Chapter 45

A STRIKE TO THE HEART

Walking into Puget Sound Realty, Sara could not help but notice the stark contrast to the atmosphere of her colleagues at Olympic Realty. Worker bees moved about at a harried pace with dogged determination and semi-permanent worry etched on their faces. No one smiled or offered "hello" or engaged in any apparent social interaction. It was a sad place, disheartening – a place of pure business devoid of happiness or joy or the satisfaction of personal engagement and accomplishment.

As she approached the receptionist desk and waited for some acknowledgement of her presence, there was a flurry of activity. Finally, the stylish but frazzled young woman with a desperate look about her freed herself from a tangle of phone calls long enough to greet her.

"Can I help you?"

"Sara Kent. I believe you're expecting me."

"Miss Kent! Yes!"

She pulled a file and a ring of keys from her desk drawer and began walking hurriedly down the hall with Sara following and wondering aloud what all the commotion was about.

"I'm so sorry, Ms. Kent. I'm Linda."

She allowed Sara to catch up and shook hands before resuming her pace. "I'm afraid you've caught us at a bad time."

They arrived at an office door as the receptionist announced: "Here we are!" She was surprised to find the door open and a gentleman waiting inside. Jimmy Longbow acknowledged her puzzlement and offered his explanation.

"I have an appointment."

"I see. Well, I have to get back to the desk. I'll send someone down as soon as possible." She took a hard look at Jimmy in his fresh blue suit and pointed to the intercom on her desk. "Give me a ring if you need any help."

"Thanks," replied Sara. "I'll be fine."

Jimmy waited as she strolled around her new desk and sat in a plush leather chair. He then walked to the door, listened and glanced outside. Sara observed him with bemused curiosity. She had a good idea who he was.

"I work for Rome," he said.

She leaned back and looked him up and down, back and forth, before responding.

"How do I know who you work for?"

"Read my mind," he smiled.

"So you're Jimmy Longbow."

He nodded and shook her hand. He knew a lot about the young attorney with the guts of a warrior.

"It's a pleasure to meet you, Ms. Kent."

"Sara. Jake thinks the world of you."

"I'll try not to let him down," he reflected. "We don't have a lot of time. Your phone is tapped and your office is bugged. I took care of it for now."

He showed her the tiny microphone attached to the underside corner of her desk, removing and then replacing the magnetic muffling device he had attached.

"Any other day they'd have someone down here to check it out. Today I doubt they even know you're here."

"What's going on, Jimmy?"

"Jazzman strikes again. Only this time it's a blow to the heart. All I can tell you is that the Sanctum is having a sudden cash flow problem."

Given her knowledge of the vast resources the Sanctum had under its control, the implications were astounding.

"That's incredible," she replied.

She remained cool, calm and collected. He saw at once what Rome had seen and what Jake had fallen in love with: the fire burned within. She was a warrior.

"It's a beginning," he said. "There will be a panic. The markets will react and businesses will fold. They'll make some phone calls they're not supposed to make. You're on the inside now. It's up to you to see what you can find out."

He handed her a matchbook. She declined.

"Thanks. I'm quitting."

He smiled as she took the matchbook in hand and opened it to look at the inside cover. He decided he liked her.

"Anglo humor. Very funny. Those are passwords we think will be useful. If you find anything, leave a message at the number on the bottom. I check it twice a day."

They shook hands once more as Jimmy prepared to take his leave.

"If anyone asks, I was here representing the Skokomish."

"They'll love that."

"Be careful, Sara. We've hit them hard. They can't risk this will happen again."

"I will. I promise."

Jimmy had promised himself not to allow his emotions to cloud his vision. He realized now it would be difficult to keep that promise. She was an extraordinary individual. He would do whatever it took to keep her safe.

Chapter 46

THE PANIC

Jazzman struck in the closing hour of trading on the New York Stock Exchange. By the time the Sanctum realized what was happening it was too late. The damage was done and it was significant. It was unprecedented. It would take days to get a full account but already they knew it ran into the billions. Not only had he managed to hurt them financially, he exploited their own crooked method. They had no assurance he could not repeat his performance. It effectively shut down their operation.

To Josh Logan, a man of enviable means and power in the New York financial circles, it was more than a matter of money. It was personal. Until now, as one of the Sanctum's most highly regarded administrators, he was on the short list for promotion. Still in his forties, his rise had been swift and dramatic. His seat on the elite inner circle, the vaunted Council of Elders, had virtually been reserved. But this catastrophe occurred on his watch. It wouldn't matter that he was powerless to avoid it. Heads would roll and his was on the top of the list. It was his responsibility to inform the Elders and make an account. He was anything but anxious to carry it out but he knew it had to be done.

In the hours after the market closed he was in communication with administrators across the country. It was not a mystery who had delivered the blow. It had all the markings of the infamous jazzman.

They had dispatched Marcel La Conte to Seattle for the express purpose of resolving the jazzman problem one way or another. They wanted to recruit him as a replacement for the deceased Bill Miner. Roger Thomason was only a temporary fix. Both La Conte and others found him wanting. If the jazzman refused, he would have to be eliminated.

Now everything changed. Logan called La Conte to deliver new orders: Liquidate. Forget recruitment, liquidate at once. This meddling jazzman had to be eliminated by any and all means. La Conte assured him the situation was under control. If all went as planned, La Conte said:

"By tomorrow morning I'll not only tell you who the jazzman is; I'll tell you where he's buried."

It was of course just what Logan wanted to hear. It provided him something positive to temper the bad news. He took a deep breath and made the most difficult phone call of his life.

"It's Logan," he began.

"This better be good," came the response.

"I'm certain when you hear what I have to report, you'll understand why I had to call."

When he delivered the crushing news, the voice on the other end of the line agreed. For the first time in more than a decade, a direct, in person meeting of the Council of Elders would have to be called.

The dominoes began to fall.

Chapter 47

ALL FALL DOWN

It was time for a little swing from the age of the big bands when the Count was King. The mood was up and coming. The sound was smooth and easy. The jazzman laid down his cards and waited for the returns, for the product of his labor, his confidence supreme and his patience wanting.

It don't mean a thing if it ain't got that swing...

The moment was pure platinum. He wondered if nirvana itself could surpass the feeling that now swallowed his soul, filling him with warmth and glory. He understood what an athlete feels in a moment of supreme victory. He understood what a commander or war chief feels looking out on a field of battle in conquest. He understood what Charlie Parker or Miles Davis felt the moment they found their styles.

He sang along, tapping his toes, snapping his fingers, when it all came together in glorious triumph. He froze, snapped once more and said: *Jazz baby jazz!*

He stared blankly at what now appeared on his computer screen. He was stunned. He had waited years, planning and researching, manipulating and brokering, spying, deceiving and maneuvering for the moment that was now at hand. But nothing could have prepared him for the grand revelation that unfolded in black and white on his computer screen.

There they were. All of them. The Inner Sanctum. The vaunted Elders of the most malevolent organization in history. The first three names told the entire story: Solomon Robert Guggenheim, Paul Mellon and David Rockefeller.

Suddenly it became clear. These were not the new

capitalists in the image of the founders; they were the direct descendants of the founders. This was a story of hereditary succession.

Rome sat back and let it filter into his mindset. In light of this revelation he would have to reevaluate the very nature of the enemy. As he did so, he felt a surge of outrage and righteous indignation. It was an insult to the very concept of democracy and a betrayal of their own capitalist creed. They did not play by their own rules. They did not believe in meritocracy. They were not the product of Social Darwinism they pretended to be. They had not acquired their positions of power because they were smarter or more devious or more calculating. They were not subject to the laws of evolution and survival. They were pretenders. It was the bloodline and the bloodline alone that crowned them kings.

It was inconceivable even for Rome, who held them accountable for some of the greatest crimes in modern history. They had the audacity to create a new aristocracy on the fertile soil of humankind's first enduring republic. It was so far beyond the scope of reason he had failed to see it. It fooled him and it fooled Maggie. It escaped the meticulous eye of Detective Jones. But here it was, plain and simple.

Each elder was retired and wealthy beyond belief. None were active in the business world. Each of them was considered a philanthropist, always ready to help the less fortunate, to build libraries and art museums, to host fundraisers and support a vast array of causes. Despite their generosity they shunned publicity. They did not run for office and sought no public recognition for their good deeds. To a man – and they were all men – they lived in relative seclusion far from the glare of Wall Street and Washington. To the cynical it seemed they hid behind the walls of their mansions and estates far from the encroachments of the society they wished to dominate.

Their names were etched not on marble statues and monuments but in simple text on a computer screen: Mellon,

Guggenheim, Rockefeller, Hanna, Morgan, Frick, Baruch, Carnegie, Gould, du Pont and Vanderbilt. The only name missing from the original "founders" was the name erased by an assassin's bullet. Kennedy alone was denied a seat at the table of power. Kennedy alone had broken the promise: To be king of kings you must decline the throne, the crown and the trappings of power. They answered to a higher call. They would be crowned by history herself. They would become the legends of the New World Order.

Eleven names remained. Eleven names that might have been as glorified as Rockefeller and Kennedy had it not been for the strange case of Bill Miner and a series of events beyond their control. A panic on Wall Street led to a series of calls and communications that would never have been allowed under normal circumstances. Now they would be revealed in infamy. History works in mysterious ways.

These were the untouchables of history. They were never to be contacted except in the case of the most extreme emergency. On the grandiose scale of the Sanctum, such an event literally had to rival the assassination of a president. Rome had arranged such an event by using their own methods to orchestrate a loss of a hundred billion dollars in the blink of a wary eye.

Something had to give and like clockwork it had. The wheels had only to be set in motion, churning and heaving like the pistons of a locomotive engine, like the westward migration in the 19th century, like the Oklahoma land rush and Manifest Destiny itself.

One call leads to another and another and another until, like dominoes, they all fall down.

Chapter 48

RAID AT THE POINT

This time they didn't wear gray suits. They wore green dungarees and combat boots along with their amber shades. They carried semiautomatic weapons, knives and explosives. They were prepared for all contingencies, including military engagement – or so they thought.

They descended on Roman Mason's estate at the Point of Arches by air, land and sea. Someone had betrayed the cause. Someone had tipped them off.

A group of four made their way from the southern tip of the Makah Reservation where an unpaved road ended in a coastal forest. It was a hard go but they were taking no chances. Reaching the point at sunset, they radioed an offshore chopper – a near silent black wind sweeper – to zero in on the estate. The chopper's sudden change of direction signaled a speedboat carrying five men and two Austrian wolfhounds to attack. Within minutes the speedboat docked, the chopper hovered above the landing bay, where two men disembarked by a rope ladder, and the overland crew greeted them. All avenues of escape were cut off.

The blast of an explosive device opened the entryway and pierced the calm of a quiet day on the secluded peninsula. They moved room-to-room, searching every corner of the expansive two-story cabin. Their efforts were in vain.

In fact, they found nothing: no furniture, no paintings on the walls, no desk, no files, no computers, no phones. The place was clean.

It was a double cross. The invaders thought they had the

jump but in fact they were duped. The jazzman had seen them coming. Even the chopper on the landing bay was an empty shell. Rome Mason was gone. He swept the place, leaving no trace that he had ever been here.

They went through the formality of searching the cabin for clues – fingerprints, a forgotten notepad, a dropped item – but they would find nothing.

Back at the office at Puget Sound Realty they followed the paper trail as far as it could take them. It took them nowhere. The estate and everything tied to it was registered to Olympic Realty. That much they had already known.

They were certain of one thing: Their man, Jake Marshall, had screwed up. He would have some explaining to do.

Chapter 49

A FISHING EXPEDITION

Detective Jones was worried. It had been too long since his encounter with Jimmy Longbow at The Monastery. He paced the aisles that formed naturally amidst the books and papers in his crowded study. It was dead midnight.

He counseled himself with Hamlet's caution: "Patience! Upon the heat and flame of thy distemper, sprinkle cool patience."

It was his habit to continue pacing until he reached a heightened awareness, a sensitivity to all things physical and spiritual. The bard provided internal dialogue for a flow of consciousness that the detective would ride to its conclusion.

"Defer no time!" he challenged. "Delay has dangerous ends."

He was still worried. In the last few days his wife had become suspicious of his retirement. She recognized the furrowed brow, the worry lines, the restlessness, insomnia and the late night pacing as a pattern of behavior belonging to a difficult case. She was not fooled by his explanation that he was having trouble adjusting to a schedule of leisure. She was less certain of his alternative explanation that he was following several cases as an intellectual pursuit – like others might play chess. Partly to ease his wife's mind and partly to maintain outward appearances, he went fishing every now and again though he had yet to bring home a fish.

It was difficult not to confide in her. He had always been open and completely forthright. He consulted her in his most challenging cases and was always impressed by her natural analytic ability. She had a mind like a database with infinite possibilities arranged in perfect harmony with his own. She never forgot a fact.

Despite all that and the knowledge that he could certainly use her help, this time he refrained. This time it was too dangerous. Through some twisted act of fate he had been entrusted with the key to the kingdom of justice. It was like being appointed keeper of the sacred pipe, protector of the Holy Grail or guardian of Excalibur. The risk was too great and he preferred to keep it to himself.

He was reticent to contact anyone even remotely connected to the case. He had taken the precaution of making copies of the nine micro-tapes and two dozen transcripts of the Sanctum's secret Council of Elders. He placed one copy in a safe deposit box in Tacoma. It seemed prudent at the time but now he wondered if it was a mistake. It could be traced. He kept the originals with the expectation that he would unload them in due time.

Just as doubt began to cloud his vision he realized the evidence was more secure with him than it would be with virtually anyone else – especially Rome Mason. He heard about the raid on Mason's peninsula estate from an unusual source: a man identifying himself as an agent from the Federal Bureau of Investigation. It was same man who was trailing Jake at the bar. He surmised that the cat was finally out of the bag. The whole world – or rather that part of the world that mattered – knew that Rome was the jazzman.

The detective took extraordinary measures to avoid suspicion. The Miner case was officially solved. He had managed to reach retirement with an unblemished record. He maintained his correspondence and made regular entries in his personal memoirs. He told his friends at the department he was writing his life's story. He went fishing and logged time at the country club.

Still a sense of anxiety surrounded his every move. Time passed like quicksand, heavy as mercury. He had far too much time to think and to review the contents of the evidence in his possession. What he had learned would astound the most cynical of minds.

"See how quickly nature falls into revolt when gold becomes the object!"

His pace quickened as he contemplated the nature of the beast. Like a council of darkness, this secret society of men had plotted, planned and paid for the execution of a president and, worse, the utter subversion of democracy. There existed no boundaries, no limits and no constraints of any kind on the actions they would take to preserve their self-appointed positions as the all-powerful kings of the planet. And yet they perceived themselves as patriots, heroes and role models for future generations.

"Let Hercules himself do what he may! Cat will mew and dog will have its day."

He turned to retrace his steps across the study and sensed the presence of the ancient one. It froze him to the spot as if paralysis had entered every muscle in his body. His wife knocked on the door and without hearing her words, though they were spoken with sufficient volume and clarity, he went to the phone and picked up the receiver.

"It's Jimmy."

"Yes?"

"It's best if I get to the point."

"Please."

"Bremerton Ferry, nine o'clock." Click.

That was it. The call of destiny finally came through. Now he sat on the ferry and waited for his contact. He did not expect to be greeted by the jazzman but there he was sporting facial hair and a ragged wig. He strode calmly to his bench and sat beside him.

The detective smiled and said: "I have had a dream past the wit of man to say what dream it was."

"Queen Mab," replied Rome.

The detective was impressed.

"What shall I call you?" he inquired.

"Mr. Smith will do."

The good detective placed the box, wrapped in plain brown paper, beside him and detailed its contents as they crossed the sound. Nearing port in Bremerton, Rome explained that a rented white Cherokee, fully stocked with fishing gear, was waiting for him. The detective nodded. It would not be wise to take the ferry across the sound only to board the return passage. Like it or not he would spend the day fishing.

"I have a message from someone claiming to be a friend of yours," the detective said. "He told me he's FBI."

"Did you believe him?"

"His ID was real."

"Did you believe him?"

"Yes."

Rome had known for some time that the FBI was involved. The Sanctum did not get to where it was without powerful connections in government. He expected them at some point but until now there had been no contact.

"What's the message?"

"Seems they've had their fill of the Sanctum. They view it as an antiquated institution that has outlasted its usefulness. They have other means of support. Safer means. Now that you've exposed their weakness, they wouldn't mind dealing with a new player. They want you to stop them. They won't help you but they won't move against you either. They'll be around but they're only interested as observers."

Rome peered at the detective with his most discerning eye. He realized the detective possessed second sight. He walked in dreams and spoke with the old one.

"You realize that's exactly what they would say if they fully intended to move against us."

"Of course."

"But you believed him?"

"I did. Aside from the fact that it makes sense, I looked

into his eyes and saw the face of his heart. I traced it to the source and I believe him."

"If you believe him, then I do," he said as he stood to breathe in the fresh ocean air. "It's a magnificent world," he confided.

The detective agreed in silence. He was relieved to have this burden lifted but he knew the adventure was anything but over. Rome read his mind.

"Do they really think we'll be content to stop once we've crushed the Sanctum?"

"History turns when kings underestimate their enemies," replied the detective. "They support you because they don't perceive you as a threat."

"One step at a time," smiled Rome.

"Cat will mew…"

"…and dog will have its day."

They shook hands to acknowledge their kinship.

"We'll be needing your services," said Rome.

"We'll see," replied the detective. "By the way, I don't know how you pulled it off but good work."

Rome didn't need to ask. The havoc his manipulations had wreaked was clearly visible to the informed eye in the daily market reports. The detective had an informed eye.

"Thanks. I still have a few tricks."

"I'm sure you do. You'll need them."

They parted company before the ferry docked. Detective Jones waited to allow Rome time to depart. He located the Cherokee in the parking lot and spent the next hour finding a fishing hole.

Chapter 50

CHRISTMAS AT TULALIP

It was Christmas eve at Tulalip, where the ocean mists roll in from the Strait of Juan de Fuca and wander in and out amongst the Douglas fur and cypress, blessing the land with a mystical, spiritual quality, like a London fog in Sherlock Holmes or the last scene of Casa Blanca.

Warmed by an open fire, Rome sipped honey wine, breathed the pine-scented air and mused over recent events with a feeling of profound contentment. At long last, all the pieces were coming together.

They had dealt a blow that reverberated like a sustained chord on a tenor sax. It shook them from top to bottom. He had denied the strong arm of vengeance, escaped their grasp and sent them scrambling in all directions.

"Too late," he thought.

They would never find him. And if they did it would not matter. He had them by the balls and his grip would only get tighter.

His theory had been confirmed. The market crash he manufactured had sent them into panic. With the assistance of Sara Kent and Joe Thomas, he was able to identify all the missing pieces. Detective Jones secured the tapes and transcripts that would support their account.

The most incredible and damaging piece of evidence was a tape of the Council of Elders dated September 9, 1963. It was more than clear the Sanctum was the central force behind Kennedy's assassination. Every voice was clearly recognizable. The lines of hereditary succession flowed directly to those who sat on today's Council. All the king's men and all the king's horses were accounted for.

"The rest," he thought, "should be a cakewalk."

It was not just the success of the cause that engaged his mind this evening. It was Maggie. She had captured his heart. The cause brought them together and for that he would be eternally grateful. In all his travels and experiences, his fantasies and sweet imaginings, there was no greater testament to womankind than Maggie. Intelligent, sensitive, alluring, attractive beyond belief, she was everything he wanted in a companion. She was his soul mate.

That no one had captured her affection before now seemed nothing short of a miracle. He mused that if he had met her earlier he might not have walked this path. He might not have felt the need to make his mark on the world. He might have been content to sit by the fire after a hard day's work, listening to Coltrane and sipping wine with Maggie by his side. Life is full of ironies.

He considered it his good fortune that the Thomas household held to the Christmas day tradition. Tonight she belonged to him and he was determined to make the most of it. The first part of the evening belonged to business. She would insist on reviewing every part of the unfolding plan. In that they were so very much alike. They would leave no stone unturned. They would make sure every detail was in its place.

The history of the Sanctum was ready for publication. Copies would be distributed to a hundred web sites, domestic and foreign, with strict instructions for its release. He would set up a meeting with Marcel La Conte to deliver their demands:

First, the Sanctum will immediately cease its illegal market operation.

The American and in turn the global economy would experience a sudden surge. Economists would scramble to explain the unexpected prosperity. Businesses would thrive, unemployment tumble, the homeless could be sheltered and the infirmed cared for.

Second, illicit profits already collected will be divided equally among tribal councils of the Indian nations in the names of anonymous donors.

Armed with trillions of dollars the tribes could begin to buy back sacred lands, including the Olympic Peninsula and the Black Hills of North Dakota. Native American culture and traditions could be preserved in perpetuity. No longer dependent on the government, the tribes could break with the Bureau of Indian Affairs and other agencies that had always exploited their lands and resources.

Third, all Sanctum business operations, including finances and communications, will be subject to continuous surveillance and inspections.

This would insure compliance with measures one and two. They would be allowed to engage in legitimate business but they would not be allowed to conduct any questionable practices.

He would explain the consequences of any deviation from the agreement or any attempt to circumvent its intent. He would provide La Conte with the materials that would be published in the event of the Sanctum's failure to honor the agreement along with the individuals with authorization to publish them. If none of those individuals could be contacted for whatever reason, the materials would be published immediately. Any attempt to contact or negotiate with individuals involved would also result in immediate publication. No one but the individuals listed would be authorized to alter the terms of the agreement and then only by unanimous consent. Any such modifications would only be carried out in person.

They had thought of everything.

La Conte would present the terms to the Council of Elders and they would have to submit. The alternative was unthinkable. Even if the history could be discredited, the inclusion of names, dates, locations, tapes and transcripts would enable the media to uncover the truth. The Elders would be subject to public scrutiny and disgrace. There would be a public investigation and no matter the outcome, the Sanctum could no longer operate in the shadows of anonymity.

At the far end of the spectrum of possibilities, some Sanctum members would serve prison terms while others would have their financial holdings seized. From the perspective of the Elders, the worst outcome would be the tarnishing of their characters. Instead of the heroes of American exceptionalism, they would go down in history as traitors and thieves. Their names would become eternal symbols of greed, avarice and corruption.

Whatever the cost, they could not allow their history to be published before its time. They would accept his terms. As a financial incentive, he would expunge their names from the account if all terms were upheld for a period of twenty-five years. By that time their market connections would be severed and their machine would be disassembled. He would personally see to it. They would either become legitimate businessmen on a level playing field or they would be the pariahs of the century.

He had enlisted Maggie's help in drafting the plan and he was pleased with the result. It required a complete list of all the names on the upper tier of the Sanctum's power structure. Any omission would become an opportunity to divert funds and rebuild the organization. It required that their operation remain undetected until the history and the supporting materials were distributed with publishing agreements signed and secured. It was costly but his latest manipulation secured a fortune in financing. They bought while the Sanctum sold and sold when the Sanctum bought. If their goal had been to make money they already had more than they could ever dream of spending.

Soon everything would be in place. The meeting would

take place shortly thereafter and the deadline for the Sanctum's acceptance would be New Year's Day. How fitting it seemed that a new era should begin with resetting the global calendar.

Rome turned on a little Billie Holiday accompanied by Harry Edison and Benny Carter and settled into a zone of consciousness where all things cease to be separate and distinct. Everything blended in harmony and grace when Maggie knocked at his door. He let her in with a comforting smile that said: "All is well. Everything is under control."

He handed her a list of names – the Council of Elders. He took great pleasure in watching her react just as he had. It was shocking and disgusting.

"They killed the Kennedy's not because they stood in the way of their plans – though that might have been sufficient – but because their father was one of them. He violated the code. He sought public recognition. He let his eldest son ascend to the American throne."

"Incredible," said Maggie. "But is it really that simple?"

"Nothing is simple with these people. The whole thing is twisted and warped beyond imagination. But it appears that it happened in just that way." He presented her with Detective Jones' package. "It's all in here."

"Explain it to me," she said.

"The good detective had a vision and it led to these materials. It includes transcripts and recordings of selected meetings of the Council of Elders. Apparently, there was a dissenter among them. His line of succession ended with Bill Miner."

Maggie insisted on reviewing each document and listening to each tape in chronological order. She analyzed the evidence with a critical mindset. She wondered if the tapes could be authenticated.

"I'm sure they can," said Rome, "but I don't think it will come to that."

She wondered about the source.

"That we may never know."

Finally, she took it all in and came to a conclusion. It was the collaboration she had requested in a more powerful form than she could ever have imagined. It was the dark history of the nation and she regretted that the story would likely never be told. She lifted her glass.

"To the revolution!"

It brought a smile to his face. He was the revolutionary in this couple.

They drank and Maggie promised to leave business behind for the rest of the evening. This was Rome's Christmas after all and he had chosen to spend it with her. He was the last of his immediate family and he had no connections with extended family members. Tomorrow he would have the memory of tonight and the anticipation of events to come. He declined Maggie's invitation to join her family gathering. They were too close. No one but Maggie would know of his whereabouts until the deed was done.

They enjoyed dinner and exchanged gifts, huddled on a plush blanket by the fire. Maggie gave Rome a rare recording of W.C. Handy from the grand age of jazz. Rome gave Maggie a beautiful necklace once worn by the Queen of Prussia, its centerpiece a heart shaped ruby surrounded by diamonds.

To the exquisite and mesmerizing voice of Billie Holiday singing *My Man*, their bodies melded into one. The movement of her hips made him wonder if she had missed her calling as a jazz musician. The pulse of the earth, the waves of the sea, the grace of flight and the power of volcanic eruption: all were a part of their unified soul. The glory of their coupling went well beyond pleasure, beyond ecstasy and beyond enchantment to the very edge of divine fulfillment. Had they not so much to look forward to, they would have been content to die in that moment.

As *My Man* gave way to *Always* and *Always* to *Say it Ain't So*, they climbed the mountain and soared to the burning height of passion before returning in a concurrent explosion of release to the sacred ground of mother earth. As they settled slowly into the profound relaxation that accompanies complete relief, Rome seized the moment. He lifted himself up, admired her classic, timeless beauty and said:

"I'd die for you, Maggie."

"Hopefully," she replied, "that won't be necessary."

She smiled in perfect contentment, profoundly satisfied. Frozen in time and filled with unspeakable emotions, it was impossible to tell how long they gazed into each other's eyes. Suddenly self-conscious from the glare of his adulation, she covered her body with a pillow. She felt like a child, innocent and shy.

"All is well," he whispered in her ear.

All is well. And she believed him. It was Christmas Eve at Tulalip and all things were possible.

Chapter 51

DANCE OF THE ANCESTORS

The soldiers passed not more than twenty yards from where he took shelter. A dog resembling a wolf sniffed the air but was distracted by a rustling of leaves and movement in the brush ahead. The old man knew where they were headed and what they would find when they arrived. The man they sought – White Man who Lives Apart and Thinks Deeply – was gone. From this time forward he would see him and his companions only in visions. He would walk with them, smoke with them, counsel them and pray with them only in dreams.

The time had come. He closed his eyes and began the journey of his youth. He awakened from his fever and followed his father to a camp where the fire burned hot like a beacon to the heavens. Warriors moved around the fire, absorbed by the raging flames, transfixed by a vision and dancing with the grace of dreams. One man broke from the circle and moved as a mountain lion around the fire. Another pounded a drum. Another wore the hide and horns of a buffalo and chanted a song of the sleeping ancestors.

Through the eyes of youth he saw the face of the Great Spirit in the cloud of smoke above the fire. When he called to it and tugged on his father's legging, his father looked long and hard in the direction of the vision but he could see nothing. He cautioned the boy to be quiet. It was a great honor to witness the Ghost Dance.

The boy watched them dance for a very long time without words. Then, when the Great Spirit saw that the boy's heart was strong and good, it lifted him from his body like a feather on an updraft. At first he was frightened but the Great Spirit gave him comfort and told him he would always walk in dreams like a song in the wind.

He saw the sacred ceremony from above. And as he rose he became the spirit of his father. He saw the numbers around the fire grow. And as he rose he became the spirit of his grandfather. He saw more fires across the plains with more warriors dancing and singing, more drums pounding, women and children among them: In the white rock mountains to the north, in the high plains to the east, in the desert canyons to the south and in the forests of the big waters to the west. And as he rose he became the spirit of his ancestors.

He saw the tribes under one tipi. He saw warriors of all nations, Cherokee and Choctaw, Hopi and Navaho, Apache and Lakota, Paiute and Pawnee, Arapaho and Cheyenne, Shoshone and Crow, Makah and Ozette, Skokomish and Hoh, take hands and dance before the fire of their ancestors. He saw fire on the clouds, on the wind and the water. He saw the sleeping ones awakening and joining in the dance.

He set his eyes upon the flames and beheld the crumbling of castles, the fall of empires, the unraveling of the rings of power. He saw thirteen towers of gold reduced to ashes, reduced to dust. One by one, the masters of darkness rose from their seats at the Council of Elders, abandoning their thrones, letting go of their empires and their ancestry of evil. He saw their names, their faces and the words printed in their holy book.

He saw and understood: The prophecy of the Ghost Dance was at hand.

Chapter 52

A PRIVATE ENGAGEMENT

What Marcel La Conte had in mind was a quiet Christmas for two. Aware that Cheryl Miner had little family to speak of and few close friends, he invited her to join him for dinner and conversation at his temporary estate. She had no choice but to cancel her plans to join the Thomas household and accept his overture.

When she telephoned Maggie to explain and offer an apology she intended to communicate by tone that it was less romance and more obligation. She was a little surprised that Maggie accepted her explanation without question. It was unlike her unless she knew more than she allowed.

La Conte didn't give her much time to think about it. He called at five and expected her at seven. She would have liked to contact Jake to let him know what was happening but things were moving too fast. She couldn't trust her own phone and even if she could, what could Jake do? What could anyone do? She was a pawn in a game of knights, bishops and kings.

She couldn't trust anyone – not even Jake or Maggie. The organization had ways of knowing things they could not possibly know. She was careful never to say anything that could be used against her. If it was a sting and she failed to report it, she knew too well the consequences. She didn't want to think about it. She wanted to go along like she always had but deep inside she knew that was no longer possible. Everything hinged on whether or not La Conte was going to be straight with her. If he kept his cover, she would make it through the night.

A uniformed servant greeted her at the door and led her to a study where La Conte sat listening to classical music and reading under an elegant lamp. He replaced his book in his expansive library while an attractive young maid in a sleek, black and white uniform served cocktails on a silver tray and departed without a word. They settled in separate chairs, sipping their drinks and enjoying small talk in the dimly lit room. Cheryl felt relief. As long as he played his part she would be allowed to play hers.

La Conte led the conversation, discussing their common acquaintances. He was struck by the charm of Maggie Thomas and looked forward to the opportunity of engaging her services. Cheryl readily agreed that Maggie was an extraordinary woman and remarked that most men were intimidated by her strength. He inquired about Maggie's relationship with Roman Mason and she smiled and confided that it was serious. La Conte seemed pleased but there was something in his smile that said he was not. She almost expected a forked tongue to emerge from his lips.

"I'll look forward to working with both of them," he said with the same double-edged smile.

It struck her as odd. He had only just met them. Why should he care one way or the other about their relationship? It occurred to her that La Conte was playing with her like a child teases a cat with a ball of twine. He was intimating that he knew more than he was willing to divulge. He wanted to watch her squirm. He enjoyed the process a little too much and it worried her.

As he led her into the dining room she told herself there was no way he could know but she knew it was all too possible. Even if she assumed Jake was on the level – a belief she held by gut instinct – she could not be sure that Jake's connections were untainted. She was walking a tightrope with a lead weight on her shoulders. Anything could happen and probably would.

Dinner was served. To her surprise it was traditional: turkey and dressing with all the trimmings. It was prepared by a master chef and served under candlelight. La Conte clearly wanted to impress.

He spoke at some length about his life in New Orleans. He admired the mysticism and raw sensuality of nightlife in the French Quarter. He spoke with warmth about the gypsies, the musicians, the strippers and the "finest prostitutes in all the world with the possible exception of Paris."

He lingered on the thought and looked at Cheryl with a longing that was new even to her. She did not doubt his power and appeal. She found herself being drawn in despite her will. She was at once attracted and repelled.

He waited until after dinner to dismiss the servants and make his play. His eyes were fixed to hers as he leaned back, sipped his cognac and declared, "You will stay the night." If she were free to refuse she was not entirely certain that she would. She decided to take things to a more familiar level. If La Conte was enthralled by strippers and whores, she would give him what he wanted.

She rose and strolled toward him, her hips moving to an inner rhythm of jazz, her eyes sleepy time seductive, her hands coursing upward across her lithe, firm body, gently caressing her firm but supple breasts. She stopped just beyond his reach and lifted the index finger of her right hand to her lips.

He remained motionless and poised, his eyes betraying a passion that burned deep within. She moistened the tip of her finger and reached, ever slowly, across the table to squeeze out the trinity of candles before him. She moved back, gliding in the same sensual manner and repeated the process until only a single candle remained lit.

She then displayed the artform that first attracted the eyes of the organization so many years ago. She turned her back to him and angled her head to observe his reaction in the corner of her eye. Her left hand still held to her breast beyond his view while her right hand edged up to draw down the zipper of her sleeveless, velvet gown.

With a serpentine writhing of her hips she teased it to the floor and turned, legs parted, revealing herself in black garters, red silk panties and a sleek black brassiere adorned with an embroidered red rose at its center.

She closed her eyes and moved to the rhythm of a gentle jazz beat, hand caressing every part of her exquisite body within reach. Again she turned in a flowing motion and unfastened her brassiere. When she turned again her eyes were open and her hands swept down to slide beneath the silk of her panties. There they remained as her body arched, eyes closed and head flung back, her face a portrait in ecstasy. Her hands spread outward beneath the silk as she lowered the last curtain of erotic mystery and settled in a crouch.

He let out a muffled cry of pleasure and she knew she had him at last. Slowly she rose and went to him. Suddenly childlike in his desperate state, he held out his hand. She placed it on her breast and leaned down to whisper a promise of sweet release in his ear. She took his hand and led him up the stairs to the master bedroom.

She owned him now. The game was on and she held all the aces. The pawn was transformed to a queen. On this playing field she was the broker. She had the tease. She was the holder of the world's most precious jewels. For this space in time, she was the object of all his desires and the surge of power, control and passion fused a bond between them and in turn aroused her own desire. She let go and let it happen.

In the late, early hours when their exhausted bodies settled into the quiet, relaxed place that follows sexual satisfaction, he promised her the world and opened his thoughts to her as he had opened to no woman before her.

Had he been capable of love, Marcel La Conte would have grasped the brass ring that would have changed his life.

As it was, he revealed too much. Beneath her beautiful, fluttering eyelashes, Cheryl listened and learned.

She feared it was already too late.

Chapter 53

SOUL SACRIFICE

Was it just paranoia? Jake could not be sure. He thought he was being followed. No, he was sure of it. He could not shake the feeling that his number was coming up. It was only a matter of time. He knew that the organization was aware that he was working for the jazzman but they did not know that he knew they knew. They were hoping he would lead them to Rome and that alone was keeping him alive.

He had a foreboding dream of a shadowed gunman with eyes that he could not quite place. He heard a voice that he could almost remember saying, "Stay out of the light."

It was sound advice but he had no clue how to take it. He had no place to hide. If he tried to go underground it was an admission of guilt. The Sanctum would hunt him down. Then there was Sara. He could not expose her to any more danger than he already had. She was absolutely committed to the cause – maybe more than he was. And they were close to their objective. He could feel it. No matter how rough things got, there would be no turning back.

His best play was to keep up the act. He had to offer the possibility that he was worth more alive than dead. He had to maintain the illusion that he would lead them to Rome.

But everything had changed with Cheryl's brief message: *Your man is tainted. Check your connections.*

It seemed clear to him that Cheryl believed with absolute certainty that Rome was a traitor to his own cause. How could that be? It was unthinkable and yet he had chosen not to contact Rome through the usual channel. He figured the lines were unsafe but now he wondered. Was it possible that somewhere in his unconscious mind he doubted the very source and spring of the cause?

Why? Why would Rome betray the cause he created? What would he stand to gain? If not for Rome he would not have moved to Seattle. Why would Rome solicit his help if he only intended to betray him? As quickly as he asked the question the answer came like a lightning bolt: In Rome's own words, he needed someone he could trust without question. In other words, he needed someone who would judge him not by his present deeds but by his character and history.

Was it possible he was looking for a fall guy and Jake fit the bill?

When he raised the question with Sara, she was quick to come up with an obvious alternative: Cheryl Miner was lying.

"Who do you believe?" she charged. "A man you've known for twenty years and never had reason to doubt or a woman you know to be an employee of the Sanctum? You took a chance in confiding with her and you shouldn't be surprised that she turned on you. This is nothing but a Sanctum ploy."

"That's just it," Jake countered. "It's too bold too soon. They wouldn't be so quick to show their hand."

"Is there another explanation?"

Jake wondered aloud: "They could be playing with Cheryl. That would be more like them. On the other hand…"

He let it lay there like the last slice of pizza, an unthinkable thought and the seed of doubt. Sara read it and welcomed it. It wasn't the first time they'd doubted Rome.

"We go way back," said Jake. "But he's changed. He's a very wealthy man. The man I knew I would never doubt. But…has it occurred to you he might be one of them?"

"An inside job? A coup d'etat?"

"Yes."

"It has occurred to me," she said bluntly. "I'm not a person to leave any stone unturned. I've thought it through but in the end I don't believe it."

A cloud of silence hovered over them like a three-day storm until Sara broke the spell.

"We have to do something, Jake, and it begins with trust. Who do you trust?"

"You."

"I can't help you. Who else?"

"Jimmy."

"Anyone else?"

He tried hard to come up with another name, another person or another idea but the stakes were too high for speculation.

"No one," he said.

"All right then," she replied decisively. "We contact Jimmy and go from there."

He ambled to the window and stared out at the endless gray skies. Raining again. It seemed they were trapped in the shadows and the shadows were the only thing between him and the danger ahead. "Stay out of the light," said the voice of his subconscious. But there was no other way. He was convinced that all electronic means of communication were corrupt and could not be trusted.

"His mother lives on the Makah reservation out on the peninsula. I'll drive out tomorrow. If we're lucky, he'll be there. If not, I'll leave him a message."

They sat in silence for a spell, allowing their fears to take root, hoping they would not suffer the royal Dane's dilemma, paralyzed in perpetual contemplation. Sara wondered if this was not the desired effect. Were they intended to stand idly by during this critical stage of the operation? What options did they have if they could not trust Rome?

It was a restless night. The uncertain days ahead hung over them like a stifling veil of fog that refused to lift. They went through the motions of conversation over dinner, small talk over wine and little else. They retired early though they knew they would not sleep.

Only their passion could free them from the drudgery and the weight of pressure and doubt and the unshakeable feeling that something unspeakable was about to happen.

They made love with a tenderness and abandon so profound it seemed they had never touched before. Gazing deeply into each other's eyes they sensed they were becoming one spirit, one body and one soul for the first time in their collective lives. For the first time Sara sensed that she had freed herself from the tarnished image of masculinity that was her father's legacy. For the first time Jake sensed that there was nothing he could hold back. For the first time they knew love without compromise.

As they held each other in the celestial glow of sexual fulfillment, their bodies sheathed in perspiration and the aroma of desire, it was as if they knew: It was the last time on this earth that they would feel and experience this treasure and divine gift. They held it with a rare intensity of awareness – as if to savor every nuance – until yielding at last to the realm of sweet and sensual dreams.

He rose at dawn and left her, still dreaming, with a gentle kiss. He admired the angelic expression on her loving face and tried to shrug off the gut feeling that returned to him with the morning light.

He took a circuitous route to the Bremerton Ferry and boarded only when he was certain he was not being trailed. He scanned the passengers briefly – construction workers and tourists on fishing trips – before allowing himself to let go of his fear and enjoy the passage.

The sky was clear and the waters of the sound – a thin veil of morning mist already lifting – were exceptionally calm. The seagulls in their perfect grace seemed to serenade the new day as his thoughts drifted back to Sara and his soul was comforted by her love.

When the ferry docked he felt invigorated, his spirit energized and his resolve renewed. As he drove down Highway 3 he should have noticed the green Toyota four-wheeler that fell in behind him at a safe distance. He should have noticed when the Toyota seemed to know where he was headed.

If he had noticed he might have altered his route south toward Shelton but his focus was dead ahead. His thoughts were on Jimmy and Sara and Cheryl and Rome, trying to separate fact from suspicion, winding his way through layers of deception, when he heard a strange pop and a whoosh at the right front of his vehicle. Before he could react he was off the road, screeching down an embankment into the southern fork of Hood Canal.

On the roadside above two men dressed in hunting gear and carrying rifles, watched and waited to be sure Jake Marshall did not survive. They were joined by two others emerging from a green Toyota four-wheeler. Only their amber vision shades betrayed them.

Back in Seattle, Sara awoke with a start. She knew without knowing and could not accept it.

"Jake!" she cried out instinctively. She shook the thought from her head. It was just a dream she told herself. It was just a bad, bad dream.

Chapter 54

CHANGE OF PLAN

It was not unusual for Rome to stop by Maggie's office before he went into hiding. When he did so now she immediately rescheduled her appointments and beckoned him inside with a clandestine kiss.

"Don't worry," he said. "Everything's fine."

Mind reading was a habit she generally found annoying but Rome was invariably accurate.

"I'm relieved," she replied. "I was afraid you'd be holed up for the duration."

"I had to see you."

Gazing at her warm expression, he marveled at how someone so sophisticated and intelligent could be read so easily. She would have been the world's worst poker player. She could no more hide her honest thoughts and feelings than a blind man could hide his lack of vision. Right now she was thinking: *I know you, Rome. You're not that romantic.*

"I took the necessary precautions," he continued.

She smiled in amusement. It was a distinct contrast in style. Like Song in the Wind, Rome didn't believe in getting straight to the point. A conversation was like a ritual or a meal with seven courses. If he treated his clients in this manner, it would drive them mad.

"What is it?" she pressed.

"The meeting is set. Nine o'clock tomorrow evening at La Conte's place."

"Why so late?" she wondered.

"He didn't want to disturb his evening meal."

They laughed. It was typical La Conte. Whatever the circumstances, he would not be inconvenienced. Etiquette would be observed. The revolution would have to wait until after desert.

"I want you to come with me," he said.

She took a moment to examine him as she would a client who had withheld pertinent information. She was his partner, his confidant, his lover and friend. They had drafted the plan together, plotted their strategy and confided their fears and worries. She assumed she would be engaged in the negotiations and was upset when she learned she had not been. She could think of no logical reason for the omission. She would be in danger whether she was there or not. Now, at the eleventh hour, he had changed his mind.

"Why?" she asked. "Can't handle it alone?"

Rome bowed his head as if in prayer. He had carefully considered his decision to exclude Maggie but he had failed to include her on his reasoning.

"I'm sorry, Maggie. I should have explained before. I guess I was concerned that you'd talk me out of it. The fact is: La Conte treats women as lesser beings. The only women he allows around him are prostitutes."

"What does that say about Cheryl?"

"It says she's in danger and I'm pretty sure she knows it."

"You're saying he considers Cheryl his whore?"

"That's exactly what I'm saying."

Sensing her increasing level of anxiety he slowed the pace of conversation and allowed her to catch up. It had to have occurred to her that Cheryl played a certain role in the organization – even if she had inherited a great deal of wealth.

"That isn't fair and you know it," she said.

"No, it's not. Nothing about it is fair," he replied. "But I hope you can see why I would have concerns."

She tried to judge the sincerity of his apologetic tone. His explanation was not entirely satisfactory and he knew it.

"Why the change of heart?" she inquired.

He smiled that sneaky, sly smile of his.

"Because we've got them by the balls. To hell with La Conte! It no longer matters what he thinks. In the end, he's just a messenger and ours is a message he will have to deliver."

Maggie took it all in and walked to her desk as if in deep contemplation. She turned to him and said: "Whatever shall I wear?"

He came to her, took her hand and graced it with a kiss.

"Black, I think," he replied.

He started out the door and said over his shoulder: "I'll pick you up at eight."

Chapter 55

THE FACE OF THE ENEMY

Maggie had a recurring dream and it was becoming more vivid every night. It began with the rhythmic sound of wind through the tall pines. In the scattered pictures of a peyote vision or an experimental film, she saw images of a coyote and heard howling on distant hills. She saw a large crow in flight and an owl with eyes glowing like pearls in a black sea.

Until now she had never found a path through the forest. She had never seen a towering mountain or the rings of power. Until now the voice she heard carried no words and the broken images defied interpretation. Now the images began coming together. The coyote appeared before her with smiling eyes and beckoned her to follow. It led her on a path through the misty forest as the sunlight faded and a thin sliver of moonlight appeared in the darkening sky. The eyes and sounds of forest life flickered in and out of her mind like images in a strobe light.

At the foot of a great mountain the owl appeared with wise and piercing eyes that drilled into her soul and pronounced her worthy. She was allowed to pass.

She followed the coyote on a steep, winding and ascending path, upward and upward, moving in and out of thick gray blankets of mist. She heard a caw and looked skyward where she saw the top of the mountain and the cloudlike rings surrounding it and forming a funnel to the stars. The coyote led on. They rounded a curve in the mist where the coyote vanished along with the path. She heard the coyote laugh nearby, hiding beyond her view.

As she gazed into the darkness she saw the haunting eyes of a pack of wolves forming a circle around her. The sight chilled her to the marrow of her bones. She stood motionless and shuddering like a fallen leaf as one howled and another answered and the circle began to close.

Again the caw of a crow rifled through the air, silencing the wolves and enveloping her senses in a great fluttering of wings. Time and motion stopped as a single black feather floated softly into her hand. At once she was lifted off the earth and found herself soaring upward on the wind.

In the voice of the old Indian, the crow said: *To catch the coyote you must be as the coyote. You must know the face of the enemy.*

She came to rest in what appeared to be a dark chamber shrouded in smoke and there, seated around a long wooden table, through the eyes of the crow, she saw the illuminated faces of the enemy. She saw and she understood. She saw and she knew the secret that would guide her actions.

Chapter 56

ALWAYS

The quiet serenity of the morning hours soon gave way to midday anxiety. No matter what had transpired Jake was supposed to have contacted her by now. He would know she was worried. Even if he had been unable to contact Jimmy, even if he had nothing to report, he was supposed to call. He was supposed to let her know he was okay.

Somewhere deep within, in a place she could not bring herself to look, she knew what happened. She bit her lip and slowly began to accept a hard, cold reality into her conscious mind. Tears welling in her eyes, she knew what she had to do. Somehow she made it to the phone and tapped out Jimmy's number. As she listened to his recorded message her hand began to quiver and her tears began to flow and they flowed like an endless waterfall. By the time of the beep, she was barely able to speak.

"Jimmy," she said struggling for control, "Something's happened to Jake. Something…something's happened."

It was all she could manage before hanging up and collapsing to the floor where she sobbed with abandon. In her hand she clutched the note he left before he walked out the door that morning. It read: *All my love. Always.*

It was not unusual for him to leave a note of affection. The first three words were expected. But as she searched her memory she could not find a single instance where he had written the last: *Always.*

He must have known. He must have realized.

She let go a cry as if sheer volume could release the pain

of her heart. She pressed her tear-stained face to the cold tiles of the kitchen floor and crumbled like an imploded tower.

"Always," she uttered between uncontrollable sobs that seemed to convulse her entire body from head to feet, leaving her in a fetal position. "Always."

Chapter 57

MOMENT OF TRUTH

Rome was their founder. A child of the sixties, he had transformed himself from a businessman to a man of the spirit world. With the guidance of his Indian teacher, he had risen to a level of consciousness that enabled him to infuse others with his passion.

They were so close. Maggie thought back on all the work and preparation, the research, surveillance, espionage, deceit and manipulation, all the effort and sacrifice that went in to this effort. They had lost a good man in Jake Marshall. They had risked many more, including themselves. But it would all be worth it if they succeeded.

They were on the precipice of toppling the most powerful and corrupt secret society in the history of the modern world. The future of everyone she knew or ever had known, the future of millions lay in the balance. The future of the world would be altered for better or worse. The moment of reckoning had arrived.

On the drive to La Conte's estate they went over every detail of the plan as if they had not done so a dozen times before. Once certain they were completely and absolutely prepared, an uncomfortable silence descended upon them like an unexpected death. Out of the corner of his eye Rome watched her in a curious manner. She noticed but said nothing.

La Conte waited in his study while his servant led them in. He laughed in what seemed a forced manner when he greeted them.

"Well," said La Conte, "which of you is the jazzman?"

"The jazzman does not exist," replied Rome. "He was always a figment of your imagination."

"Was he indeed? Well, Mr. Mason, you must be a very clever man. You have interfered in our business affairs, evaded detection and generally asserted yourself as a major inconvenience. The situation is intolerable."

He spoke as he wiped clean three glasses, poured from a fresh bottle of wine and drank to ease their suspicions.

"I'm told you are a clever man as well," said Rome as he opened his briefcase and pulled out the incriminating file. "Let's get down to business."

He lowered the file to La Conte's desk and watched as he leafed through the contents, lingering a moment too long on the page where his own name appeared on a graphic of the Sanctum's power structure. He closed the file and smiled.

"It's an interesting work of fiction but you did not request this meeting for literary criticism. Or am I mistaken?"

Rome pressed the play button on the recorder in his pocket and let the assassination tape roll long enough for recognition to register on La Conte's face. It did not take long.

"We have the entire collection," said Maggie. "It covers 1963 to the present. We believe that lifts our manuscript from the realm of fiction to the realm of history. We also believe that its publication would mark the end of the Sanctum as it currently exists. We believe that a public inquiry would be inevitable and the implications of that inquiry are what should concern you."

La Conte maintained an air of dignity. He seemed unaffected. His demeanor was beginning to wear on her.

"If you believe all this, why not publish and be done with it? Why bring this to me?"

Maggie answered with equal amounts of confidence and contempt.

"If by our actions we were able to destroy you and all of

the individuals named herein, we suspect that others would emerge or rise from the ranks to take your places. The machinery would remain intact. We would prefer that you and your colleagues retain your positions and, to a large degree, your wealth, under certain conditions of conduct."

"I am relieved," said La Conte. "I was afraid I was dealing with individuals who did not care for personal compensation. Now I can see I am dealing with reasonable people, business people. Indeed, Ms. Thomas, I also believe that we would prefer to retain our positions and wealth."

He sipped his wine and took a moment to appreciate his own arrogance. If he considered himself at risk, he would not let it show.

"Let me be frank," he said. "We are kings among kings, rulers of the ruling class. We are more powerful than your president of the United States. Surely you are not so naïve as to believe we would allow an insignificant group of electronic pirates and renegades to bend us to our knees! Surely you do not believe we would hand over our holdings or make anything but the most token of concessions."

Maggie made sure he had finished before she replied.

"I appreciate your frankness and will respond in kind. You will comply with our demands because your colleagues and co-conspirators in the shadow government – yes, we know all about them – have begun to think of you as a liability. You will comply because our demands are more than reasonable. We are not ambitious. We do not seek to destroy you utterly though you should be utterly destroyed. We do not seek your heads on a platter though that is precisely where they belong. We do not seek to imprison you or strip from you the financial empires you have built on the backs of common people. We do not even wish to expose you. We only want a little property and the capital to procure it. Consider it your philanthropic penance. You will survive. You will carry on. You may even prosper. But you will do so on the level playing field you purport to champion.

261

What could be more fitting?"

La Conte was impressed despite himself. He sighed and refilled his wine.

"Do not be so sure of yourselves. Our partners will not abandon us. We have survived crises before and we will survive this one. After all, they prefer dealing with a known entity. We go way back."

Rome stepped into the fray with growing distaste for the man before them. He never liked smug people and La Conte was bathing in it.

"The Sanctum has blundered, La Conte. You've placed them all at risk. You're like an old rusted machine. They no longer need you. They have other ways to raise money without all the drama."

La Conte nodded and calculated his moves.

"What if I refused to relay your demands?"

"You'll pay for it when the story hits."

"If that's the best you can offer, I must say I'm less than impressed."

Maggie was tired of his act and decided to try a more aggressive line.

"I wonder," she said. "Is it the size of your penis?"

His reaction was only just perceptible – a slight stiffening, a restrained glance at Rome. He started playing with his pen.

"Is that it?" she pressed. "Is that why you're such an insolent little jerk?"

Rome was taken back and wondered if her tactic was wise. He broke in quietly but firmly: "Maggie."

But she continued to press, defiantly, eyes blazing, boring into the space behind the man's stunned expression.

"Cheryl was right on the mark in her assessment of your finer assets: Inadequate. Have we made an impression yet?"

"Maggie!" interrupted Rome with a little more urgency. He feared La Conte would act on impulse. He was afraid of what he might do.

She stood and turned to Rome.

"Let's get out of here. This...thing is not interested in anything we have to say."

He took her arm as gently as he could and pulled her aside to express his alarm.

"I don't think that would be in our best interest."

"No," she said with a degree of disappointment. "You wouldn't."

Rome was stunned and the air had a sudden heaviness, a grim pall, a dark cloud of remorse and a stifling, choking presence that waited for her next words.

Beneath it all, her heart had already broken. She was operating on strength of character, pride and the moral indignation that accompanies a betrayal of trust. It was not easy to fight back the flood of tears that promised to soothe the pain of her heart but she managed on pure grit and determination.

"Why did you want me here, Rome?" She didn't wait for his response. "Don't give me that crap about La Conte's attitude toward women. You wanted a witness. You wanted to erase any doubt that might arise concerning the legitimacy of this meeting."

He glared at her but said nothing.

"I don't know which of you is more disgusting," she went on. "I suppose it would be you, Rome, with your shroud of virtue and decency. The stench of mendacity is almost too much to take."

Rome stayed silent and motionless as if in shock. His eyes were glazed and she could see his anger rising.

"I'm curious," she pressed. "Did the two of you discuss which role you would play or did you just naturally assume the roles that best suited you?"

La Conte remained inexplicably smug despite his apparent paralysis. He clearly did not know how to respond to this unexpected turn. His eyes darted back and forth between them as if watching a tennis match at some distance.

He seemed almost amused.

Striking a contrast, Rome's eyes flared as if *he* had been betrayed. When he finally spoke it was with frightening intensity. It made her wonder. It made her doubt her own conviction. Was it possible she was wrong?

"Would you care to explain what you're talking about?" he challenged.

She took a moment to recompose. The scene had to be played out. There was no other way. She took a breath and gathered all the strength she could summon.

"The cause, Rome? Remember the cause? It wasn't a war against the capitalist beast, was it? It wasn't a revolution or a rebellion or even a protest. It was a straightforward coup d'etat, an inside job, a power play – like Capone taking over the Chicago mob. You were afraid the Elders wouldn't select you to succeed them so you took matters into your own hands."

Rome shook his head emphatically, his eyes still burning with apparent outrage, staring at Maggie with disbelief and contempt.

"You're making a grave mistake," he said.

"Am I?"

She met his contempt with her own, ultimately unshaken and decisive in resolve.

"Your grandfather invested as much as twenty thousand dollars over a period of ten years. He saw the crash of '87 coming and transferred most of his investment into high yield, low risk bonds and utilities. His losses were relatively small."

She allowed Rome to sift through the information and observed him calculating his response, like a desperate man down to his last bet. He fought most of his adult life to stand at this threshold; he would not give up without a fight.

"Did you really think I wouldn't check it out?" she pushed. "It was you who told me not to trust anyone. Well, maybe I wouldn't have given it another thought but your friend got a little careless in the heat of passion."

"My friend?" Rome challenged. His eyes narrowed and his brow creased as he seemed determined to explain his way free of accusation. "What friend is that?"

La Conte shrugged and for all appearances gave up the charade.

"The bitches are all the same," he said. "You can make love to them but you cannot trust them."

Maggie did not delay. "What an astute observation, La Conte. Was it a happy childhood?"

Rome remained determined despite it all. He could see he was losing her but his eyes still carried the fire of conviction. He pressed on.

"Maggie, please! This man is hardly my friend. He's certainly not my partner in this or any other endeavor. If I exaggerated my grandfather's loss it's because my family exaggerated. Families do. The effect was the same. He was devastated."

He paced the room and spoke with force. She could not tell if he had anticipated this development but even if he had it was an impressive performance.

"Cheryl works for the Sanctum and you're going to take her word over mine? Jake has been playing both sides against the middle. I warned you not to trust him. He's useful but who knows what side he's on today. If you don't believe me, ask Jimmy."

"Jake's dead," she said quietly.

It stopped his flow of words and froze his thoughts. Clearly this was something he had not anticipated.

"Didn't you think we'd know?"

"I didn't know."

Rome glared with scorn at La Conte who looked back with indifference. Business is business, he seemed to say. Don't take it personally.

Maggie did not buy it. This performance was meant to convince her that Rome had nothing to do with Jake's murder, that this was La Conte's doing alone. But she knew how convincing he could be in deception. She struggled to keep her mind focused. She had already considered all the evidence and made her decision.

"You think I ordered Jake's death?" he asked in utter disbelief.

She nodded without any indication of doubt or remorse. She would not be moved. She had been fooled by him before and would not allow it to happen again.

"You can't believe that. After all we've been through and all we've meant to each other."

"You, La Conte, the Sanctum: What difference does it make who gave the order? Jake's dead. But for your actions he wouldn't be. There's blood on your hands. Jake, Bill, Kramer, God knows who else."

Rome just shook his head. He'd run dry of words to defend himself.

"You almost pulled it off," continued Maggie. "We didn't want to believe it. Jake was your good friend – or at least we thought he was. Jimmy was like a brother to you. Sara all but worshiped you. We were all emotionally blind which is exactly what you counted on. If it hadn't been for Jake, who knows what might have been?"

La Conte cleared his throat and smiled.

"I can see you two have a few differences to work out. If you don't mind, I have business to attend to." He rose and motioned for them to leave.

"Sit down, La Conte," fired Maggie. "You don't want to miss this."

La Conte complied like a gentle lamb and Rome sat and prepared to listen.

"Let me acquaint you with what has taken place over the last twenty-four hours. Cheryl sent a message to Jake questioning your loyalty, Rome. Jake didn't trust the phone lines so he decided to drive out to the reservation and contact Jimmy. As you've gathered, he never made it. When he didn't return, Sara left a message on Jimmy's machine. She didn't know what else she could do. Jimmy found out what happened and came to me.

"By that time I was not entirely surprised by what he had to say. You'll appreciate this part, Rome. I had a dream. I dreamed about a crow, a coyote and the rings of power. I won't bore you with the details. You already know them and La Conte wouldn't understand. But I saw the faces of the enemy and yours was among them. That's what convinced me. But Jimmy still wasn't convinced. After all, the two of you had shared a vision and smoked from the sacred pipe. He needed more evidence. So we went to work. We began with phone records and credit accounts. There it was. It was as if we only had to ask and the answers came pouring in like coins on a jackpot. You made seven trips to New Orleans in the last eighteen months. Dozens of phone calls to and from La Conte, Kramer, Bates and Logan. This was before you were supposed to know who they were. Why, Mr. Mason? That's the only question that remains."

Rome lowered his eyes and sighed before answering: "I can explain."

"I'm not surprised," she replied. "You're very good at explaining things. But no explanation will get you out of this one. You see, Jimmy still wasn't convinced. He realized there were explanations. You represented Bill Miner. You were investigating the case. Who knows? So we set up a little trap. He alerted you that something was up. He told you his plan was to link up with Jake and meet Cheryl at the cabin by Lake Goesiger. He made sure no one knew but you. When the gray suits arrived with the semi-automatic weapons that was confirmation enough for everyone, including Jimmy."

La Conte sized up the silence and took notice of Rome's resignation. His cover was blown and he knew it.

"Well," said La Conte, "now that we know what we know, let us proceed. Shall we?"

Maggie waited to see if Rome would make one last attempt at explanation. When none was forthcoming, she obliged.

"As you wish, Mr. La Conte. The plan remains the same with a few necessary modifications."

"Aren't you forgetting something," interrupted Rome. His tone was altered, reflecting La Conte's manner of detached confidence. It seemed he was dropping the last vestige of pretense.

"What's that?" inquired Maggie.

"The history, the tapes, the transcripts and accounts: You don't have them."

He looked like a man who just played his trump card, smug and filled with venom. Maggie did not respond. She stood motionless and allowed them to think they had an out. Finally, she spoke.

"Honestly, I didn't know until now."

Rome went blank, his eyes inward as if looking for the rationalization that would justify his betrayal.

"I never meant to hurt you," he said. "Believe me, you wouldn't have known the difference. The tribes would have been endowed though the amount might have been a little disappointing. I would have explained that we overestimated the Sanctum's holdings. There would have been a few administrative problems. I would have explained that the effect of a few billion dollars wasn't that dramatic on a multi-trillion dollar economy. We'd have gone on. We'd have done good work and we'd have been happy together."

Maggie turned to him with renewed resolve, composed, calm, confident and prepared.

"And Jake? Would Jake have been happy, too?"

Again Rome summoned what appeared to be sincere remorse, if not guilt, before he replied: "You must believe I had nothing to do with Jake's death. Jake was my friend."

She looked to La Conte who seemed to have recovered his sadistic sense of amusement.

"Off the record?"

Maggie nodded and La Conte continued.

"I'm afraid I did have something to do with it. The man was too curious. He was becoming an annoyance. With so much at stake, I could not allow him to interfere. It was an executive decision and one I would surely make again. Mr. Mason was not contacted and would surely not have approved."

Still unable to reconcile the man that sat before her with the man she thought she knew, she returned her focus to Rome. He was a child of the sixties and a founding father. It was inconceivable that he should choose to join hands with the likes of La Conte.

"What happened to you?"

Rome sighed. He appeared almost relieved. At last he would be able to shed the burden of deception he had carried too long. Maybe he had begun to believe it himself. Now he would say what he wanted to say all along: the truth.

"Do you remember the sixties? No, how could you? You only read about it in books and newspapers. Tom Hayden, Jerry Ruben, Abbie Hoffman, Timothy Leary and all the others. A pack of fools, idiots and clowns of which I was proud to be one. We followed the great unknown cause on the promise of free love, acid dreams and a magic bus ride. We got exactly what we deserved.

"Vietnam wasn't a cause. It was an excuse. We didn't care about civil rights, free speech, higher consciousness or love thy neighbor. We just wanted to have a good time. Of course, the system loved our anti-materialism because it meant we would never have what they had: Power and wealth. A piece of the American pie.

"We weren't the solution, Maggie. We were a part of the problem. We were the opium that holds the masses down. No one was more betrayed than those within the movement who naively believed we could actually change the world.

"So I faced the same choice we all faced. Wake up or

die. Hayden woke up and joined the system. Ruben followed. Leary became a mockery of himself. Hoffman chose the noble path. As you might have gathered, I'm not the noble type. I chose to wake up and join the fold. So I became a rich man with a rich man's appetite and I make no apologies."

Maggie was perplexed.

"Is it really that simple? A conservative backlash? You actually believe that *you* were betrayed?"

She felt a rising wave of indignation and rage.

"That is truly pathetic. You're a walking enigma. You can't win for losing. You were blessed to be a part of one of the great cultural protests of modern history and you choose to become the enemy. Even when you were finally in a position to make the changes you dreamed about...look at you. You'd have sold us all out."

Her voice trailed off and she fought back the powerful emotions that threatened to reduce her to tears. She would not let that happen. She would remain strong. She would not allow herself to doubt. Not yet. Not now.

"I didn't really expect you to understand," he mumbled with a hint of sarcasm. "You weren't there. You don't know. Like every snot-nosed kid of the eighties you have this idealized notion of what went down. It was all bullshit."

"You know, Rome, maybe I wasn't there. I was a little too young and a little too sheltered by my privileged upbringing. But in my own way I was a part of it, too. And I swore that I would never forget what that cause stood for. It was about human rights and peace and justice and common decency. It was an awakening of the spirit and soul of the human race. Thank God there are people who remember and who keep the dream alive! Thank God I'm one of them!"

Again La Conte cleared his throat and smiled.

"While all this is very amusing, I'm sure there will be other opportunities to discuss our philosophies. I believe we have more pressing matters at hand."

She lifted her gaze from the pathetic figure her lover had become and resisted the strange impulse to embrace him as a mother would a wayward child. There might come a time for forgiveness but that time would wait.

"It's true," she said. "We don't have the official history. Rome was careful to keep it out of my hands. He said it was for my own protection. Now we know the real reason."

She had recovered her legal persona and proceeded with the precision and confidence of an experienced trial lawyer.

"But I'm certain you'll agree, gentlemen, that what we do have is more than sufficient. The good detective took the precaution of making copies of the tapes and transcripts. In addition, we've put together a detailed account of what I call The Jazzman Insurrection. It's about two high-ranking members of a secret, powerful organization and their attempt to overthrow its leadership.

"You know me, Rome. You know my work. I assure you it's quite convincing. If our demands are not met, it will be sent to every known member of the Sanctum. Rest assured, gentlemen, your fate is sealed. You can either cooperate with us or face the judgment of the Council of Elders. Since we all now by now you're not the noble kind, you have very little choice. But you're more than welcome to exercise it."

La Conte looked to Rome whose eyes had turned inward where they remained. He was the portrait of a beaten man and Maggie read him like an open book. He was wondering how he could have failed to see it coming. He was so close to his goal. Maybe he realized now it was the old Indian who outwitted him. La Conte was ready to toss over his king.

"She is very persuasive, Mr. Mason. I can see why you were so taken with her."

Rome looked up as if awakening from a dream but he could find no words.

"May we have some time to discuss it?" inquired La Conte.

"What is there to discuss?" replied Maggie. "We've got you by the proverbial balls. You take the deal or not. We don't care. With you or without you, we proceed with our plan this evening."

Rome finally found his bearings enough to talk in a halting, uncertain manner: "Did you mention certain modifications?"

"Yes, I did. Your names will be listed in the account and on the protected list so that your protection will be contingent on ours. In short, you can't betray us without betraying yourselves."

Both Rome and an equally despondent La Conte nodded in resignation.

"The contributions to the tribal councils of Native Americans will be fixed for now at a trillion dollars over a period of ten years. The Olympic Peninsula Project under the control of Sara Kent, Jimmy Longbow, Joe Thomas and myself, will administer the fund.

"You, Mr. La Conte, will surrender all holdings and investments in Puget Sound Realty to the Olympic Peninsula Project. You, Mr. Mason, will surrender all holdings and investments in Olympic Realty to the project. You will become an employee.

"The terms of your protection, gentlemen, will be tied to your continued and faithful employment. You will fulfill your responsibilities to the cause you have served so well.

"I believe that covers it."

She sat, leaned back and crossed her legs in celebration of a triumphant moment despite the fall of her prince. She struck a pose of defiance and pride while Rome was a study in shame and humility.

Oddly, La Conte seemed amused. He stood and walked around his desk where he extended his hand and Maggie grasped it firmly.

"It is a rare pleasure, Ms. Thomas, to be beaten by someone of your charm and intellect. Please give my apologies to Mrs. Miner. I was actually quite fond of her."

He turned to Rome and spoke with a measure of distaste. "I believe this is the fruit of your labor, Mr. Mason. It is time, is it not, to face your ultimate defeat?"

Rome nodded in agreement and spoke as if drained of all energy.

"I'm sorry. You've won."

Again she felt a sudden urge to pity, a slight tug on the strings of her heart, but she held it at bay. She would not allow emotional distractions until the last brick was in place.

"Gentlemen, let's go to work."

Chapter 58

COUNCIL OF ELDERS

The ancient one, known to his friends as Song of the Wind, stood atop Mount Olympus flaming a fire with a mixture of sacred herbs.

"Great Spirit," he pleaded, eyes closed and hands to heaven. "You have given me the eyes of the crow and the power of the wolf to teach! I ask you now to bless my children with clarity of vision and second sight that they may see the moment of their triumph! That they might hold it in their hearts! That this may give them the strength they need for the many battles to come!"

He tended the fire and swept the smoke into his lungs.

"This I ask for they have proven worthy. They have fought for the cause that belongs to you and the earth mother and father sky and to all beings who walk the path of the good and the true!"

He breathed in the clean fresh air and absorbed the beauty of his surroundings.

"This I ask knowing that soon I will ask no more for I will be letting go this earthly plane to join the ancestors who hold a place for me in the great fire circle of the spirit world above. Let it be so."

He clutched the earth in his hands and cast it in the four directions, then above, then below, then to his heart and then he began to chant in a tongue that was not his own.

The location of the meeting of the Council of Elders was as remote as exists on the North American continent.

Somewhere on the high desert plains of the Southwest there is an expansive underground network of living quarters, green houses, communication centers and security installations fully supplied with tools, weapons, clean water and generators. In the event of a nuclear holocaust it would shelter the Inner Sanctum for a hundred years. It is invisible from the sky and inaccessible by road. Anyone who came within twenty miles of the facility would be deterred by dead cattle and warning signs of military testing.

Members of the Council of Elders were escorted to the center by silent black helicopters in the dead of night. After a night's sleep and breakfast in their chambers, they were fully briefed before being guided to the conference room.

It was an expansive room with blue velvet on the walls, highlighting classic works of art from around the world. The only furnishings were a large round table with twelve chairs. A placard bearing the family name of each member was placed before each chair.

With Mr. Rockefeller serving as chairman, the meeting was called to order when the members were seated. An empty chair belonged to the Kennedy family and would always be vacant out of respect and as a reminder of what happens to those who betray the sacred trust.

The chairman presented the issue before them.

"Gentlemen, it has been a decade since we last gathered. That alone conveys the gravity of the situation. You have read the transcripts. You have listened to the tapes. We are all aware of this organization's history. You have also, I trust, examined the demands of this...terrorist group. The floor is open to discussion."

An eerie silence gave way to bickering and grumblings of discontent. These were the most powerful men in the world reduced to petty quarrel. Whose idea was that history anyway? How had they allowed the situation to get so out of hand? Du Pont noted that his family had voted against the assassination.

The chair pounded his gavel.

"Gentlemen, please! We cannot alter the past!"

"The hell we can't!" protested Mellon.

"There are options!" asserted Baruch.

They grew quiet in anticipating that someone somehow had figured a way out. Baruch's face was contorted with worry and fatigue.

"The chair recognizes the House of Baruch."

Mr. Baruch cleared his voice.

"First option: We accept defeat and go our separate ways. We can absorb the loss and our reputations will remain intact."

"Never!" said the House of Carnegie.

"We don't negotiate with terrorists!" added Vanderbilt.

"We already have," countered Baruch.

Rockefeller pounded his gavel.

"Option two: We allow them to publish and deny the allegations. We own much of the media and can mitigate the harm. There will be a series of investigations but it is unlikely we will ever be called to account by any court or agent of government. We would, however, be forced to cease operations and risk the revenge of history."

"Inconceivable!" said Morgan.

Baruch continued. "Third option: We continue the negotiations and hope they will settle for..."

"There is a deadline!" Rockefeller interjected. "We have less than twenty-four hours, the very start of the new millennium."

"Will they yield?" inquired Baruch.

"According to La Conte, they will not. They are not businessmen. They are ideologues and revolutionaries. They accomplish their objective whether we accept their terms or not."

A darker and more foreboding silence lowered upon their heads before Baruch went on.

"Our fourth and final option, gentlemen: Retaliation.

We kill every last one of them, quickly and as prudently as possible. We pull the trigger and don't look back."

The elders were stunned. Some of them might have seen this day coming but most considered the days of violent reprisal behind them.

"Can we do it?" demanded Gould.

"Why haven't we done it already?" inquired Vanderbilt.

The chair pounded the gavel and spoke with the full weight of gravity.

"I assure you, as I am myself assured, if it were possible, we would have done it and we would not be here today. I am further advised, as we all are aware, that our allies in the military and in the government will not assist us in this matter. We are accountable for our own mess and I suggest we look to it."

Another spell of profound silence while the gentleman from the House of Hanna lit a cigar and the gentleman from the House of Guggenheim shifted uneasily in his seat.

"If there is no more discussion, gentlemen, the chair will entertain the question: Shall we accept the demands or not?"

"So moved," said Baruch.

"Second," said Mellon.

"The chair reminds you that we will all be bound by the majority and we will all share the consequences in equal measures. Understood?"

Ten heads nodded in assent.

"The chair calls on the House of du Pont. How say you?"

"The House of du Pont votes aye."

"The chair calls on the House of Vanderbilt. How say you?"

"The House of Vanderbilt votes nay."

"The chair calls on the House of Gould. How say you?"

"The House of Gould says aye."

"The chair calls on the House of Hanna. How say you?"

"The House of Hanna votes aye."

"The chair calls on the House of Morgan. How say

you?"

"The House of Morgan votes nay."

"The chair calls on the House of Carnegie. How say you?"

"The House of Carnegie votes aye."

"The chair calls on the House of Frick. How say you?"

"The House of Frick votes nay."

"The chair calls on the House of Guggenheim. How say you?"

"The House of Guggenheim votes nay."

"The chair calls on the House of Mellon. How say you?"

"The House of Mellon votes nay."

"The chair calls on the House of Baruch. How say you?"

"The House of Baruch votes aye."

All eyes turned to the chairman, who sat motionless, paralyzed with the realization that it came down to him. He recalled the decades of unchallenged authority. He thought of fortunes and empires and pages of history left unturned. He thought of Kennedy and Camelot and his eyes settled on the empty chair to his left. Somehow he knew, as they all must have known, there would come a time for the debt to be repaid. He thought of Caesar and Brutus and he felt a sharp pain deep in his gut. He felt emptiness within his soul and sensed eyes upon him, eyes beyond those of his partners in high crime, beyond the circle of power. For a fleeting moment he glimpsed a chance at redemption and he grasped it with both hands.

"The chair," he said in a voice quivering with emotion, "in behalf of the House of Rockefeller casts the deciding vote: Aye."

And the weight of eternal history came crashing down upon them. And the towers fell. And the rings of power came tumbling down.

"By a vote of six to five with one abstention, the conditions are accepted. This council is disbanded and any further business – namely, in compliance with the terms of agreement – will be conducted by our representatives and theirs. Gentlemen of the Inner Sanctum, for the very last time, this council is adjourned."

A thousand miles away to the north and west, a celebration began in the hearts of the triumphant rebels. After all their trials and sacrifices, they had won the war.

Chapter 59

FINAL REDEMPTION

The dream did not end with the Council of Elders' decision to accept the insurgent demands. It continued upward on the wings of the crow as the towers and the rings of power crumbled below. It continued upward on the wings of the hawk, soaring and spiraling, and upward still on the wings of the great thunderbird, the majestic eagle, upward to the land of the Overworld among the stars, where the great fire circle of spirit beings reigned and raged in glory, where the drums beat to the heart of all beings and where the Ghost Dancers danced.

There in the heavens, in the land beyond this land, in the land of virgin forests and endless plains and clear, flowing rivers and streams, where the buffalo and the wolf and the bear roamed freely, where the rebels regained their human form and joined the circle in celebration.

There Maggie joined hands with the ancient one who went by many names, among them Song in the Wind and Crow Dog and Sitting Bull, the Hunkpapa warrior and Ghost Dance leader at Wounded Knee.

There they danced in a shuffling step around and around in a great circle, chanting praise to the earth mother and father sky and the Great Spirit and the medicine wheel of life. And as they danced they witnessed the changeling crow transform into the hawk and the hawk into the eagle and the eagle into the crow once more.

They chanted praise to the brave earth warriors who confronted the beast, the enemy of all, who confronted their own demons to bring this victory home.

They danced and chanted words in another language, a language of the spirits and the stars, and as they danced and chanted the earth warriors appeared and joined the circle: Jimmy Longbow, Cheryl Miner, Detective Jones and Sara Kent. Jake Marshall and Bill Miner appeared and joined them for this was a circle of the living and the dead, a sacred line connecting the earth to its living past, present and future. They were at last joined by Rome Mason, dancing at Maggie's side, holding her hand and giving praise.

"This is the way of the medicine wheel," announced the old one in a voice that sprang from within. "The crow gives way to the hawk, the hawk to the eagle, the eagle to the human and the human to the crow. All is one in harmony as the wheel turns in perfect balance.

"This is the war we fight. It is the war against imbalance. It goes by many names: greed and evil and tyranny. It is a war that cannot be won for it must always be.

"In this war you will find many enemies. You will know them by the darkness in their eyes and the emptiness in their hearts. In this war you will also find many friends and allies, some of this world and some beyond, and you will know them by your dreams.

"This is the gift I leave you. You will know them by your dreams. Mitakuye Oyasin. Let it be so."

His voice faded into images of earth changes, images of earthquakes and floods, fire and famine, locusts and pestilence. The images were as familiar as the daily news. But each image of horror and destruction gave way like the Phoenix to new fire circles across the land, where drums pounded and warriors danced. The change had begun: A fundamental and all-encompassing change that reaches the lower depths of the human heart and leaves its imprint on all facets of life.

Maggie awakened with new understanding and she set out at once for the Point of Arches on Olympic Peninsula.

Somehow she knew that is where she would find him, counting waves on his balcony of dreams.

Rome did not greet her when she arrived at his coastal estate. She walked through an empty house, recalling evenings they had spent plotting and gazing into each other's eyes before climbing the stairs to the balcony overlooking the Pacific. There he stood immobile and gazing at the sea.

"You planned it this way, didn't you?"

Leaning over the railing, he tilted his head to the side to acknowledge her presence and measure her understanding.

"The ocean is the greatest jazz master," he said. "It soothes even the most troubled soul."

As Maggie looked at him her understanding grew and her soul reached out.

"I'm not sure why but you wanted La Conte to think you betrayed us. You set it up. You arranged for us to discover you."

"If I'd have made it any easier," Rome smiled, "La Conte would have seen through it. As it was he almost didn't buy it. Your performance convinced him. He wrote it all off to the folly of love."

"Why couldn't you have told me?"

He sighed. "Dear Maggie. I don't know if it's a flaw or a virtue or a little bit of both but you're a terrible liar. La Conte may be a poor judge of character but he's not a fool. If you had tried to play that scene knowing that it was a charade, he'd have seen it. I couldn't take that chance."

"What difference would it have made? We had the history. We had the evidence. We could document his betrayal of the Sanctum. We held all the cards."

"All but one: the vengeance card. I know La Conte. If he knew I betrayed him, it would have become personal. He'd have tried to kill us all without regard to the consequences. It was too late for Jake. I'll always regret that. La Conte ordered the hit because he knew Cheryl liked him. She was attracted to him and he was jealous. It became a personal thing."

"Could you have stopped him before?"

"I tried. I told him Jake was critical to the operation. I was sure we could wrap it up before La Conte took action. I was wrong and Jake paid for it."

"You could have told Jimmy."

She could sense his pain and guilt building. Reliving his decisions was more difficult than he imagined.

"I thought about it. But Jimmy has a soft spot. He would have told you and everything would have been altered. Your performance would have been different and less convincing. I did what I thought was best even if it meant I would have to live with it forever."

Maggie understood and tears swelled in her eyes.

"What if we hadn't found out?" she managed to ask.

"That was the gamble I had to take. I had faith in you."

"What if I hadn't figured it out? Would you have told me?"

Rome shook his head.

"Would you have believed me? I wouldn't expect you to. I did put in a word with the old man and he told me you would know when the time came."

She shook her head in mock disbelief.

"Damn you! That was a pretty convincing speech you gave about the lost cause of the sixties!"

"It was well rehearsed."

He went to her and wiped away the tears that ran down her cheeks. He held her close and looked deep into her eyes, his expression pensive, neither relieved nor celebratory.

"Stay strong, Maggie. It's not over. We've got them for now but if we give them half a chance, they'll try to regain what they've lost. It's one thing to seize control and another to hold it. You understand that, don't you?"

"Of course," she said. "It's the day after the revolution."

"Exactly."

"Can you still read my thoughts?" she asked with a tantalizing smile.

"Like a book," he answered with a kiss.

In a moment they knew their love had not wavered. If anything it grew stronger.

"Come on," she said. "It's time to rejoin the world. There's a celebration in town."

They embraced as lovers do when they make up after their first fight. At Rome's insistence, they counted seven waves and then they descended the stairs.

"Detective Jones has a message," she said with a wink.

"What's that?"

"Rejoice beyond a common joy and set it down with gold on lasting pillars!"

"As You Like It," he smiled.

"All's Well that Ends Well," replied Maggie.

It would not be necessary to explain Rome's return to good graces except to write the story that could never be told – not unless the Sanctum failed to live up to the terms of their agreement.

It would not be necessary to explain how he became a trusted employee of the Sanctum, serving as a consultant and advisor. It was not necessary to explain that he enlisted La Conte in a secret partnership to depose them. He was discontent with the pace of change and the likelihood of being passed over by the Council of Elders.

La Conte had been of invaluable assistance in uncovering resources, revealing names and misleading the organization's army of investigators. The plan could not have succeeded without him. Yet La Conte had never known Rome's true intent. Had he known it would have been a matter of honor to destroy them all. It was far easier for the Sanctum to yield to the cause than for La Conte to accept his partner's betrayal.

The Miner case took the Sanctum by surprise. The

history, the tapes and the documents, though their rumored existence attracted attention, was an unanticipated source of ammunition. Miner had taken possession of the history and paid for it with his life.

The greater mystery was the tapes and supporting documents. If Miner was responsible, why hadn't he packaged them with the history? It was as if they simply appeared and Detective Jones received the call. Had the old one worked his magical ways? Who among them could doubt?

It no longer mattered. Each of them had dreamed the dream of the Ghost Dance. They had joined hands and danced around the sacred fire. They knew and understood that each of them held a place in the circle and none within the circle could betray the others.

Guided by the mysterious Indian, a spirit being that walked in their dreams, the pieces had fallen into place. It was Song of the Wind that Rome sought when he set out for the Point of Arches days ago. But the old one had vanished, leaving nothing behind but the faint caw of a crow and a message of hope.

Now it was up to them.

Epilogue

PROPHECY FULFILLED

The end of the second millennium was marked by disaster after disaster on an unprecedented scale. Tornados roamed the continent like the buffalo once roamed the plains. Weather patterns changed, scorching some parts of the earth while flooding others. Quakes struck with increasing frequency and intensity. More than half the United States was declared a disaster area at one time or another over the last few years. Volcanoes worldwide sent plumes of ash into the atmosphere. Thundering storms wreaked havoc on all things electrical, triggering horrendous collisions on the air, land and sea. Communication systems broke down, crops failed and diseases spread with increasing alarm.

To the spiritual eye these were all signs of revolutionary change to come. The white buffalo had returned. People of all tribes, be they racial, cultural, religious or economic, returned to the old ways and called upon the elders for guidance. Native Americans were increasingly regarded by the greater society with reverence and remorse for the sins of the past.

Against this backdrop of despair and hopelessness, as well as repentance and spiritual rebirth, the nation welcomed the dawn of the third millennium and prayed in one voice for a new beginning. The prayer was received and answered in kind.

On the seventh day of January the first of many extraordinary contributions was received anonymously and distributed to tribal councils across the continent.

Inspired by strange dreams and visions, the elders of each tribe proclaimed the prophecy of the Ghost Dance at hand. The Great Spirit had blessed the Indian for his patience, courage, wisdom and perseverance.

From the Skokomish and Makah to the Iroquois and Lakota, from the Seminoles and Cherokee to the Apache, Navaho, Miwok and Hopi, the tribes celebrated in song and danced the Ghost Dance.

The skies were brilliant over the northern Pacific. From where the old Indian sat on a granite overhang on Mount Olympus, the whole of the earth seemed to glow with an inner radiance. He did not need to be told: A new age was dawning in the land of the setting sun.

He closed his eyes and he saw the rings of power tumble to the earth. The Ghost Dancers had begun the sacred ceremony. The ancestors rejoiced.

He opened his eyes and a decade had passed. The whole of the Olympic Peninsula was now a sanctuary of native culture. He closed his eyes and became the crow, soaring over herds of buffalo and forests filled with wildlife, the hunting grounds of plenty and fields of abundant growth.

He saw his people take hands with the white man, the brown, the black and the yellow, not as masters and captives, not as conquerors and conquered, but as human beings of equal worth and value. He saw that all men and women and all beings of the earth had a place in the grace and the glory of God – in the infinite wisdom of the Great Spirit.

The change was gradual – so gradual that it would not be noticed for many years – but Native Americans were buying back their lands, putting an end to a century of strip mining, toxic waste and clear-cut deforestation. The earth would begin to work her miracles of healing. Gradual but sure.

The silent revolution had come and gone. There were no

accounts in the daily news. There would be no references in the history books. Yet an era of unparalleled good will had dawned.

The old man on the mountain listened contented to the song of the wind through the tall trees. He saw that it was good and gave thanks to those who had accomplished it.

To the one called Maggie with the seeing eyes, to Jimmy Longbow, his native grandson, to Jake and Sara and the good detective, and to the White Man Who Sits Apart and Thinks Deeply. He had taught them well and well had he been taught. To all he gave his blessings.

"The Great Spirit has used us well," he observed.

In the radiant light of a new day, Maggie, Rome and Jimmy hiked out to where the old one had spoken his words of wisdom. They found no one. The hut, the fire pit and all signs of his existence were gone except for a small leather pouch filled with herbs and charms.

Rome wondered how he had not seen it before. He clutched it to his heart and offered it to Jimmy who respectfully declined.

"It's yours, white man. Give thanks."

He did so with a silent prayer. And as he placed it around his neck a large crow cawed loudly, circled four times in the sky above and vanished without a trace.

ABOUT THE AUTHOR

Jack Random has lived a rich and diverse life. His roots firmly planted in the fertile central valley of California, he has marched the streets in protest, haunted jazz town bars, read poetry in cafes and town squares, strutted his hour upon the stage, crisscrossed the country by air, rail, highway and thumb, mourned at Wounded Knee, gazed into the eyes of the crow at Grand Canyon, and paid tribute at the grave of Geronimo. He has labored in the fields of plenty, toiled on the assembly line, pursued higher education and attempted to enlighten children in the public schools. He has been a pilgrim and a seeker of truth. He is married to the love of his life. All the while he has chronicled his thoughts and revelations in words: plays, poetry, novels, stories and essays.

OTHER BOOKS FROM CROW DOG PRESS

Wasichu: The Killing Spirit – A Novel by Jack Random. A modern telling of the life of Crazy Horse recalls the history of Native America and its most revered leader.

Number Nine: The Adventures of Jake Jones and Ruby Daulton – A Novel by Jack Random. Jake & Ruby on an adventure to New Orleans in the summer of Katrina.

A Patriot Dirge – A Novel by Jack Random. Roman Mason takes on the political and economic forces that rule over our lives (Jazzman Series).

Jazzman Chronicles: Volumes I–X – Essays by Jack Random. Political commentaries from 2000 to 2014.

***A Mother's Story* – Stories, Art and Reflections** by Artis Brown Miller. A mother of eight reflects on a life of hardship and love.

Pawns to Players: The Stairway Scandal – A Novel by Jack Random. An aristocrat and a billionaire play a chess match to determine the fate of the American government.

The Grand Canyon Zen Golf Tour – A Memoir by Jack Random. Two friends embark on a journey of golf, music, poetry and family in the summer of 1993.

Hard Times: The Wrath of an Angry God – A Novel by Jack Random. Not with a bang but a whimper the end of days comes.

Pawns to Players: A Match for the White House – A Novel by Jack Random. Part two of the Chess Series.

Apache Jack: Native Visions & Stories by Jack Random. A collection of short works surrounding Indian culture.

Random Jack: Tales from Jazztown & Beyond by Jack Random. A collection of short stories.

D'Arc Underground & Other Plays by Jack Random. The first of two volumes of plays.

Aphrodite House & Other Plays by Jack Random. A second volume of plays.

Crow Dog Press